Simulations

Simulations

15 Tales of Virtual Reality

Edited by Karie Jacobson

A CITADEL PRESS BOOK
Published by Carol Publishing Group

A Citadel Press Book
Published by Carol Publishing Group
Citadel Press is a registered trademark of Carol Communications, Inc.
Editorial Offices: 600 Madison Avenue, New York, N.Y. 10022
Sales and Distribution Offices: 120 Enterprise Avenue, Secaucus, N.J. 07094
In Canada: Canadian Manda Group, P.O. Box 920, Station U, Toronto, Ontario M8Z 5P9
Queries regarding rights and permissions should be addressed to Carol Publishing Group, 600 Madison Avenue, New York, N.Y. 10022

Carol Publishing Group books are available at special discounts for bulk purchases, for sales promotions, fund raising, or educational purposes. Special editions can be created to specifications. For details, contact Special Sales Department, Carol Publishing Group, 120 Enterprise Avenue, Secaucus, N.J. 07094

Manufactured in the United States of America
10 9 8 7 6 5 4 3 2 1

Library of Congress Cataloging-in-Publication Data

Jacobson, Karie.
Simulations : 15 tales of virtual reality / by Karie Jacobson.
p. cm.
"A Citadel Twilight book."
ISBN 0-8065-1406-X
1. Science fiction, American. 2. Virtual reality—Fiction.
I. Title.
PS3560.A268S57 1993
813′.54—dc20 92-39509
CIP

TO MY MOTHER

PERMISSIONS ACKNOWLEDGMENTS

All good ideas have been thought of by somebody before they are realized.

—ARTHUR C. CLARKE

Reality isn't enough anymore.

—JOHN WALKER,
founder of Autodesk,
a California company working
on virtual reality

Thanks to all the editors, writers, and others who took time away from their busy schedules to help me with this project. I'm especially grateful to George Zebrowski, who took me under his wing and told me what I needed to know as a first-time anthologist; to Sam Dickers, who showed me how they wreck a nice beach; to Kevin Moore for saving my crashed disks; and to Randy Walser for checking my facts.

Thanks to my friends Chas Fuhrman, Sweet Allison James, Grandma, Justin, Molly Mac, Rebecca, Leif, Diana, and Keja. Also thanks to Rachel Steiner, "sister," for being the antithesis of beige.

Contents

Introduction

Like atomic energy, spaceships, and test tube babies, artificial reality is a science fiction concept that is being made actual. The literary movement known as "cyberpunk" that emerged in the early eighties took it as an integral theme, and early science fiction writers such as Aldous Huxley, Frederick Pohl, Ray Bradbury, Isaac Asimov, and Arthur C. Clarke all wrote about it.

The artificial worlds in fiction, however, don't always bear close resemblance to the current technology of VR, or virtual reality. VR enables you to "enter" a 3-D computer-simulated world by putting on an electronic helmet and gloves. Fictional artificial realities range from Aldous Huxley's "feelies," which you experience by grasping the knob of your theatre chair, to William Gibson's "cyberspace," which you enter via neural inputs in your brain. But the questions and possibilities raised by VR are often the same as those raised in fiction.

Some people think that virtual reality will be an addictive, passive form of entertainment; others believe it could be used to expand human consciousness. The stories in this anthology explore many views on the subject. Most were written before virtual reality was actually invented and focus less on machinery than on the moral, social, political, and metaphysical effects virtual reality may have on human beings. For a brief, factual overview of current VR technology, read ahead.

A Practical Guide to Virtual Reality

Virtual reality isn't overhyped, only mishyped. The focus has been on VR as "electronic LSD," sex toy, or fantasy game. What the media usually neglects to mention is that virtual reality will soon be entering many facets of our daily lives, the way computers already have. Just as computers are much more than an advanced form of typewriter, and are essential to everything from ATM machines to international communications, so VR is more than a new form of entertainment. It's a practical tool which will be used in communications, design, warfare, surgery, and manufacturing.

How It Works

Remember stereoscopes, those viewphones displaying faded 3-D pictures of truck stops and bikini girls? Stereoscopes contain two pictures of the same subject from slightly different angles; your eyes fuse the pictures together and create the illusion of three-dimensionality. Virtual reality operates on the same simple premise, except that the pictures are moving on a screen. When you turn your head in your VR headset, the perspective shifts accordingly.

Every movement triggers a complex reaction from the computer. The more detailed the virtual landscape, the more changes the computer has to make, and the slower the reaction time is, creating a lag between your actual movement and the movement of the virtual "you." This is why virtual worlds are presently cartoonish at their best, choppy and digitized at their worst, even though computer graphics are capable of convincing realism. (Many special effects in movies are achieved with computer graphics; it's nearly impossible to tell where the graphics and video pictures fuse.)

Three-D or "holographic" sound has already been perfected. A fairly realistic sound can be gotten from speakers, but with headphones, the sound can be "placed" in relation to the shape of a human head. The result is eerie; I was fully prepared when I put on holographic headphones, but I still jumped and turned around when I heard someone rustling papers behind me. "Hello, hello," a voice said softly, and I could have sworn I felt warm breath on the back of my neck. The way our eyes create the illusion of depth from two flat pictures, our imagination creates sensation from sound. Even cartoonish-looking virtual worlds will seem more convincing with the addition of 3-D sound.

TELEPRESENCE

Telepresence is a close relative of VR. Instead of feeding your senses input from a simulated world, your headset feeds you the point of view of a teleoperator, a robot in another location. Thus, you can see the world from the perspective of a two-foot-tall dog or an eighteen-foot giant, or you could feel as if you were walking on the surface of Mars.

ENTERTAINMENT

In our century, we have so many choices of stimuli that reality is often the least appealing option. Why experience adventure when we can watch it on TV? Why simply *be* when we can be stimulated by video, stereo, advertising, or mind-altering drugs? In science fiction, the ultimate symbol for our media-saturated age is often machine-created reality. Many people, wary of the new technology, agree. It's bad enough, they say, that we're addicted to TV; now we have a new machine that replaces reality itself. If we're already manipulated by politicians and advertisers through television, then virtual reality will be even worse.

VR's proponents call these fears misguided. They say that virtual reality is fundamentally different than TV because VR is interactive rather than passive. This means it could shake us out of our stupor and encourage creativity and play. Because a virtual world can theoretically contain any number of people, there is room for socialization. VR even has the potential to be "electronic LSD": a mind-expanding device that doesn't damage brain cells.

The advantage a virtual world has over the real world is that it has no boundaries. As long as VR is used as a supplement and not a substitute for the real world, it could be a positive force. Of course, the same thing was said about TV...

COMMUNICATIONS

Computers can translate images from the physical world into computer graphics, and virtual reality will put those images in three dimensions. This means that a person in Tokyo can feel as if she's dancing in a New York club. Video-telephones have never gained widespread use because they are expensive and impractical, but telepresence-telephones, when they are perfected and mass-produced will be much more viable.

Virtual reality could enable people to exchange simulations the way we now exchange words. Figures and numbers—the stock market charts, for instance—may be represented by colors, shapes, and images.

All of this adds up to a shift in the way we will receive information: concepts conveyed with images instead of letters, "face-to-face" connections instead of telephone conversations. Ideally, VR will help repersonalize an increasingly linear world.

VIRTUAL SEX ("Teledildonics")

Jaron Lanier of VPL Research summed up the feelings of most people working with VR when he called virtual sex "a ridiculous idea [that] will probably exist only to the level of those blowup party dolls."

The idea is being pursued anyway. There is already virtual pornography; a Playboy party featured a visit with Virtual Valerie. Howard Rheingold described telepresence sex in his recent book *Virtual Reality:* ". . . you slip into a lightweight . . . bodysuit . . . Embedded in the inner surface of the suit, using a technology that does not yet exist, is an array of intelligent sensor-detectors . . . that can receive and transmit a realistic sense of tactile presence . . . you can run your cheek over (virtual) satin, feel the difference when you encounter (virtual) flesh . . ." One of the more interesting aspects of this, says Rheingold, is that the sensors could be switched around, so that, for instance, you could have direct genital contact with someone by shaking hands in VR. The key phrase here, though, is that the technology does not yet exist.

VIRTUAL REAL ESTATE

A backyard of virtual trees sounds pretty unappealing now, but if the population of the world continues to grow at its present rate, it may be the closest most people get to having their own property. In overcrowded Tokyo, virtual offices already exist. Strangely—considering the endless possibilities—they are just as drab as the real thing.

VIRTUAL SURGERY

Wearing sophisticated goggles, surgeons will perceive a three-dimensional image of the desired result superimposed on the patient's body. Delicate microsurgery will be done through an enlarged model; as the surgeon cuts an instrument into the virtual layout, a tiny teleoperated instrument will cut into the real body.

EDUCATION AND RESEARCH

VR could help students learn by doing, instead of being passive receptors of information. Abstract concepts such as algebra or quantum mechanics could be turned into concrete images for students to play with. Chemical researchers will work with computer models of molecules that they can actually pick up and handle. When a poor bond is formed the researcher will feel resistance from the molecule, and when a better position is found the molecule will slide easily into place. Astronomers will be able to test Newton's laws in a simulated solar system, and mechanics and surgeons will practice on computer-generated models. Simulators are already used to train pilots and new drivers, but instead of consisting of a flat screen and a joystick, VR simulators will surround the trainee in three dimensions.

DESIGN

Instead of laying out a two-dimensional blueprint, or painstakingly constructing a model, designers can view a virtual representation of their proposed house, airplane, or automobile. They can walk down the hallways or sit in the cockpit, and see for themselves if what works on paper works in three dimensions. In Japan, housewives are able to custom-design their dream kitchens in virtual displays.

WAR

The military has been using simulators to train pilots and others for years, but the simulators have always consisted of a flat screen and a joystick. In preparation for the Gulf War, United States soldiers were accustomed to foreign terrain and trained to fly fighting planes in a simulated desert. Tanks are being perfected in which the driver, instead of looking through a window or portal, sees a visual representation of the surrounding landscape on a screen. Human targets would be shown as computer graphics. Telepresence brings the possibility of fighting from afar via robots.

War simulation is the only major theme in VR fiction which is not represented in this anthology. I recommend the novels *Ender's Game* by Orson Scott Card (Tor, 1985) and *On My Way to Paradise* by Dave Wolverton (Bantam Spectra, 1989) for those who wish to explore the possible ramifications of simulated warfare.

MANUFACTURING

Workers and factories who now monitor temperatures via numbers on a screen could return to a more direct method: through a telerobot, they could stick their hands directly into the vat. Workers who construct products may do so with the aid of a three-dimensional display instead of a blueprint.

For more information on virtual reality, read Howard Rheingold's book *Virtual Reality: The Revolutionary Technology of Computer Generated Artificial Worlds—and How It Promises and Threatens to Transform Business and Society* (Summit Books, 1991.) The periodicals *Whole Earth Review* and *Mondo 2000* frequently feature articles on the subject. The following companies are working on virtual reality: Autodesk, Sense8, Telepresence Research, Fake Space Labs,

Pop Optix, Polhemus Navigation Systems, RPI, Enter, Division, VPL Research, and Simmgraphics.

If you're interested in tracing the roots of VR in science fiction, check out the annotated bibliography at the back of this book. It lists most of the early VR stories and novels and highlights a few of the more notable recent ones. Meanwhile, this anthology is a good place to start.

Most of the major themes which run through virtual reality fiction appear in this anthology. The stories included represent a wide range in time, from Ray Bradbury's 1950 classic "The Veldt" to previously unpublished new stories such as Daniel Pearlman's "From Here to Eternitape." A few, like Vonda McIntyre's "Steelcollar Worker," are based on hard science; others stretch the concept of artificial worlds to the limits of the imagination. The stories have the common bond of strong writing and original and provocative ideas, but differ in style from cyberpunk to satire. All are entertaining, many are bizarre, and most will make you think about the possibilities and implications of the new technology of virtual reality.

Simulations

Ray Bradbury

The Veldt

Ray Bradbury's beautifully written stories have won him acclaim both in and outside of the field of science fiction. He has won too many awards to list, including the Nebula Grand Master and the Bram Stoker Life Achievement awards, and has written some of the only science fiction to be regularly taught in schools.

Artificial realities make several appearances in Bradbury's works. In Farenheit 451, *Mrs. Morgan spends hours in an empty, plotless interactive soap opera; in* Dandelion Wine, *a man builds a Happiness Machine that makes its users unhappy when they have to return to the comparative drabness of day-to-day life. "The Veldt," written in 1950, has since become a classic artificial reality story.*

"George, I wish you'd look at the nursery."

"What's wrong with it?"

"I don't know."

"Well, then."

"I just want you to look at it, is all, or call a psychologist in to look at it."

"What would a psychologist want with a nursery?"

"You know very well what he'd want." His wife paused in the middle of the kitchen and watched the stove busy humming to itself, making supper for four.

"It's just that the nursery is different now than it was."

"All right, let's have a look."

They walked down the hall of their soundproofed, Happylife Home, which had cost them thirty thousand dollars installed, this house which clothed and fed and rocked them to sleep and played and sang and was good to them. Their approach sensitized a switch somewhere and the nursery light flicked on when they came within ten feet of it. Similarly, behind them, in the halls, lights went on and off as they left them behind, with a soft automaticity.

"Well," said George Hadley.

They stood on the thatched floor of the nursery. It was forty feet across by forty feet long and thirty feet high; it had cost half again as much as the rest of the house. "But nothing's too good for our children," George had said.

The nursery was silent. It was empty as a jungle glade at hot high noon. The walls were blank and two dimensional. Now, as George and Lydia Hadley stood in the center of the room, the walls began to purr and recede into crystalline distance, it seemed, and presently an African veldt appeared, in three dimensions, on all sides, in color, reproduced to the final pebble and bit of straw. The ceiling above them became a deep sky with a hot yellow sun.

George Hadley felt the perspiration start on his brow.

"Let's get out of this sun," he said. "This is a little too real. But I don't see anything wrong."

"Wait a moment, you'll see," said his wife.

Now the hidden odorophonics were beginning to blow a wind of odor at the two people in the middle of the baked veldtland. The hot straw smell of lion grass, the cool green smell of the hidden water hole, the great rusty smell of animals, the smell of dust like a red paprika in the hot air. And now the sounds: the thump of distant antelope feet on grassy sod, the papery rustling of vultures. A shadow passed through the sky. The shadow flickered on George Hadley's upturned, sweating face.

"Filthy creatures," he heard his wife say.

"The vultures."

"You see, there are the lions, far over, that way. Now they're on their way to the water hole. They've just been eating," said Lydia. "I don't know what."

"Some animal." George Hadley put his hand up to shield off the burning light from his squinted eyes. "A zebra or a baby giraffe, maybe."

"Are you sure?" His wife sounded peculiarly tense.

"No, it's a little late to be *sure*," he said, amused. "Nothing over there I can see but cleaned bone, and the vultures dropping for what's left."

"Did you hear that scream?" she asked.

"No."

"About a minute ago?"

"Sorry, no."

The lions were coming. And again George Hadley was filled with admiration for the mechanical genius who had conceived this room. A miracle of efficiency selling for an absurdly low price. Every home should have one. Oh, occasionally they frightened you with their clinical accuracy, they startled you, gave you a twinge, but most of the time what fun for everyone, not only your own son and daughter, but for yourself when you felt like a quick jaunt to a foreign land, a quick change of scenery. Well, here it was!

And here were the lions now, fifteen feet away, so real, so feverishly and startlingly real that you could feel the prickling fur on your hand, and your mouth was stuffed with the dusty upholstery smell of their heated pelts, and the yellow of them was in your eyes like the yellow of an exquisite French tapestry, the yellows of lions and summer grass, and the sound of the matted lion lungs exhaling on the silent noontide, and the smell of meat from the panting, dripping mouths.

The lions stood looking at George and Lydia Hadley with terrible green-yellow eyes.

"Watch out!" screamed Lydia.

The lions came running at them.

Lydia bolted and ran. Instinctively, George sprang after her. Outside, in the hall, with the door slammed, he was laughing and she was crying, and they both stood appalled at the other's reaction.

"George!"

"Lydia! Oh, my dear poor sweet Lydia!"

"They almost got us!"

"Walls, Lydia, remember; crystal walls, that's all they are. Oh, they look real, I must admit—Africa in your parlor—but it's all dimensional superreactionary, supersensitive color film and mental tape film behind glass screens. It's all odorophonics and sonics, Lydia. Here's my handkerchief."

"I'm afraid." She came to him and put her body against him and cried steadily. "Did you see? Did you *feel*? It's too real."

"Now, Lydia . . ."

"You've go to tell Wendy and Peter not to read any more on Africa."

"Of course—of course." He patted her.

"Promise?"

"Sure."

"And lock the nursery for a few days until I get my nerves settled."

"You know how difficult Peter is about that. When I punished him a month ago by locking the nursery for even a few hours—the tantrum he threw! And Wendy too. They *live* for the nursery."

"It's got to be locked, that's all there is to it."

"All right." Reluctantly he locked the huge door. "You've been working too hard. You need a rest."

"I don't know—I don't know," she said, blowing her nose, sitting down in a chair that immediately began to rock and comfort her. "Maybe I don't have enough to do. Maybe I have time to think too much. Why don't we shut the whole house off for a few days and take a vacation?"

"You mean you want to fry my eggs for me?"

"Yes." She nodded.

"And darn my socks?"

"Yes." A frantic, watery-eyed nodding.

"And sweep the house?"

"Yes, yes—oh, yes!"

"But I thought that's why we bought this house, so we wouldn't have to do anything?"

"That's just it. I feel like I don't belong here. The house is wife and mother now and nursemaid. Can I compete with an African veldt? Can I give a bath and scrub the children as efficiently or quickly as the automatic scrub bath can? I cannot. And it isn't just me. It's you. You've been awfully nervous lately."

"I suppose I have been smoking too much."

"You look as if you didn't know what to do with yourself in this house, either. You smoke a little more every morning and drink a little more every afternoon and need a little more sedative every night. You're beginning to feel unnecessary too."

"Am I?" He paused and tried to feel into himself to see what was really there.

"Oh, George!" She looked beyond him, at the nursery door. "Those lions can't get out of there, can they?"

He looked at the door and saw it tremble as if something had jumped against it from the other side.

"Of course not," he said.

At dinner they ate alone, for Wendy and Peter were at a special plastic carnival across town and had televised home to say they'd be late, to go ahead eating. So George Hadley, bemused, sat watching the dining-room table produce warm dishes of food from its mechanical interior.

"We forgot the ketchup," he said.

"Sorry," said a small voice within the table, and ketchup appeared.

As for the nursery, thought George Hadley, it won't hurt for the children to be locked out of it awhile. Too much of anything isn't good for anyone. And it was clearly indicated that the children had been spending a little too much time on Africa. That *sun*. He could feel it on his neck, still, like a hot paw. And the *lions*. And the smell of blood. Remarkable how the nursery caught the telepathic emanations of the children's minds and created life to fill their every desire. The children thought lions, and there were lions. The children thought zebras, and there were zebras. Sun—sun. Giraffes—giraffes. Death and death.

That *last*. He chewed tastelessly on the meat that the table had cut for him. Death thoughts. They were awfully young, Wendy and Peter, for death thoughts. Or, no, you were never too young, really. Long before you knew what death was you were wishing it on someone else. When you were two years old you were shooting people with cap pistols.

But this—the long, hot African veldt—the awful death in the jaws of a lion. And repeated again and again.

"Where are you going?"

He didn't answer Lydia. Preoccupied, he let the lights glow softly on ahead of him, extinguish behind him as he padded to the nursery door. He listed against it. Far away, a lion roared.

He unlocked the door and opened it. Just before he stepped inside, he heard a faraway scream. And then another roar from the lions, which subsided quickly.

He stepped into Africa. How many times in the last year had he opened this door and found Wonderland, Alice, the Mock Turtle, or Aladdin and his Magical Lamp, or Jack Pumpkinhead of Oz, or Dr. Doolittle, or the cow jumping over a very real-appearing moon—all the delightful contraptions of a make-believe world. How often had he seen Pegasus flying in the sky ceiling, or seen fountains of red fireworks, or heard angel voices singing. But now, this yellow hot Africa, this bake oven with murder in the heat. Perhaps Lydia was right. Perhaps they needed a little vacation from the fantasy which was growing a bit too real for ten-year-old children. It was all right to exercise one's mind with gymnastic fantasies, but when the lively child mind settled on *one* pattern . . . ? It seemed that, at a distance, for the past month, he had heard lions roaring, and smelled their strong odor seeping as far away as his study door. But, being busy, he had paid it no attention.

George Hadley stood on the African grassland alone. The lions looked up from their feeding, watching him. The only flaw to the illusion was the open door through which he could see his wife, far down the dark hall, like a framed picture, eating her dinner abstractedly.

"Go away," he said to the lions.

They did not go.

He knew the principle of the room exactly. You sent out your thoughts. Whatever you thought would appear.

"Let's have Aladdin and his lamp." he snapped.

The veldtland remained; the lions remained.

"Come on, room! I demand Aladdin!" he said.

Nothing happened. The lions mumbled in their baked pelts.

"Aladdin!"

He went back to dinner. "The fool room's out of order," he said. "It won't respond."

"Or—"

"Or what?"

"Or it *can't* respond," said Lydia, "because the children have thought about Africa and lions and killing so many days that the room's in a rut."

"Could be."

"Or Peter's set it to remain that way."

"*Set* it?"

"He may have got into the machinery and fixed something."

"Peter doesn't know machinery."

"He's a wise one for ten. That I.Q. of his—"

"Nevertheless—"

"Hello, Mom. Hello, Dad."

The Hadleys turned. Wendy and Peter were coming in the front door, cheeks like peppermint candy, eyes like bright blue agate marbles, a smell of ozone on their jumpers from their trip in the helicopter.

"You're just in time for supper," said both parents.

"We're full of strawberry ice cream and hot dogs," said the children, holding hands. "But we'll sit and watch."

"Yes, come tell us about the nursery," said George Hadley.

The brother and sister blinked at him and then at each other. "Nursery?"

"All about Africa and everything," said the father with false joviality.

"I don't understand," said Peter.

"Your mother and I were just traveling through Africa with rod and reel; Tom Swift and his Electric Lion," said George Hadley.

"There's no Africa in the nursery," said Peter simply.

"Oh, come now, Peter. We know better."

"I don't remember any Africa," said Peter to Wendy. "Do you?"

"No."

"Run see and come tell."

She obeyed.

"Wendy, come back here!" said George Hadley, but she was gone. The house lights followed her like a flock of fireflies. Too late, he realized he had forgotten to lock the nursery door after his last inspection.

"Wendy'll look and come tell us," said Peter.

"She doesn't have to tell *me.* I've seen it."

"I'm sure you're mistaken, Father."

"I'm not, Peter. Come along now."

But Wendy was back. "It's not Africa," she said breathlessly.

"We'll see about this," said George Hadley, and they all walked down the hall together and opened the nursery door.

There was a green, lovely forest, a lovely river, a purple mountain, high voices singing, and Rima, lovely and mysterious, lurking in the trees with colorful flights of butterflies, like animated bouquets, lingering in her long hair. The African veldtland was gone. The lions were gone. Only Rima was here now, singing a song so beautiful that it brought tears to your eyes.

George Hadley looked in at the changed scene. "Go to bed," he said to the children.

They opened their mouths.

"You heard me," he said.

They went off to the air closet, where a wind sucked them like brown leaves up the flue to their slumber rooms.

George Hadley walked through the singing glade and picked up something that lay in the corner near where the lions had been. He walked slowly back to his wife.

"What is that?" she asked.

"An old wallet of mine," he said.

He showed it to her. The smell of hot grass was on it and the smell of a lion. There were drops of saliva on it, it had been chewed and there were blood smears on both sides.

He closed the nursery door and locked it, tight.

In the middle of the night he was still awake and he knew his wife was awake. "Do you think Wendy changed it?" she said at last, in the dark room.

"Of course."

"Made it from a veldt into a forest and put Rima there instead of lions?"

"Yes."

"Why?"

"I don't know. But it's staying locked until I find out."

"How did your wallet get there?"

"I don't know anything," he said, "except that I'm beginning to be sorry we bought that room for the children. If children are neurotic at all, a room like that—"

"It's supposed to help them work off their neuroses in a healthful way."

"I'm starting to wonder." He stared at the ceiling.

"We've given the children everything they ever wanted. Is this our reward—secrecy, disobedience?"

"Who was it said, 'Children are carpets, they should be stepped on occasionally'? We've never lifted a hand. They're insufferable—let's admit it. They come and go when they like; they treat us as if *we* were offspring. They're spoiled and we're spoiled."

"They've been acting funny every since you forbade them to take the rocket to New York a few months ago."

"They're not old enough to do that alone, I explained."

"Nevertheless, I've noticed they've been decidedly cool toward us since."

"I think I'll have David McClean come tomorrow morning to have a look at Africa."

"But it's not Africa now, it's Green Mansions country and Rima."

"I have a feeling it'll be Africa again before then."

A moment later they heard the screams.

Two screams. Two people screaming from downstairs. And then a roar of lions.

"Wendy and Peter aren't in their rooms," said his wife.

He lay in his bed with his beating heart. "No," he said. "They've broken into the nursery."

"Those screams—they sound familiar."

"Do they?"

"Yes, awfully."

And although their beds tried very hard, the two adults couldn't be rocked to sleep for another hour. A smell of cats was in the night air.

"Father?" said Peter.

"Yes."

Peter looked at his shoes. He never looked at his father any more, nor at his mother. "You aren't going to lock up the nursery for good, are you?"

"That all depends."

"On what?" snapped Peter.

"On you and your sister. If you intersperse this Africa with a little variety—oh, Sweden perhaps, or Denmark or China—"

"I thought we were free to play as we wished."

"You are, within reasonable bounds."

"What's wrong with Africa, Father?"

"Oh, so now you admit you have been conjuring up Africa, do you?"

"I wouldn't want the nursery locked up," said Peter coldly. "Ever."

"Matter of fact, we're thinking of turning the whole house off for about a month. Live sort of a carefree one-for-all existence."

"That sounds dreadful! Would I have to tie my own shoes instead of letting the shoe tier do it? And brush my own teeth and comb my hair and give myself a bath?"

"It would be fun for a change, don't you think?"

"No, it would be horrid. I didn't like it when you took out the picture painter last month."

"That's because I wanted you to learn to paint all by yourself, son."

"I don't want to do anything but look and listen and smell; what else *is* there to do?"

"All right, go play in Africa."

"Will you shut off the house sometime soon?"

"We're considering it."

"I don't think you'd better consider it any more, Father."

"I won't have any threats from my son!"

"Very well." And Peter strolled off to the nursery.

"Am I on time?" said David McClean.

"Breakfast?" asked George Hadley.

"Thanks, had some. What's the trouble?"

"David, you're a psychologist."

"I should hope so."

"Well, then, have a look at our nursery. You saw it a year ago when you dropped by; did you notice anything peculiar about it then?"

"Can't say I did; the usual violences, a tendency toward a slight paranoia here or there, usual in children because they feel persecuted by parents constantly, but, oh, really nothing."

They walked down the hall. "I locked the nursery up," explained the father, "and the children broke back into it during the night. I let them stay so they could form the patterns for you to see."

There was a terrible screaming from the nursery.

"There it is," said George Hadley. "See what you make of it."

They walked in on the children without rapping.

The screams had faded. The lions were feeding.

"Run outside a moment, children," said George Hadley. "No, don't change the mental combination. Leave the walls as they are. Get!"

With the children gone, the two men stood studying the lions clustered at a distance, eating with great relish whatever it was they had caught.

"I wish I knew what it was," said George Hadley. "Sometimes I can almost see. Do you think if I brought high-powered binoculars here and—"

David McClean laughed dryly. "Hardly." He turned to study all four walls. "How long as this been going on?"

"A little over a month."

"It certainly doesn't *feel* good."

"I want facts, not feelings."

"My dear George, a psychologist never saw a fact in his life. He only hears about feelings; vague things. This doesn't feel good, I tell you. Trust my hunches and my instincts. I have a nose for something bad. This is very bad. My advice to you is to have the whole damn room torn down and your children brought to me every day during the next year for treatment."

"Is it that bad?"

"I'm afraid so. One of the original uses of these nurseries was so that we could study the patterns left on the walls by the child's mind, study at our leisure, and help the child. In this case, however, the room has become a channel toward—destructive thoughts, instead of a release away from them."

"Didn't you sense this before?"

"I sensed only that you had spoiled your children more than most. And now you're letting them down in some way. What way?"

"I wouldn't let them go to New York."

"What else?"

"I've taken a few machines from the house and threatened them, a month ago, with closing up the nursery unless they did their homework. I did close it for a few days to show I meant business."

"Ah, ha!"

"Does that mean anything?"

"Everything. Where before they had a Santa Claus now they have a Scrooge. Children prefer Santas. You've let this room and this house replace you and your wife in your children's affections. This room is their mother and father, far more important in their lives than their real parents. And now you come along and want to shut it off. No wonder there's hatred here. You can feel it coming out of the sky. Feel that sun. George, you'll have to change your life. Like too many others, you've built it around creature comforts. Why, you'd starve tomorrow if something went wrong in your kitchen. You wouldn't know how to tap an egg. Nevertheless, turn everything off. Start new. It'll take time. But we'll make good children out of bad in a year, wait and see."

"But won't the shock be too much for the children, shutting the room up abruptly, for good?"

"I don't want them going any deeper into this, that's all."

The lions were finished with their red feast.

The lions were standing on the edge of the clearing watching the two men.

"Now *I'm* feeling persecuted," said McClean. "Let's get out of here. I never have cared for these damned rooms. Makes me nervous."

"The lions look real, don't they?" said George Hadley. "I don't suppose there's any way—"

"What?"

"—that they could *become* real?"

"Not that I know."

"Some flaw in the machinery, a tampering or something?"

"No."

They went to the door.

"I don't imagine the room will like being turned off," said the father.

"Nothing ever likes to die—even a room."

"I wonder if it hates me for wanting to switch it off?"

"Paranoia is thick around here today," said David McClean. "You can follow it like a spoor. Hello." He bent and picked up a bloody scarf. "This yours?"

"No." George Hadley's face was rigid. "It belongs to Lydia."

They went to the fuse box together and threw the switch that killed the nursery.

The two children were in hysterics. They screamed and pranced and threw things. They yelled and sobbed and swore and jumped at the furniture.

"You can't do that to the nursery, you can't!"

"Now, children."

The children flung themselves onto a couch, weeping.

"George," said Lydia Hadley, "turn on the nursery, just for a few moments. You can't be so abrupt."

"No."

"You can't be so cruel."

"Lydia, it's off, and it stays off. And the whole damn house dies as of here and now. The more I see of the mess we've put ourselves in, the more it sickens me. We've been contemplating our mechanical, electronic navels for too long. My God, how we need a breath of honest air!"

And he marched about the house turning off the voice clocks, the stoves, the heaters, the shoe shiners, the shoe lacers, the body scrubbers and swabbers and massagers, and every other machine he could put his hand to.

The house was full of dead bodies, it seemed. It felt like a mechanical cemetery. So silent. None of the humming hidden energy of machines waiting to function at the tap of a button.

"Don't let them do it!" wailed Peter at the ceiling, as if he was talking to the house, the nursery. "Don't let Father kill everything." He turned to his father. "Oh, I hate you!"

"Insults won't get you anywhere."

"I wish you were dead!"

"We were, for a long while. Now we're going to really start living. Instead of being handled and massaged, we're going to *live*."

Wendy was still crying and Peter joined her again. "Just a moment, just one moment, just another moment of nursery," they wailed.

"Oh, George," said the wife, "it can't hurt."

"All right—all right, if they'll only just shut up. One minute, mind you, and then off forever."

"Daddy, Daddy, Daddy!" sang the children, smiling with wet faces.

"And then we're going on a vacation. David McClean is coming back in half an hour to help us move out and get to the airport. I'm going to dress. You turn the nursery on for a minute, Lydia, just a minute, mind you."

And the three of them went babbling off while he let himself be vacuumed upstairs through the air flue and set about dressing himself. A minute later Lydia appeared.

"I'll be glad when we get away," she sighed.

"Did you leave them in the nursery?"

"I wanted to dress too. Oh, that horrid Africa. What can they see in it?"

"Well, in five minutes we'll be on our way to Iowa. Lord, how did we ever get in this house? What prompted us to buy a nightmare?"

"Pride, money, foolishness."

"I think we'd better get downstairs before those kids get engrossed with those damned beasts again."

Just then they heard the children calling, "Daddy, Mommy, come quick—quick!"

They went downstairs in the air flue and ran down the hall. The children were nowhere in sight. "Wendy? Peter!"

They ran into the nursery. The veldtland was empty save for the lions waiting, looking at them. "Peter, Wendy?"

The door slammed.

"Wendy, Peter!"

George Hadley and his wife whirled and ran back to the door.

"Open the door!" cried George Hadley, trying the knob. "Why, they've locked it from the outside! Peter!" He beat at the door. "Open up!"

He heard Peter's voice outside, against the door.

"Don't let them switch off the nursery and the house," he was saying.

Mr. and Mrs. George Hadley beat at the door. "Now, don't be ridiculous, children. It's time to go. Mr. McClean'll be here in a minute and . . ."

And then they heard the sounds.

The lions on three sides of them, in the yellow veldt grass, padding through the dry straw, rumbling and roaring in their throats.

The lions.

Mr. Hadley looked at his wife and they turned and looked back at the beasts edging slowly forward, crouching, tails stiff.

Mr. and Mrs. Hadley screamed.

And suddenly they realized why those other screams had sounded familiar.

"Well, here I am," said David McClean in the nursery doorway. "Oh, hello." He stared at the two children seated in the center of the open glade eating a little picnic lunch. Beyond them was the water hole and the yellow veldtland; above was the hot sun. He began to perspire. "Where are your father and mother?"

The children looked up and smiled. "Oh, they'll be here directly."

"Good, we must get going." At a distance Mr. McClean saw the lions fighting and clawing and then quieting down to feed in silence under the shady trees.

He squinted at the lions with his hand up to his eyes.

Now the lions were done feeding. They moved to the water hole to drink.

A shadow flickered over Mr. McClean's hot face. Many shadows flickered. The vultures were dropping down the blazing sky.

"A cup of tea?" asked Wendy in the silence.

John Varley

Overdrawn at the Memory Bank

Inventive, optimistic, and colorful, John Varley's works have won him six Locus awards, two Nebulas, the Jupiter, the Science Fiction Chronicle, the Prix Apollo, and the Hugo Awards. His complex characters, including strong, independent women, are the glue that holds together a dazzling display of unique ideas.

The concept of being stuck in a fantasy world goes back to daydreams of being trapped on a tropical island. But the scenario is somewhat different when the world is entirely in your head, as it is in the following story.

It was schoolday at the Kenya disneyland. Five nine-year-olds were being shown around the medico section where Fingal lay on the recording table, the top of his skull removed, looking up into a mirror. Fingal was in a bad mood (hence the trip to the disneyland) and could have done without the children. Their teacher was doing his best, but who can control five nine-year-olds?

"What's the big green wire do, teacher?" asked a little girl, reaching out one grubby hand and touching Fingal's brain where the main recording wire clamped to the build-in terminal.

"Lupus, I told you you weren't to touch anything. And look at you, you didn't wash your hands." The teacher took the child's hand and pulled it away.

"But what does it matter? You told us yesterday that the reason no one cares about dirt like they used to is dirt isn't dirty anymore."

"I'm sure I didn't tell you exactly *that*. What I said was that when humans were forced off Earth, we took the golden opportunity to wipe out all harmful germs. When there were only three thousand people alive on the moon after the Occupation it was easy for us to sterilize everything. So the medico doesn't need to wear gloves like surgeons used to, or even wash her hands. There's no danger of infection. But it isn't polite. We don't want this man to think we're being impolite to him, just because his nervous system is disconnected and he can't do anything about it, do we?"

"No, teacher."

"What's a surgeon?"

"What's 'infection'?"

Fingal wished the little perishers had chosen another day for their lessons, but like the teacher has said, there was very little he could do. The medico had turned his motor control over to the computer while she took the reading. He was paralyzed. He eyed the little boy carrying the carved stick, and hoped he didn't get a notion to poke him in the cerebrum with it. Fingal was insured, but who needs the trouble?

"All of you stand back a little so the medico can do her work. That's better. Now, who can tell me what the big green wire is? Destry?"

Destry allowed as how he didn't know, didn't care, and wished he could get out of here and play spat ball. The teacher dismissed him and went on with the others.

"The green wire is the main sounding electrode," the teacher said. "It's attached to a series of very fine wires in the man's head, like the ones you have, which are implanted at birth. Can anyone tell me how the recording is made?"

The little girl with the dirty hands spoke up.

"By tying knots in string."

The teacher laughed, but the medico didn't. She had heard it all before. So had the teacher, of course, but that was why he was a teacher. He had the patience to deal with children, a rare quality now that there were so few of them.

"No, that was just an analogy. Can you all say analogy?"

"*Analogy*," they chorused.

"Fine. What I told you is that the chains of FPNA are very much *like* strings with knots tied in them. If you make up a code with every millimeter and every knot having a meaning, you could write words in string by tying knots in it. That's what the machine does with the FPNA. Now . . . can anyone tell me what FPNA stands for?"

"Ferro-Photo-Nucleic Acid," said the girl, who seemed to be the star pupil.

"That's right, Lupus. It's a variant on DNA, and it can be knotted by magnetic fields and light, and made to go through chemical changes. What the medico is doing now is threading long strings of FPNA into the tiny tubes that are in the man's brain. When she's done, she'll switch on the machine and the current will start tying knots. And what happens then?"

"All his memories go into the memory cube," said Lupus.

"That's right. But it's a little more complicated than that.

You remember what I told you about a divided cipher? The kind that has two parts, neither of which is any good without the other? Imagine two of the strings, each with a lot of knots in them. Well, you try to read one of them with your decoder, and you find out that it doesn't make sense. That's because whoever wrote it used two strings, with knots tied in different places. They only make sense when you put them side-by-side and read them that way. That's how this decoder works, but the medico uses twenty-five strings. When they're all knotted the right way and put into the right openings in that cube over there," he pointed to the pink cube in the medico's bench, "they'll contain all this man's memories and personality. In a way, he'll be in the cube, but he won't know it, because he's going to be an African lion today."

This excited the children, who would much rather be stalking the Kenya savanna than listening to how a multi-holo was taken. When they quieted down the teacher went on, using analogies that got more strained by the minute.

"When the strings are in . . . class, pay attention. When they're in the cube, a current sets them in place. What we have then is a multi-holo. Can anyone tell me why we can't just take a tape-recording of what's going on in this man's brain, and use that?"

One of the boys answered, for once.

"Because memory isn't . . . what's that word?"

"Sequential?"

"Yeah, that's it. His memories are stashed all over his brain and there's no way to sort them out. So this recorder takes a picture of the whole thing like a hologram. Does that mean you can cut the cube in half and have two people?"

"No, but that's a good question. This isn't that sort of hologram. This is something like . . . like when you press your hand into clay, but in four dimensions. If you chip off a part of the information, right? Well, this is sort of like that. You can't see the imprint because it's too small, but everything the man ever did and saw and heard and thought will be in the cube."

"Would you move back a little?" asked the medico. The children in the mirror over Fingal's head shuffled back and became more than just heads with shoulders sticking out. The medico adjusted the last strand of FPNA suspended in his cortex to the close tolerances specified by the computer.

"I'd like to be a medico when I grow up," said one boy.

"I thought you wanted to go to college and study to be a scientist."

"Well, maybe. But my friend is teaching me to be a medico. It looks a lot easier."

"You should stay in school, Destry. I'm sure your parent will want you to make something of yourself." The medico fumed silently. She knew better than to speak up—education was a serious business and interference with the duties of a teacher carried a stiff fine. But she was obviously pleased when the class thanked her and went out the door, leaving dirty footprints behind them.

She viciously flipped a switch, and Fingal found he could breath and move the muscles in his head.

"Lousy conceited college graduate," she said. "What the hell's wrong with getting your hands dirty, I ask you?" She wiped the blood from her hands onto her blue smock.

"Teachers are the worst," Fingal said.

"Ain't it the truth? Well, being a medico is nothing to be ashamed of. So I didn't go to college, so what? I can do my job, and I can see what I've done when I'm through. I always did like working with my hands. Did you know that being a medico used to be one of the most respected professions there was?"

"Really?"

"Fact. They had to go to college for years and years, and they made a hell of a lot of money, let me tell you."

Fingal said nothing, thinking she must be exaggerating. What was so tough about medicine? Just a little mechanical sense and a steady hand, that was all you needed. Fingal did a lot of maintenance on his body himself, going to the shop only for major work. And a good thing, at the prices they charged. It was not the sort of thing one discussed while lying helpless on the table, however.

"Okay, that's done." She pulled out the modules that contained the invisible FPNA and set them in the developing solution. She fastened Fingal's skull back on and tightened the recessed screws set into the bone. She turned his motor control back over to him while she sealed his scalp back into place. He stretched and yawned. He always grew sleepy in the medico's shop; he didn't know why.

"Will that be all for today, sir? We've got a special on blood changes, and since you'll just be lying there while you're out doppling in the park, you might as well . . ."

"No, thanks. I had it changed a year ago. Didn't you read my history?"

She picked up the card and glanced at it. "So you did. Fine. You can get up now, Mr. Fingal." She made a note on the card and set it down on the table. The door opened and a small face peered in.

"I left my stick," said the boy. He came in and started looking under things, to the annoyance of the medico. She attempted to ignore the boy as she took down the rest of the information she needed.

"And are you going to experience this holiday now, or wait until your double has finished and play it back then?"

"Huh? Oh, you mean . . . yes. I see. No, I'll go right into the animal. My psychist advised me to come out here for my nerves, so it wouldn't do me much good to wait it out, would it?"

"No, I suppose it wouldn't. So you'll be sleeping here while you dopple in the park. Hey!" She turned to confront the little boy, who was poking his nose into things he should stay away from. She grabbed him and pulled him away.

"You either find what you're looking for in one minute or

you get out of here, you see?" He went back to his search, giggling behind his hand and looking for more interesting things to fool around with.

The medico made a check on the card, glanced at the glowing numbers on her thumbnail and discovered her shift was almost over. She connected the memory cube through a machine to a terminal in the back of his head.

"You've never done this before, right? We do this to avoid blank spots, which can be confusing sometimes. The cube is almost set, but now I'll add the last ten minutes to the record at the same time as I put you to sleep. That way you'll experience no disorientation, you'll move through a dream state to full awareness of being in the body of a lion. Your body will be removed and taken to one of our slumber rooms while you're gone. There's nothing to worry about."

Fingal wasn't worried, just tired and tense. He wished she would go on and do it and stop talking about it. And he wished the little boy would stop pounding his stick against the table leg. He wondered if his headache would be transferred to the lion.

She turned him off.

They hauled his body away and took his memory cube to the installation room. The medico chased the boy into the corridor and hosed down the recording room. Then she was off to a date she was already late for.

The employees of Kenya disneyland installed the cube into a metal box set into the skull of a full-grown African lioness. The social structure of lions being what it was, the proprietors charged a premium for the use of a male body, but Fingal didn't care one way or the other.

A short ride in an underground railroad with the sedated body of the Fingal-lioness, and he was deposited beneath the blazing sun of the Kenya savanna. He awoke, sniffed the air, and felt better immediately.

The Kenya disneyland was a total environment buried twenty kilometers beneath Mare Moscoviense on the far-side of Luna. It was roughly circular with a radius of two hundred kilometers. From the ground to the "sky" was two kilometers except over the full-sized replica of Kilimanjaro, where it bulged to allow clouds to form in a realistic manner over the snowcap.

The illusion was flawless. The ground curved away consistent with the curvature of the Earth, so that the horizon was much more distant than anything Fingal was used to. The trees were real, and so were all the animals. At night an astronomer would have needed a spectroscope to distinguish the stars from the real thing.

Fingal certainly couldn't spot anything wrong. Not that he wanted to. The colors were strange but that was from the limitations of feline optics. Sounds were much more vivid, as were smells. If he'd thought about it, he would have realized the gravity was much too weak for Kenya. But he wasn't thinking; he'd come here to avoid that necessity.

It was hot and glorious. The dry grass made no sound as he walked over it on broad pads. He smelled antelope, wildebeest, and . . . was that baboon? He felt pangs of hunger but he really didn't want to hunt. But he found the lioness body starting on a stalk anyway.

Fingal was in an odd position. He was in control of the lioness, but only more or less. He could guide her where he wanted to go, but he had no say at all over instinctive behaviors. He was as much a pawn to these as the lioness was. In one sense, he *was* the lioness; when he wished to raise a paw or turn around, he simply did it. The motor control was complete. It felt great to walk on all fours, and it came as easily as breathing. But the scent of the antelope went on a direct route from the nostrils to the lower brain, made a connection with the rumblings of hunger, and started him on the stalk.

The guidebook said to surrender to it. Fighting it wouldn't do anyone any good, and could frustrate you. If you were paying to be a lion, read the chapter on "Things to Do," you might as well *be* one, not just wear the body and see the sights.

Fingal wasn't sure he liked this as he came up downwind and crouched behind a withered clump of scrub. He pondered it while he sized up the dozen or so antelope grazing just a few meters from him, picking out the small, the weak, and the young with a predator's eye. Maybe he should back out now and go on his way. These beautiful creatures were not harming him. The Fingal part of him wished mostly to admire them, not eat them.

Before he quite knew what had happened, he was standing triumphant over the bloody body of a small antelope. The others were just dusty trails in the distance.

It had been incredible!

The lioness was fast, but might as well have been moving in slow-motion compared to the antelope. Her only advantage lay in surprise, confusion, and quick, all-out attack. There had been the lifting of a head, ears had flicked toward the bush he was hiding in, and he had exploded. Ten seconds of furious exertion and he bit down on a soft throat, felt the blood gush and the dying kicks of the hind legs under his paws. He was breathing hard and the blood coursed through his veins. There was only one way to release the tension.

He threw his head back and roared his bloodlust.

He'd had it with lions at the end of the weekend. It wasn't worth it for the few minutes of exhilaration at the kill. It was a life of endless stalking, countless failures, then a pitiful struggle to get a few bites for yourself from the kill you had made. He found to his chagrin that his lioness was very low in the dominance-order. When he got his kill back to the pride—he didn't know why he had dragged it back but the lioness seemed to know—it was promptly stolen from him. He/she sat back helplessly and watched the dominant male take his share, followed by the rest of the pride. He was left with a dried haunch four hours later, and had to contest even that with vultures and hyenas. He saw what the premium payment was for. That male had it *easy*.

But he had to admit that it had been worth it. He felt better; his psychist had been right. It did one good to leave the insatiable computers at his office for a weekend of simple living. There were no complicated choices to be made out here. If he was in doubt, he listened to his instincts. It was just that the next time, he'd go as an elephant. He'd been watching them. All the other animals pretty much left them alone and he could see why. To be a solitary bull, free to wander where he wished with food as close as the nearest tree branch . . .

He was still thinking about it when the collection crew came for him.

He awoke with the vague feeling that something was wrong. He sat up in bed and looked around him. Nothing seemed to be out of place. There was no one in the room with him. He shook his head to clear it.

It didn't do any good. There was still something wrong. He tried to remember how he had gotten there, and laughed at himself. His own bedroom! What was so remarkable about that?

But hadn't there been a vacation, a week-end trip? He remembered being a lion, eating raw antelope, being pushed around within the pride, fighting it out with the other females and losing. Retiring to rumble to him/herself.

Certainly he should have come back to human consciousness in the disneyland medical section. He couldn't remember it. He reached for his phone, not knowing who he wished to call. His psychist, perhaps, or the Kenya office.

"I'm sorry, Mr. Fingal," the phone told him. "This line is no longer available for outgoing calls. If you'll . . ."

"Why not?" he asked, irritated and confused. "I paid my bill."

"That is of no concern to this department, Mr. Fingal. And please do not interrupt. It's hard enough to reach you. I'm fading, but the message will be continued if you look to your right." The voice and the power hum behind it faded. The phone was dead.

Fingal looked to his right and jerked in surprise. There was a hand, a woman's hand, writing on his wall. The hand faded out at the wrist.

"*Mene, Mene* . . ." it wrote, in thin letters of fire. Then the hand waved in irritation and erased that with its thumb. The wall was smudged with soot where the words had been.

"You're projecting, Mr. Fingal." the hand wrote, quickly etching out the words with a manicured nail. "That's what you expected to see." The hand underlined the word "expected" three times. "Please cooperate, clear your mind, and see what is *there,* or we're not going to get anywhere. Damn, I've about exhausted this medium."

And indeed it had. The writing had filled the wall and the hand was now down near the floor. The apparition wrote smaller and smaller in an effort to get it all in.

Fingal had an excellent grasp on reality, according to his psychist. He held tightly onto that evaluation like a talisman as he leaned closer to the wall to read the last sentence.

"Look on your bookshelf," the hand wrote. "The title is *Orientation in Your Fantasy World.*"

Fingal knew he had no such book, but could think of nothing better to do.

His phone didn't work, and if he was going through a psychotic episode he didn't think it wise to enter the public corridor until he had some idea of what was going on. The hand faded out, but the writing continued to smoulder.

He found that book easily enough. It was a pamphlet, actually, with a gaudy cover. It was the sort of thing he had seen in the outer office of the Kenya disneyland, a promotional booklet. At the bottom it said, "Published under the auspices of the Kenya computer; A. Joachim, operator." He opened it and began to read.

CHAPTER ONE
"Where Am I?"

You're probably wondering by now where you are. This is an entirely healthy and normal reaction, Mr. Fingal. Anyone would wonder, when beset by what seems to be paranormal manifestations, if his grasp on reality had weakened. Or, in simple language, "Am I nuts, or what?"

No. Mr. Fingal, you are not nuts. But you are not, as you probably think, sitting on your bed, reading a book. It's all in your mind. You are still in the Kenya disneyland. More specifically, you are contained in the memory cube we took of you before your weekend on the savanna. You see, there's been a big goof-up.

CHAPTER TWO
"What Happened?"

We'd like to know that, too, Mr. Fingal. But here's what we do know. Your body has been misplaced. Now, there's nothing to worry about, we're doing all we can to locate it and find out how it happened but it will take some time. Maybe it's small consolation, but this has never happened before in the seventy-five years we've been operating, and as soon as we find out how it happened this time, you can be sure we'll be careful not to let it happen again. We're pursuing several leads at this time, and you can rest easy that your body will be returned to you intact just as soon as we locate it.

You are awake and aware right now because we have incorporated your memory cube into the workings of our H-210 computer, one of the finest holo-memory systems available to modern business. You see, there are a few problems.

CHAPTER THREE
"*What* Problems?"

It's kind of hard to put in terms you'd understand, but let's take a crack at it, shall we?

The medium we use to record your memories isn't the one you've probably used yourself as insurance against accidental death. As you must know, that system will store your memories for up to twenty years with no degradation or loss of information, and is quite expensive. The system we use is a temporary one, good for two, five, fourteen, or twenty-eight days, depending on the length of your stay. Your memories are put in the cube, where you might expect them to remain static and unchanging, like they do in your insurance-recording. If you thought that, you would be wrong, Mr. Fingal. Think about it. If you die, your bank will immediately start a clone from the plasma you stored along with the memory cube. In six months your memories would be played back into the clone and you would awaken, missing the memories that were accumulated in your body from the time of your last recording. Perhaps this has happened to you. If it has, you know the shock of wakening from the recording process to be told that it is three or four years later, and that you died in that time.

In any case, the process we use is an *ongoing* one, or it would be worthless to you. The cube we install in the African animal of your choice is capable of adding the memories of your stay in Kenya to the memory cube. When your visit is over, these memories are played back into your brain and you leave the disneyland with the exciting, educational, and refreshing experiences you had as an animal, though your body never left our slumber room. This is known as "doppling," from the German *doppelganger*.

Now, to the problems we talked about. Thought we'd *never* get around to them, didn't you?

First, since you registered for a week-end stay, the medico naturally used one of the two-day cubes as part of our budget-excursion fare. These cubes have a safety factor, but aren't much good beyond three days at best. At the end of that time the cube would start to deteriorate. Of course, we fully expect to have you installed in your own body before then. Additionally, there is the problem of storage. Since these ongoing memory cubes are intended to be in use all the time your memories are stored in them, it presents certain problems when we find ourselves in the spot we are now in. Are you following me, Mr. Fingal? While the cube has already passed its potency for use in co-existing with a live host, like the lioness you just left, it *must* be kept in constant activation at all times or loss of information results. I'm sure you wouldn't want that to happen, would you? Of course not. So what we have done is to "plug you in" to our computer, which will keep you aware and healthy and guard against the randomizing of your memory nexi. I won't go into that; let it stand that randomizing is not the sort of thing you'd like to have happen to you.

CHAPTER FOUR
"So What Gives, Huh?"

I'm glad you asked that. (Because you *did* ask that, Mr. Fingal. This booklet is part of the analogizing process that I'll explain further down the page.)

Life in a computer is not the sort of thing you could just jump into and hope to retain the world-picture-compatibility so necessary for sane functioning in this complex society. This has been tried, so take our word for it. Or, rather, my word. Did I introduce myself? I'm Apollonia Joachim, First Class Operative for the Data-Safe computer trouble-shooting firm. You've probably never heard of us, even though you do work with computers.

Since you can't just come aware in the baffling, on-and-off world that passes for reality in a data system, your mind, in cooperation with an analogizing program I've given your computer, interprets things in ways that seem safe and comfortable to it. The world you see around you is a figment of your imagination. Of course, it looks real to you because it comes from the same part of the mind that you normally use to interpret reality. If we wanted to get philosophical about it, we could probably argue all day about what constitutes reality and why the one you are perceiving now is any less real than the one you are used to. But let's not get into that, all right?

The world will likely continue to function in ways you are accustomed for it to function. It won't be exactly the same. Nightmares, for instance. Mr. Fingal, I hope you aren't the nervous type, because your nightmares can come to life where you are. They'll seem quite real. You should avoid them if you can, because they can do you real harm. I'll say more about this later if I need to. For now, there's no need to worry.

CHAPTER FIVE
"What Do I Do Now?"

I'd advise you to continue with your normal activities. Don't be alarmed at anything unusual. For one thing, I can only communicate with you by means of paranormal phenomena. You see, when a message from me is fed into the computer it reaches you in a way your brain is not capable of dealing with. Naturally, your brain classifies this as an unusual event and fleshes the communication out in unusual fashion. Most of the weird things you see, if you stay calm and don't let your own fears out of the closet to persecute you, will be me. Otherwise, I anticipate that your world should look, feel, taste, sound, and smell pretty normal. I've talked to your psychist. He assures me that your world-grasp is strong. So sit tight. We'll be working hard to get you out of there.

CHAPTER SIX
"Help!"

Yes, we'll help you. This is a truly unfortunate thing to have happened, and of course we will refund all your money promptly. In addition, the lawyer for Kenya wants me to ask you if a lump sum settlement against all future damages is a topic worthy of discussion. You can think about it, there's no hurry.

In the meantime, I'll find ways to answer your questions. It might become unwieldy the harder your mind struggles to normalize my communications into things you are familiar with. That is both your greatest strength—the ability of your mind to bend the computer world it doesn't wish to see into media you are familiar with—and my biggest handicap. Look for me in tea-leaves, on billboards, on holovision; anywhere! It could be exciting if you get into it.

Meanwhile, if you have received this message you can talk to me by filling in the attached coupon and dropping it in the mailtube. Your reply will probably be waiting for you at the office. Good luck!

Yes! I received your message, and am interested in the exciting opportunities in the field of *computer living*! Please send me, without cost or obligation, your exciting catalog telling me how I can *move up* to the big, wonderful world outside!

NAME ....
ADDRESS ....
I.D. ....

Fingal fought off the urge to pinch himself. If what this booklet said was true—and he might as well believe it—it would hurt and he would *not* wake up. He pinched himself anyway. It hurt.

If he understood this right, everything around him was the product of his imagination. Somewhere, a woman was sitting at a computer input and talking to him in normal language, which came to his brain in the form of electron pulses it could not cope with and so edited into forms he was conversant with. He was analogizing like mad. He wondered if he had caught it from the teacher, if analogies were contagious.

"What the hell's wrong with a simple voice from the air?" he wondered aloud. He got no response, and was rather glad. He'd had enough mysteriousness for now. And on second thought, a voice from the air would probably scare the pants off him.

He decided his brain must know what it was doing. After all, the hand startled him but he hadn't panicked. He could *see* it, and he trusted his visual sense more than he did voices from the air, a classical sign of insanity if ever there was one.

He got up and went to the wall. The letters of fire were gone, but the black smudge of the erasure was still there. He sniffed it: carbon. He fingered the rough paper of the pamphlet, tore off a corner, put it in his mouth and chewed it. It tasted like paper.

He sat down and filled out the coupon and tossed it to the mailtube.

Fingal didn't get angry about it until he was at the office. He was an easy-going person, slow to boil. But he finally reached a point where he had to say something.

Everything had been so normal he wanted to laugh. All his friends and acquaintances were there, doing exactly what he would have expected them to be doing. What amazed and bemused him was the number and variety of spear-carriers, minor players in this internal soap-opera. The extras his mind had cooked up to people the crowded corridors; like the man he didn't know who had bumped into him on the tube, apologized, and disappeared, presumably back into the bowels of his imagination.

There was nothing he could do to vent his anger but test the whole absurd set-up. There was doubt lingering in his mind that the whole morning had been a fugue, a temporary lapse into dreamland. Maybe he'd never gone to Kenya, after all, and his mind was playing tricks on him. To get him there, or keep him away? He didn't know, but he could worry about that if the test failed.

He stood up at his desk-terminal, which was in the third column of the fifteenth row of other identical desks, each with its diligent worker. He held up his hands and whistled. Everyone looked up.

"I don't believe in you," he screeched. He picked up a stack of tapes on his desk and hurled them at Felicia Nahum at the desk next to his. Felicia was a good friend of his, and she registered the proper shock until the tapes hit her. Then she melted. He looked around the room and saw that everything had stopped like a freeze-frame in a motion picture.

He sat down and drummed his fingers on his desk top. His heart was pounding and his face was flushed. For an awful moment he had thought he was wrong. He began to calm down, glancing up every few seconds to be sure the world really *had* stopped.

In three minutes he was in a cold sweat. What the hell had he *proved*? That this morning had been real, or that he really was crazy? It dawned on him that he would never be able to test the assumptions under which he lived. A line of print flashed across his terminal.

"But when could you ever do so, Mr. Fingal?"

"Ms. Joachim?" he shouted, looking around him. "Where are you? I'm afraid."

"You mustn't be," the terminal printed. "Calm yourself. You have a strong sense of reality, remember? Think about this: even before today, how could you be sure the world you saw was not the result of catatonic delusions? Do you see what I mean? The question 'What is reality?' is, in the end, unanswerable. We all must accept at some point what we see and are told, and live by a set of untested and untestable assumptions. I ask you to accept the set I gave you this morning because, sitting here in the computer room where you cannot see me, my world-picture tells me that they are the true set. On the other hand, you could believe that I'm deluding myself, that there's nothing in the pink cube I see and that you're a spear-carried in *my* dream. Does that make you more comfortable?"

"No," he mumbled, ashamed of himself. "I see what you mean. Even if I am crazy, it would be more comfortable to go along with it than to keep fighting it."

"Perfect, Mr. Fingal. If you need further illustrations you could imagine yourself locked in a strait-jacket. Perhaps there are technicians laboring right now to correct your condition, and they are putting you through this psycho-drama as a first step. Is that any more attractive?"

"No, I guess it isn't."

"The point is that it's as reasonable an assumption as the set of facts I gave you this morning. But the main point is that you should behave the same if either set is true. Do you see? To fight it in the one case will only cause you trouble, and in the other, would impede the treatment. I realize I'm asking you to accept me on faith. And that's all I can give you."

"I believe in you," he said. "Now, can you start everything going again?"

"I told you I'm not in control of your world. In fact, it's a considerable obstacle to me, seeing as I have to talk to you in these awkward ways. But things should get going on their own as soon as you let them. Look up."

He did, and saw the normal hum and bustle of the office. Felicia was there at her desk, as though nothing had happened. Nothing had. Yes, something had, after all. The tapes were scattered on the floor near his desk, where they had fallen. They had unreeled in an unruly mess.

He started to pick them up, then saw they weren't as messy as he had thought. They spelled out a message in coils of tape.

"You're back on the track," it said.

For three weeks Fingal was a very good boy. His co-workers, had they been real people, might have noticed a certain standoffishness in him, and his social life at home was drastically curtailed. Otherwise, he behaved exactly as if everything around him were real.

But his patience had limits. This had already dragged on far beyond what he had expected of it. He began to fidget at his desk, let his mind wander. Feeding information into a computer can be frustrating, unrewarding, and eventually stultifying. He had been feeling it even before his trip to Kenya; it had been the *cause* of his trip to Kenya. He was sixty-eight years old, with centuries ahead of him, and stuck in a ferro-magnetic rut. Longlife could be a mixed blessing when you felt boredom creeping up on you.

What was getting to him was the growing disgust with his job. It was bad enough when he merely sat in a real office with two hundred real people shoveling slightly unreal data into a much-less-than-real-to-his senses computer. How much worse now, when he knew that the data he handled had no meaning to anyone but himself, was nothing but occupational therapy created by his mind and a computer program to keep him busy while Joachim searched for his body?

For the first time in his life he began punching some buttons for himself. Under slightly less stress he would have gone to see his psychist, the approved and perfectly normal thing to do. Here, he knew he would only be talking to himself. He failed to perceive the advantages of such an idealized psychoanalytic process; he'd never really believed that a psychist did little but listen in the first place.

He began to change his own life when he became irritated with his boss. She pointed out to him that his error-index was on the rise, and suggested that he shape up or begin looking for another source of employment.

This enraged him. He'd been a good worker for twenty-five years. Why should she take that attitude when he was just not feeling himself for a week or two?

Then he was angrier than ever when he thought about her being merely a projection of his own mind. Why should he let *her* push him around?

"I don't want to hear it," he said. "Leave me alone. Better yet, give me a raise in salary."

"Fingal," she said promptly, "you've been a credit to your section these last weeks. I'm going to give you a raise."

"Thank you. Go away." She did, by dissolving into thin air. This really made his day. He leaned back in his chair and thought about his situation for the first time since he was young.

He didn't like what he saw.

In the middle of his ruminations, his computer screen lit up again.

"Watch it, Fingal," it read. "That way lies catatonia."

He took the warning seriously, but didn't intend to abuse the newfound power. He didn't see why judicious use of it now and then would hurt anything. He stretched, and yawned broadly. He looked around, suddenly hated the office with its rows of workers indistinguishable from their desks. Why not take the day off?

On impulse, he got up and walked the few steps to Felicia's desk.

"Why don't we go to my house and make love?" he asked her.

She looked at him in astonishment, and he grinned. She was almost as surprised as when he had hurled the tapes at her.

"Is this a joke? In the middle of the day? You have a job to do, you know. You want to get us fired?"

He shook his head slowly. "That's not an acceptable answer."

She stopped, and rewound from that point. He heard her repeat her last sentences backwards, then she smiled.

"Sure, why not?" she said.

Felicia left afterwards in the same, slightly disconcerting way his boss had left earlier; by melting into the air. Fingal sat quietly in his bed, wondering what to do with himself. He felt he was getting off to a bad start if he intended to edit his world with care.

His telephone rang.

"You're damn right," said a woman's voice, obviously irritated with him. He sat up straight.

"Apollonia?"

"Ms. Joachim to you, Fingal. I can't talk long, this is quite a strain on me. But listen to me, and listen hard. Your navel is very deep, Fingal. From where you're standing, it's a pit I can't even see the bottom of. If you fall into it I can't guarantee to pull you out."

"But do I have to take *everything* as it is? Aren't I allowed some self-improvement?"

"Don't kid yourself. That wasn't self-improvement. That was sheer laziness. It was nothing but masturbation, and while there's nothing wrong with that, if you do it to the exclusion of all else your mind will grow in on itself. You're in grave danger of excluding the external universe from your reality."

"But I thought there was no external universe for me here."

"Almost right. But I'm feeding you external stimuli to keep you going. Besides, it's the attitude that counts. You've never had trouble finding sexual partners; why do you feel compelled to alter the odds now?"

"I don't know," he admitted. "Like you said, laziness, I guess."

"That's right. If you want to quit your job, feel free. If you're serious about self-improvement, there are opportunities available to you there. Search them out. Look around you, explore. But don't try to meddle in things you don't understand. I've got to go now. I'll write you a letter if I can, and explain more."

"Wait! What about my body? Have they made any progress?"

"Yes, they've found out how it happened. It seems . . ." her voice faded out, and he switched off the phone.

The next day he received a letter explaining what was known so far. It seemed that the mix-up had resulted from the visit of the teacher to the medico section on the day of his recording. More specifically, the return of the little boy after the others had left. They were sure now that he had tampered with the routine card that told the attendants what to do with Fingal's body. Instead of moving it to the slumber room, which was a green card, they had sent it somewhere—no one knew where yet—for a sex change, which was a blue card. The medico, in her haste to get home for her date, had not noticed the switch. Now the body could be in any of several thousand medico shops in Luna. They were looking for it, and for the boy.

Fingal put the letter down and did some hard thinking.

Joachim had said there were opportunities for him in the memory banks. She had also said that not everything he saw was his own projections. He was receiving, was capable of receiving, external stimuli. Why was that? Because he would tend to randomize without them, or some other reason? He wished the letter had gone into that.

In the meantime, what did he do?

Suddenly he had it. He wanted to learn about computers. He wanted to know what made them tick, to feel a sense of power over them. It was particularly strong when he thought about being a virtual prisoner inside one. He was like a worker on an assembly line. All day long he labors, taking small parts off a moving belt and installing them on larger assemblies. One day, he happens to wonder who puts the parts on the belt? Where do they come from? How are they made? What happens after he installs them?

He wondered why he hadn't thought of it before.

The admissions office of the Lunar People's Technical School was crowded. He was handed a form and told to fill it out. It looked bleak. The spaces for "previous experience" and "aptitude scores" were almost blank when he was through with them. All in all, not a very promising application. He went to the desk and handed the form to the man sitting at the terminal.

The man fed it into the computer, which promptly decided Fingal had no talent for being a computer repairperson. He started to turn away, when his eye was caught by a large poster behind the man. It had been there on the wall when he came in, but he hadn't read it.

LUNA NEEDS
COMPUTER TECHNICIANS
THIS MEANS YOU
MR. FINGAL!

Are you dissatisfied with your present employment? Do you feel you were cut out for better things? Then today may be your lucky day. You've come to the right place, and if you grasp this golden opportunity you will find doors opening that were closed to you.

Act, Mr. Fingal. This is the time. Who's to check up on you? Just take that stylus and fill it in any old way you want. Be grandiose, be daring! The fix is in, and you're on your way to

BIG MONEY!

The secretary saw nothing unusual about Fingal coming to the desk a second time, and didn't even blink when the computer decided he was eligible for the accelerated course.

It wasn't easy at first. He really did have little aptitude for electronics, but aptitude is a slippery thing. His personality matrix was as flexible now as it would ever be. A little effort at the right time would go a long way toward self-improvement. What he kept telling himself was that everything that made him what he was was etched in that tiny cube wired in to the computer, and if he was careful he could edit it.

Not radically, Joachim told him in a long, helpful letter later in the week. That way led to complete disruption of the FPNA matrix and catatonia, which in this case would be distinguishable from death only to a hair-splitter.

He thought a lot about death as he dug into the books. He was in a strange position. The being known as Fingal would not die in any conceivable outcome of this adventure. For one thing, his body was going toward a sex change and it was hard to imagine what could happen to it that would kill it. Whoever had custody of it now would be taking care of it just as well as the medicos in the slumber room would have. If Joachim was unsuccessful in her attempt to keep him aware and sane in the memory bank, he would merely awake and remember nothing from the time he fell asleep on the table.

If, by some compounded unlikelihood, his body *was* allowed to die, he had an insurance recording safe in the vault of his bank. The recording was three years old. He would awaken in the newly-grown clone body knowing nothing of the last three years, and would have a fantastic story to listen to as he was brought up to date.

But none of that matter to *him*. Humans are a time-binding species, existing in an eternal *now*. The future flows through them and becomes the past, but it is always the present that counts. The Fingal of three years ago was *not* the Fingal in the memory bank. The simple fact about immortality by memory recording was that it was a poor solution. The three-dimensional cross-section that was the Fingal of now must always behave as if his life depended on his actions, for he would feel the pain of death if it happened to him. It was small consolation to a dying man to know that he would go on, several years younger and less wise. If Fingal lost out here, he would *die*, because with memory recording he was three people: the one who lived now, the one lost somewhere on Luna, and the one potential person in the bank vault. They were really no more than close relatives.

Everyone knew this, but it was so much better than the alternative that few people rejected it. They tried not to think about it and were generally successful. They had recordings made as often as they could afford them. They heaved a sigh of relief as they got onto the table to have another recording taken, knowing that another chunk of their lives was safe for all time. But they awaited the awakening nervously, dreading being told that it was now twenty years later because they had died sometime after the recording and had to start all over. A lot can happen in twenty years. The person in the new clone body might have to cope with a child he or she had never seen, a new spouse, or the shattering news that his or her employment was now the function of a machine.

So Fingal took Joachim's warnings seriously. Death was death, and though he could cheat it, death still had the last laugh. Instead of taking your whole life from you death now only claimed a percentage, but in many ways it was the most important percentage.

He enrolled in classes. Whenever possible he took the ones that were available over the phone lines so he needn't stir from his room. He ordered his food and supplies by phone and paid his bills by looking at them and willing them out of existence. It could have been intensely boring, or it could have been wildly interesting. After all, it was a dream-world, and who doesn't think of retiring into fantasy from time to time? Fingal certainly did, but firmly suppressed the idea when it came. He intended to get out of this dream.

For one thing, he missed the company of other people. He waited for the weekly letters from Apollonia (she now allowed him to call her by her first name) with a consuming passion and devoured every word. His file of such letters bulged. At lonely moments he would pull one out at random and read it again and again.

On her advice, he left the apartment regularly and stirred around more or less at random. During these outings he had wild adventures. Literally. Apollonia hurled the external stimuli at him during these times and they could be anything from The Mummy's Curse to Custer's Last Stand with the original cast. It beat hell out of the movies. He would just walk down the public corridors and open a door at random. Behind it might be King Solomon's mines or the sultan's harem. He endured them all stoically. He was unable to get any pleasure from sex. He knew it was a one-handed exercise, and it took all the excitement away.

His only pleasure came in his studies. He read everything he could about computer science and came to stand at the head of his class. And as he learned, it began to occur to him to apply his knowledge to his own situation.

He began seeing things around him that had been veiled before. Patterns. The reality was starting to seep through his illusions. Every so often he would look up and see the faintest shadow of the real world of electron flow and fluttering circuits he inhabited. It scared him at first. He asked Apollonia about it on one of his dream journeys, this time to Coney Island in the mid-twentieth century. He liked it there. He could lie on the sand and talk to the surf. Overhead, a skywriter's plane spelled out the answers to his questions. He studiously ignored the brontosaurus rampaging through the roller coaster off to his right.

"What does it mean, O Goddess of Transistoria, when I begin to see circuit diagrams on the walls of my apartment? Overwork?"

"It means the illusion is beginning to wear thin," the plane spelled out over the next half-hour. "You're adapting to the reality you have been denying. It could be trouble, but we're hot on the trail of your body. We should have it soon and get you out of there." This had been too much for the plane. The sun was going down now, the brontosaurus vanished, and the plane ran out of gas. It spiraled into the ocean and the crowds surged closer to the water to watch the rescue. Fingal got up and went back to the boardwalk.

There was a huge billboard. He laced his fingers behind his back and read it.

"Sorry for the delay. As I was saying, we're almost there. Give us another few months. One of our agents thinks he will be at the right medico shop in about one week's time. From there it should go quickly. For now, avoid those places where you see the circuits showing through. They're no good for you, take my word for it."

Fingal avoided the circuits as long as he could. He finished his first courses in computer science and enrolled in the intermediate section. Six months rolled by.

His studies got easier and easier. His reading speed was increasing phenomenally. He found that it was more advantageous for him to see the library as composed of books instead of tapes. He could take a book from the shelf, flip through it rapidly, and know everything that was in it. He knew enough now to realize that he was acquiring a facility to interface directly with the stored knowledge in the computer, bypassing his senses entirely. The books he held in his hands were merely the sensual analogs of the proper terminals to touch. Apollonia was nervous about it, but let him go on. He breezed through the intermediate and graduated into the advanced classes.

But he was surrounded by wires. Everywhere he turned, in the patterns of veins beneath the surface of a man's face, in a plate of french fries he ordered for lunch, in his palmprints, overlaying the apparent disorder of a head of blonde hair on the pillow beside him.

The wires were analogs of analogs. There was little in a modern computer that consisted of wiring. Most of it was made of molecular circuits that were either embedded in a crystal lattice or photographically reproduced on a chip of silicon. Visually, they were hard to imagine, so his mind was making up these complex circuit diagrams that served the same purpose but could be experienced directly.

One day he could resist it no longer. He was in the bathroom, on the traditional place for the pondering of the imponderable. His mind wandered, speculating on the necessity of moving his bowels, wondering if he might safely eliminate the need to eliminate. His toe idly traced out the pathways of a circuit board incorporated in the pattern of tiles on the floor.

The toilet began to overflow, not with water, but with coins. Bells were ringing happily. He jumped up and watched in bemusement as his bathroom filled with money.

He became aware of a subtle alteration in the tone of the bells. They changed from the merry clang of jackpot to the tolling of a death knell. He hastily looked around for a manifestation. He knew that Apollonia would be angry.

She was. Her hand appeared and began to write on the wall. This time the writing was in his blood. It dripped menacingly from the words.

"What are you doing?" the hand wrote, and having writ, moved on. "I told you to leave the wires along. Do you know what you've done? You may have wiped the financial records for Kenya. It could take *months* to straighten them out."

"Well what do I care?" he exploded. "What have they done for me lately? It's *incredible* that they haven't located my body by now. It's been a full *year*."

The hand was bunched up in a fist. Then it grabbed him around the throat and squeezed hard enough to make his eyes bulge out. It slowly relaxed. When Fingal could see straight, he backed warily away from it.

The hand fidgeted nervously, drummed its fingers on the floor. It went to the wall again.

"Sorry," it wrote, "I guess I'm getting tired. Hold on."

He waited, more shaken than he remembered being since his odyssey began. There's nothing like a dose of pain, he reflected, to make you realize that it *can* happen to you.

The wall with the words of blood slowly dissolved into a heavenly panorama. As he watched, clouds streamed by his vantage point and mixed beautifully with golden rays of sunshine. He heard organ music from pipes the size of sequoias.

He wanted to applaud. It was so overdone, and yet so convincing. In the center of the whirling mass of white mist an angel faded in. She had wings and a halo, but lacked the traditional white robe. She was nude, and hair floated around her as if she were underwater.

She levitated to him, walking on the billowing clouds, and handed him two stone tablets. He tore his eyes away from the apparition and glanced down at the tablets:

Thou shalt not screw around with
things you do not understand.

"All right, I promise I won't," he told the angel. "Apollonia, is that you? Really you, I mean?"

"Read the Commandments, Fingal. This is hard on me."

He looked back at the tablets.

Thou shalt not meddle in the hardware systems of the Kenya Corporation, for Kenya shall not hold him indemnifiable who taketh freedoms with its property.

Thou shalt not explore the limits of thy prison. Trust in the Kenya Corporation to extract thee.

Thou shalt not program.

Thou shalt not worry about the location of thy body, for it has been located, help is on the way, the cavalry has arrived, and all is in hand.

Thou shalt meet a tall, handsome stranger who will guide thee from thy current plight.

Thou shalt stay tuned for further developments.

He looked up and was happy to see that the angel was still there.

"I won't, I promise. But where is my body, and why has it taken so long to find it? Can you . . ."

"Know thee that appearing like this is a great taxation upon me, Mr. Fingal. I am undergoing strains the nature of which I have not time to reveal to thee. Hold thy horses, wait it out, and thou shalt soon see the light at the end of the tunnel."

"Wait, don't go." She was already starting to fade out.

"I cannot tarry."

"But . . . Apollonia, this is charming, but why do you appear to me in these crazy ways? Why all the pomp and circumstance? What's wrong with letters?"

She looked around her at the clouds, the sunbeams, the tablets in his hand, and at her body, as if seeing them for the first time. She threw her head back and laughed like a symphony orchestra. It was almost too beautiful for Fingal to bear.

"Me?" she said, dropping the angelic bearing. "Me? I don't pick 'em, Fingal. I told you, it's *your* head, and I'm just passing through." She arched her eyebrows at him. "And really, sir, I had no idea you felt this way about me. Is it puppy love?" And she was gone, except for the grin.

The grin haunted him for days. He was disgusted with himself about it. He hated to see a metaphor overworked so. He decided his mind was just an inept analogizer.

But everything had its purpose. The grin forced himself to look at his feelings. He was in love; hopelessly, ridiculously, just like a teenager. He got out all his old letters from her and read through them again, searching for the magic words that could have inflicted this on him. Because it was *silly*. He'd never met her except under highly figurative circumstances. The one time he saw her, most of what he saw was the product of his own mind.

There were no clues in the letters. Most of them were as impersonal as a textbook, though they tended to be rather chatty. Friendly, yes; but intimate, poetic, insightful, revealing? No. He failed utterly to put them together in any way that should add up to love, or even a teenage crush.

He attacked his studies with renewed vigor, awaiting the next communication. Weeks dragged by with no word. He called the post office several times, placed personal advertisements in every periodical he could think of, took to scrawling messages on public building, sealed notes in bottles and flushed them down the disposal, rented billboards, bought television time. He screamed at the empty walls of his apartment, buttonholed strangers, tapped Morse Code on the water pipes, started rumors in skid row taprooms, had leaflets published and distributed all over the solar system. He tried every medium he could think of, and could not contact her. He was alone.

He considered the possibility that he had died. In his present situation, it might be hard to tell for sure. He abandoned it as untestable. That line was hazy enough already without his efforts to determine which side of the life/death dichotomy he inhabited. Besides, the more he thought about existing as nothing more than kinks in a set of macromolecules plugged into a data system, the more it frightened him. He'd survived this long by avoiding such thoughts.

His nightmares moved in on him, set up housekeeping in his apartment. They were a severe disappointment, and confirmed his conclusion that his imagination was not as vivid as it might be. They were infantile boogeyman, the sort that might scare him when glimpsed hazily through the fog of a nightmare, but were almost laughable when exposed to the full light of consciousness. There was a large, talkative snake that was crudely put together, fashioned from the incomplete picture a child might have of a serpent. A toy company could have done a better job. There was a werewolf whose chief claim to dread was a tendency to shed all over Fingal's rugs. There was a woman who consisted mostly of breasts and genitals, left over from his adolescence, he suspected. He groaned in embarrassment every time he looked at her. If he had ever been that infantile he would rather have left the dirty traces of it buried forever.

He kept booting them into the corridor but they drifted in at night like poor relations. The talked incessantly, and always about him. The things they knew! They seemed to have a very low opinion of him. The snake often expressed the opinion that Fingal would never amount to anything because he had so docilely accepted the results of the aptitude tests he took as a child. That hurt, but the best salve for the wound was further study.

Finally a letter came. He winced as soon as he got it open. The salutation was enough to tell him he wasn't going to like it.

Dear Mr. Fingal,

I won't apologize for the delay this time. It seems that most of my manifestations have included an apology and I feel I deserved a rest this time. I can't be always on call. I have a life of my own.

I understand that you have behaved in an exemplary manner since I last talked with you. You have ignored the inner workings of the computer just as I told you to do. I haven't been completely frank with you, and I will explain my reasons.

The hook-up between you and the computer is, and always has been, two-way. Our greatest fear at this end had been that you would begin interfering with the workings of the computer, to the great discomfort of everyone. Or that you would go mad and run amuck, perhaps wrecking the entire data system. We installed you in the computer as a humane necessity, because you would have died if we had not done so, though it would have cost you only two days of memories. But Kenya is in the business of selling memories, and holds them to be a sacred trust. It was a mix-up on the part of the Kenya Corporation that got you here in the first place, so we decided we should do everything we could for you.

But it was at great hazard to our operations at this end.

Once, about six months ago, you got tangled in the weather-control sector of the computer and set off a storm over Kilimanjaro that is still not fully under control. Several animals were lost.

I have had to fight the Board of Directors to keep you on-line, and several times the program was almost terminated. You know what that means.

Now, I've leveled with you. I wanted to from the start, but the people who own things around here were worried that you might start fooling around out of a spirit of vindictiveness if you knew these facts, so they were kept from you. You could still do a great deal of damage before we could shut you off. I'm laying it on the line now, with Directors chewing their nails over my shoulder. *Please* stay out of trouble.

On to the other matter.

I was afraid from the outset that what has happened might happen. For over a year I've been your only contact with the world outside. I've been the only other person in your universe. I would have to be an extremely cold, hateful, awful person—which I am not—for you *not* to feel affection for me under those circumstances. You are suffering from intense sensory-deprivation and it's well-known that someone in that state becomes pliable, suggestible, and lonely. You've attached your feelings to me as the only thing around worth caring for.

I've tried to avoid intimacy with you for that reason, to keep things firmly on the last-name basis. But I relented during one of your periods of despair. And you read into my letters some things that were not there. Remember, even in the printed medium it is your mind that controls what you see. Your censor has let through what it wanted to see and maybe even added some things of its own. I'm at your mercy. For all I know, you may be reading this letter as a passionate affirmation of love. I've added every reinforcement I know of to make sure the message comes through on a priority channel and is not garbled. I'm sorry to hear that you love me. I do not, repeat not, love you in return. You'll understand why, at least in part, when we get you out of there.

It will never work, Mr. Fingal. Give up.

Apollonia Joachim

Fingal graduated first in his class. He had finished the required courses for his degree during the last long week after his letter from Apollonia. It was a bitter victory for him, marching up to the stage to accept the sheepskin, but he clutched it to him fiercely. At least he had made the most of his situation, at least he had not meekly let the wheels of the machine chew him up like a good worker.

He reached out to grasp the hand of the college president and saw it transformed. He looked up and saw the bearded, robed figure flow and writhe and become a tall, uniformed woman. With a surge of joy, he knew who it was. Then the joy became ashes in his mouth, which he hurriedly spit out.

"I always knew you'd choke on a figure of speech," she said, laughing tiredly.

"You're here," he said. He could not quite believe it. He stared dully at her, grasping her hand and the diploma with equal tenacity. She was tall, as the prophecy had said, and handsome. Her hair was cropped short over a capable face, and the body beneath the uniform was muscular. The uniform was open at the throat, and wrinkled. There were circles under her eyes, and the eyes were bloodshot. She swayed slightly on her feet.

"I'm here, all right. Are you ready to go back?" She turned to the assembled students. "How about it, gang? Do you think he deserves to go back?"

The crowd went wild, cheering and tossing mortarboards into the air. Fingal turned dazedly to look at them, with a dawning realization. He looked down at the diploma.

"I don't know," he said. "I don't know. Back to work at the data room?"

She clapped him on the back.

"No. I promise you that."

"But how could it be different? I've come to think of this piece of paper as something . . . real. Real! How could I have deluded myself like that? Why did I accept it?"

"I helped you along," she said. "But it wasn't all a game. You really did learn all the things you learned. It won't go away when you return. That thing in your hand is imaginary, for sure, but who do you think prints the real ones? You're registered where it counts—in the computer—as having passed all the courses. You'll get a real diploma when you return."

Fingal wavered. There was a tempting vision in his head. He'd been here for over a year and had never really exploited the nature of the place. Maybe that business about dying in the memory bank was all a shuck, another lie invented to keep him in his place. In that case, he could remain here and satisfy his wildest desires, become king of the universe with no opposition, wallow in pleasure no emperor ever imagined. Anything he wanted here he could have, anything at all.

And he really felt he might pull it off. He'd noticed many things about this place, and now had the knowledge of computer technology to back him up. He could squirm around and evade their attempts to erase him, even survive if they removed his cube by programming himself into other parts of the computer. He could do it.

With a sudden insight he realized that he had no desires wild enough to keep him here in his navel. He had only one major desire right now, and she was slowly fading out. A lap-dissolve was replacing her with the old college president.

"Coming?" she asked.

"Yes." It was as simple as that. The stage, president, students, and auditorium faded out and the computer room at Kenya faded in. Only Apollonia remained constant. He held onto her hand until everything stabilized.

"Whew," she said, and reached around behind her head. She pulled out a wire from her occipital plug and collapsed into a chair. Someone pulled a similar wire from Fingal's head, and he was finally free of the computer.

Apollonia reached out for a steaming cup of coffee, on a table littered with empty cups.

"You were a tough nut," she said. "For a minute I thought you'd stay. It happened once. You're not the first to have this happen to you, but you're no more than the twentieth. It's an unexplored area. Dangerous."

"Really?" he said. "You weren't just saying that?"

"No," she laughed. "Now the truth can be told. It *is* dangerous. No one had ever survived more than three hours in that kind of cube, hooked into a computer. You went for six. You *do* have a strong world-picture."

She was watching him to see how he reacted to this. She was not surprised to see him accept it readily.

"I should have known that," he said. "I should have thought of it. It was only six hours out here, and more than a year for me. Computers think faster. Why didn't I see that?"

"I helped you not see it," she admitted. "Like the push I gave you not to question why you were studying so hard. Those two orders worked a lot better than some of the orders I gave you."

She yawned again, and it seemed to go on forever.

"See, it was pretty hard for me to interface with you for six hours straight. No one's ever done it before, it can get to be quite a strain. So we've both got something to be proud of."

She smiled at him but it faded when he did not return it.

"Don't look so hurt, Fingal . . . what *is* your first name? I knew it, but erased it early in the game."

"Does it matter?"

"I don't know. Surely you must see why I haven't fallen in love with you, though you may be a perfectly lovable person. I haven't had *time.* It's been a very long six hours, but it was still only six hours. What can I do?"

Fingal's face was going through awkward changes as he absorbed that. Things were not so bleak after all.

"You could go to dinner with me."

"I'm already emotionally involved with someone else, I should warn you of that."

"You could still go to dinner. You haven't been exposed to my new determination. I'm going to really make a case."

She laughed warmly and got up. She took his hand.

"You know, it's possible that you might succeed. Just don't put wings on me again, all right? You'll never get anywhere like that."

"I promise. I'm through with visions—for the rest of my life."

Jonathan Lethem

Walking the Moons

Jonathan Lethem has published short fiction in Asimov's, Interzone, Universe 2, Journal Wired, Fantasy and Science Fiction, Pulphouse, *and* New Pathways. *He works in a bookstore in Berkeley, California, and has written lyrics for three rock bands.*

This story "struck a nerve," as the author put it, winning a place in Gardner Dozois' Best of the Year. *A lot of stories portray virtual reality as flashy and romantic and indistinguishable from real life. This isn't one of them.*

"Look," says the mother of The Man Who Is Walking Around The Moons Of Jupiter, "he's going so fast." She snickers to herself and scuttles around the journalist to a table littered with wiring tools and fragmented mechanisms. She loops a long, tangled cord over her son's intravenous tube and plugs one end into his headset, jostling him momentarily as she works it into the socket. His stride on the treadmill never falters. She runs the cord back to a modified four-track recorder sitting in the dust of the garage floor, then picks up the recorder's microphone and switches it on.

"Good morning, Mission Commander," she says.

"Yes," grunts The Man Who, his slack jaw moving beneath the massive headset. It startles the journalist to hear the voice of The Man Who boom out into the tiny garage.

"Interview time, Eddie."

"Who?"

"Mr. Kaffey. *Systems* Magazine, remember?"

"O.K.," says Eddie, The Man Who. His weakened, pallid body trudges forward. He is clothed only in jockey undershorts and orthopedic sandals, and the journalist can see his heart beat beneath the skin of his chest.

The Mother Of smiles artificially and hands the journalist the microphone. "I'll leave you boys alone," she says. "If you need anything, just yodel."

She steps past the journalist, over the cord, and out into the sunlight, pulling the door shut behind her.

The journalist turns to the man on the treadmill.

"Uh, Eddie?"

"Yeah."

"Uh, I'm Ron Kaffey. Is this O.K.? Can you talk?"

"Mr. Kaffey, I've got nothing but time." The Man Who smacks his lips and tightens his grip on the railing before him. The tread rolls away steadily beneath his feet, taking him nowhere.

The journalist covers the mike with the palm of his hand and clears his throat, then begins again. "So you're out there now. On Io. Walking."

"Mr. Kaffey, I'm currently broadcasting my replies to your questions from a valley on the northwestern quadrant of Io, yes. You're coming in loud and clear. No need to raise your voice. We're fortunate in having a pretty good connection, a good Earth-to-Io hookup, so to speak." The journalist watches as The Man Who moistens his lips, then dangles his tongue in the open air. "Please feel free to shoot with the questions, Mr. Kaffey. This is pretty uneventful landscape even by Io standards and I'm just hanging on your every word."

"Explain to me," says the journalist, "what you're doing."

"Ah. Well, I designed the rig myself. Took pixel satellite photographs and fed them into my simulator, which gives me a steadily unfolding virtual-space landscape." He reaches up and taps at his headset. "I log the equivalent mileage at the appropriate gravity on my treadmill and pretty soon I've had the same experience an astronaut would have. If we could afford to send them up anymore. Heh." He scratches violently at his ribs, until they flush pink. "Ask me questions," he says. "I'm ready at this end. You want me to describe what I'm seeing?"

"Describe what you're seeing."

"The desert, Mr. Kaffey. God, I'm so goddamned bored of the desert. That's all there is, you know. There isn't any atmosphere. We'd hope for some atmosphere, we had some hopes, but it didn't turn out that way. Nope. The dust all lays flat here, because of that. I try kicking it up, but there isn't any wind." The Man Who scuffs in his Dr. Scholl's sandals at the surface of the treadmill, booting imaginary pebbles, stirring up nonexistent dust. "You probably know I can't see Jupiter right now. I'm on the other side, so I'm pretty much out here alone under the stars. There isn't any point in my describing *that* to you."

The Man Who scratches again, this time at the patch where the intravenous tube intersects his arm, and the journalist is afraid he'll tear it off. "Bored?" asks the journalist.

"Yeah. Next time I think I'll walk across a grassy planet. What do you think of that? Or across the Pacific Ocean. On the bottom, I mean. 'Cause they're mapping it with ultrasound. Feed it into the simulator. Take me a couple of weeks. Nothing like this shit.

"I'm thinking more in terms of smaller scale walks from here on in, actually. Get back down to earth, find ways to make it count for more. You know what I mean? Maybe even the ocean isn't such a good idea, actually. Maybe my fans can't really identify with my off-world walks, maybe they're feeling, who knows, a little, uh, alienated by this Io thing. I know I am. I feel out of touch, Mr. Kaffey. Maybe I ought to walk across the cornbelt or the sunbelt or something. A few people in cars whizzing past, waving at me, and farmer's wives making me picnic lunches, because they've heard I'm passing through. I could program that. I could have every goddamn Mayor from Pinole to Akron give me the key to their goddamn city."

"Sounds O.K., Eddie."

"Sounds O.K.," echoes The Man Who. "But maybe even that's a little much. Maybe I ought to walk across the street to the drugstore for a pack of gum. You don't happen to have a stick of gum in your pocket, Mr. Journalist? I'll just open my mouth and you stick it in. I trust you. We don't have to tell my mother. If you hear her coming you just let me know, and I'll swallow it. You won't get in any trouble."

"I don't have any," says the journalist.

"Ah well."

The Man Who walks on, undaunted. Only now something is wrong. There's a hiss of escaping liquid, and the journalist is certain that The Man Who's nutrient serum is leaking from his arm. Then he smells the urine and sees the undershorts of The Man Who staining dark, and adhering to the cave-white flesh of his thigh.

"What's the matter, Kaffey? No more questions?"

"You've wet yourself," says the journalist.

"Oh, damn. Uh, you better call my mom."

But The Mother Of has already sensed that something is amiss. She steps now back into the garage, smoking a cigarette and squinting into the darkness at her son. She frowns as she discerns the stain, and takes a long drag on her cigarette, closing her eyes.

"I guess you're thinking that there might not be a story here," says The Man Who. "Least not the story you had in mind."

"Oh no, I wouldn't say that," says the journalist quickly. He's not sure if he hasn't detected a note of sarcasm in the voice of The Man Who by now. "I'm sure we can work something up."

"Work something up," parrots The Man Who. The Mother Of has his shorts down now, and she's swabbing at his damp flank with a paper towel. The Man Who sets his mouth in a grim smile and trudges forward. He's not here, really. He's out on Io, making tracks. He's going to be in the Guiness Book of World Records.

The journalist sets the microphone back down in the dust and packs his bag. As he walks the scrubby driveway back to the street he hears The Man Who Is Walking Around The Moons Of Jupiter, inside the garage, coughing on cigarette fumes.

Michael Kandel

Virtual Reality

Michael Kandel has gained critical acclaim for his translations of Stanislaw Lem's works—two of which were nominated for National Book Awards—and was a finalist in 1991 for the John W. Campbell Award for Best New Writer. His third and most recent novel, Captain Jack Zodiac, *a hilarious satire on all the ills of our century, was described by Paul D. Philippo a having a "consistency of craziness and synergy of riffs." Kandel currently works as an editor for Harcourt Brace Jovanovich, where he has worked with such writers as Umberto Eco, Mark Helprin, and James Morrow.*

The following story gives new meaning to the old cliche, "This is not what it looks like."

James Pokelogan came home early one day and found his wife, Louise, in bed with a large man.

"This is not what it looks like," she said, smoothing her hair with one hand, smoothing the sheet with the other. She was a little out of breath. "José," she explained, "is a simulation."

"A what?" asked James.

"A simulation. He's not real."

"He looks real to me."

José, sitting up in bed, had the shoulders of a wrestler but was rather flabby, saggy, in the chest, belly, and hip areas. There was a mole on his neck. He gave James a grin, as if the two men were old buddies and their unexpected meeting like this a terrific joke.

The room smelled a little like a gym.

"He looks real to me," James repeated.

"That's because of all the pixels," said Louise Pokelogan.

"Pixels?"

"He's computer-generated."

"You could have fooled me," said James.

"Yes, I know. It's amazing. The technology."

James was so discombobulated by all this that he forgot to ask his wife later, at the supper table, what she had been doing, anyway, in bed with a computer simulation, and why the simulation's name was José.

José didn't exactly have a computer ring to it.

Was Louise happy with her marriage? he asked himself that night, staring at the ceiling. Perhaps they should go out more. Perhaps he should buy her candy now and then, or flowers. Put a little romance back in their life.

The next day, he came home with a bunch of red carnations. Suddenly suspicious, however, he let himself in quietly and tiptoed to the bedroom.

Sure enough: there they were again, and going at it hammer and tongs. This is what porno movies were probably like, James Pokelogan thought. Grunts, moans, the bed creaking, the usual piston action. In and out, in and out. Except the man wasn't José.

"What the hell," said James in the doorway, holding the red carnations and feeling like the world's biggest jerk.

"Oh," said Louise. She had difficulty untangling herself, this time apparently caught right *in medias res.*

There was drool on her cheek, drool on one of her breasts, and as the couple hurriedly, awkwardly disengaged, James couldn't help seeing out of the corner of his eye, amid the confusion of limbs, the kind of whang you might expect to see on a camel or a yak at the zoo, but not on a human being. Enormous.

"This is Caetano," Louise told her husband, swallowing hard. She dimpled her cheeks so she wouldn't pant as she spoke. "He's the exterminator. That problem we've been having with squirrels, then wasps, in the crawlspace?"

"I come home—" James began.

"Please don't jump," his wife said, "to conclusions. There's a very simple explanation."

"You're not going to tell me this guy is a—"

"Caetano is here, I'm not."

James opened his mouth, closed his mouth, squinted. "What do you mean?"

"Caetano's here to do the exterminating. I'm not here."

"You're not here?"

"No, my simulation let him in."

"Your simulation?"

"Yes."

As James, frowning, puzzled this over, Caetano pulled up his drawers and said: "Look, Mr. Pokelogan, I can come back later."

"You're not here?" James asked his wife.

"No," she said. "I'm out shopping. I can't be in two places at the same time, you know."

James nodded slowly. That was perfectly true. But, then, what the hell was the exterminator doing in bed with a simulation of James's wife? A very lifelike simulation, too. Every detail correct, even the pale appendectomy scar.

The technology certainly was amazing. Today's computers.

"Maybe we should go to a marriage counselor," he muttered into the air, to no one in particular, since his wife, as she said, was not there, was only virtually there, and he didn't know this Caetano character from Adam.

Did she get him out of the Yellow Pages or what?

James went to see Frances Hogben, Louise's lifelong friend.

"Tell me honestly," he asked. "Do you think Louise, well, do you think maybe she no longer loves me?"

Frances smoked with an unusually long pink cigarette holder that made James think of whangs in flagrante, and she wore lots of trendy Third World bead things. He had never really liked Frances, but she knew Louise thoroughly, since Girls' State, if not before, and it was a point of honor with her always to call a spade a spade.

"Of course she loves you," she said, puffing, lifting her arm in one of those meaningless theatrical gestures typical of her. Frances didn't shave her armpits or use a deodorant. An arch, ironic smile. Light blue lipstick.

"Thanks, Frances," he said.

James Pokelogan bought his wife a box of imported assorted chocolates the following day.

This time, too, on a sudden stab of suspicion, he didn't knock or ring the bell but let himself in, turning the key slowly-slowly, and held his breath as he approached the bedroom on tiptoe. Such silence was completely unnecessary. Over the noise they were making, they wouldn't have heard him if he had come clomping in with hobnail boots or wood sandals.

They didn't hear him gasp, didn't hear him drop the box of chocolates in the doorway.

They were not two. Five, no, six of them, maybe seven filled the bed, spilled off the bed, and Louise Pokelogan was right in the thick of it, doing everything imaginable X-rated and all at the same time, with whangs everywhere you looked, all larger than life by a factor of ten.

James blinked, stunned.

His wife noticed him finally. A flicker of alarm. Then she managed a slight apologetic smile. Pulled herself together. Went to smooth her hair—but there was jism all over her hand. In her hair, too. Yuck.

The room smelled like a barn.

"And how do you explain *this*?" James asked in a squeak.

"Dear," Louise said, clearing her throat. She could speak only with an effort. "Dear, this is, ah, Dragomir, Paul . . . Zeke, Josh . . . Boffo."

Each man, as he was introduced, nodded and watched James gravely, as if this were a lecture hall.

"And I suppose you're going to tell me—"

"Oh no," said Louise, "we're all here."

"You're all here."

"Yes, this time you're the one that's not."

James had to run that one past himself three or four times. "I'm not here."

"No."

"How is it that I'm not here," he asked carefully, "if I think I am?"

"Simple," said his wife. "You're a simulation."

"I'm a simulation?"

"Yes."

He flexed his fingers, wriggled his toes in their shoes. "I don't feel like a simulation." He looked at and touched his wedding ring. "This certainly doesn't feel like a simulation." It felt like gold. And the chocolates scattered on the floor, one of them crushed and oozing cherry syrup, were they supposed to be—what was it—pixels? 3-D graphics? But how were 3-D graphics possible? Didn't you need special glasses?

His wife smiled. "Simulations are wraparound now, dear. All the companies, following Japan's lead, have gone laser holo."

"Yes," said the naked man called Dragomir, annoyingly lean and rugged. "I know a little about it. They have these feedback interfacing devices that respond to the direction your eyes move. It's very sophisticated programming."

"Heuristic algorithms," said another of the lovers, Paul, who evidently knew more than a little about it.

Zeke and Boffo nodded, smiled. They were up on it too.

And the whangs on them.

What whangs.

"I have just one question," said James Pokelogan in a choked voice, feeling within himself a rising frustration, an aggrieved exasperation. "If I'm not here, but you and these men all are, then what the holy hell are you doing, Louise, in bed with them?"

But what really hurt, what really rankled, was the fact that everyone nowadays seemed so damned comfortable with this virtual reality stuff, while he still had trouble, even broke into a sweat, when it was necessary to change numbers in the memory of his telephone or set up the VCR to record a show the following evening if they were going out.

It made a man feel . . . well, it made a man feel awfully inadequate.

Michael Swanwick and William Gibson

Dogfight

This tightly woven story is the collaboration of two intense, visionary writers. Michael Swanwick recently won the Nebula Award for his novel Stations of the Tide *(1992), and has also received the Theodore Sturgeon Memorial Award. His beautifully crafted works have gotten high praise for their originality and diversity—his books have been classified in genres from cyberpunk to fantasy.*

William Gibson received the Nebula and the Philip K. Dick Memorial Award for his high-tech, dizzyingly complex first novel, Neuromancer *(1984), which is generally acknowledged to be the definitive cyberpunk novel. Gibson's work has inspired many real-life programmers, hackers, and virtual reality innovators.*

Virtual reality games already exist, so it's only a matter of time before they become available and affordable. "Dogfight" is a disturbing look at games of the future; as you'll see, it's also a story about choices.

He meant to keep on going, right down to Florida. Work passage on a gunrunner, maybe wind up conscripted into some ratass rebel army down in the war zone. Or maybe, with that ticket good as long as he didn't stop riding, he'd just never get off—Greyhound's Flying Dutchman. He grinned at his faint reflection in cold, greasy glass while the downtown lights of Norfolk slid past, the bus swaying on tired shocks as the driver slung it around a final corner. They shuddered to a halt in the terminal lot, concrete lit gray and harsh like a prison exercise yard. But Deke was watching himself starve, maybe in some snowstorm out of Oswego, with his cheek pressed up against that same bus window, and seeing his remains swept out at the next stop by a muttering old man in faded coveralls. One way or the other, he decided, it didn't mean shit to him. Except his legs seemed to have died already. And the driver called a twenty-minute stopover—Tidewater Station, Virginia. It was an old cinder-block building with two entrances to each rest room, holdover from the previous century.

Legs like wood, he made a halfhearted attempt at ghosting the notions counter, but the black girl behind it was alert, guarding the sparse contents of the old glass case as though her ass depended on it. *Probably does,* Deke thought, turning away. Opposite the washrooms, an open doorway offered GAMES, the word flickering feebly in biofluorescent plastic. He could see a crowd of the local kickers clustered around a pool table. Aimless, his boredom following him like a cloud, he stuck his head in. And saw a biplane, wings no longer than his thumb, blossom bright orange flame. Corkscrewing, trailing smoke, it vanished the instant it struck the green-felt field of the table.

"Tha's right, Tiny," a kicker bellowed, "you *take* the sumbitch!"

"Hey," Deke said. "What's going on?"

The nearest kicker was a bean pole with a black mesh

Peterbilt cap. "Tiny's defending the Max," he said, not taking his eyes from the table.

"Oh, yeah? What's that?" But even as he asked, he saw it: a blue enamel medal shaped like a Maltese cross, the slogan *Pour le Mérite* divided among its arms.

The Blue Max rested on the edge of the table, directly before a vast and perfectly immobile bulk wedged into a fragile-looking chrome-tube chair. The man's khaki work shirt would have hung on Deke like the folds of a sail, but it bulged across that bloated torso so tautly that the buttons threatened to tear away at any instant. Deke thought of southern troopers he'd seen on his way down; of that weird, gut-heavy endotype balanced on gangly legs that looked like they'd been borrowed from some other body. Tiny might look like that if he stood, but on a larger scale—a forty-inch jeans inseam that would need a woven-steel waistband to support all those pounds of swollen gut. If Tiny were ever to stand at all—for now Deke saw that that shiny frame was actually a wheelchair. There was something disturbingly childlike about the man's face, an appalling suggestion of youth and even beauty in features almost buried in fold and jowl. Embarrassed, Deke looked away. The other man, the one standing across the table from Tiny, had bushy sideburns and a thin mouth. He seemed to be trying to push something with his eyes, wrinkles of concentration spreading from the corners. . . .

"You dumbshit or what?" The man with the Peterbilt cap turned, catching Deke's Indo proleboy denims, the brass chains at his wrists, for the first time. "Why don't you get your ass lost, fucker. Nobody wants your kind in here." He turned back to the dogfight.

Bets were being made, being covered. The kickers were producing the hard stuff, the old stuff, liberty-headed dollars and Roosevelt dimes from the stamp-and-coin stores, while more cautious bettors slapped down antique paper dollars laminated in clear plastic. Through the haze came a trio of red planes, flying in formation. Fokker D VIIs. The room fell silent. The Fokkers banked majestically under the solar orb of a two-hundred-watt bulb.

The blue Spad dove out of nowhere. Two more plunged from the shadowy ceiling, following closely. The kickers swore, and one chuckled. The formation broke wildly. One Fokker dove almost to the felt, without losing the Spad on its tail. Furiously, it zigged and zagged across the green flatlands but to no avail. At last it pulled up, the enemy hard after it, too steeply—and stalled, too low to pull out in time.

A stack of silver dimes was scooped up.

The Fokkers were outnumbered now. One had two Spads on its tail. A needle-spray of tracers tore past its cockpit. The Fokker slip-turned right, banked into an Immelmann, and was behind one of its pursuers. It fired, and the biplane fell, tumbling.

"Way to go, Tiny!" The kickers closed in around the table.

Deke was frozen with wonder. It felt like being born all over again.

Frank's Truck Stop was two miles out of town on the Commercial Vehicles Only route. Deke had tagged it, out of idle habit, from the bus on the way in. Now he walked back between the traffic and the concrete crash guards. Articulated trucks went slamming past, big eight-segmented jobs, the wash of air each time threatening to blast him over. CVO stops were easy makes. When he sauntered into Frank's, there was nobody to doubt that he'd come in off a big rig, and he was able to browse the gift shop as slowly as he liked. The wire rack with the projective wetware wafers was located between a stack of Korean cowboy shirts and a display for Fuzz Buster mudguards. A pair of Oriental dragons twisted in the air over the rack, either fighting or fucking, he couldn't tell which. The game he wanted was there: a wafer labeled SPADS&FOKKERS. It took him three seconds to boost it and less time to slide the magnet—which the cops in D.C. hadn't even bothered to confiscate—across the universal security strip.

On the way out, he lifted two programming units and a little Batang facilitator-remote that looked like an antique hearing aid.

He chose a highstack at random and fed the rental agent the line he'd used since his welfare rights were yanked. Nobody ever checked up; the state just counted occupied rooms and paid.

The cubicle smelled faintly of urine, and someone had scrawled Hard Anarchy Liberation Front slogans across the walls. Deke kicked trash out of a corner, sat down, back to the wall, and ripped open the wafer pack.

There was a folded instruction sheet with diagrams of loops, rolls, and Immelmanns, a tube of saline paste, and a computer list of operational specs. And the wafer itself, white plastic with a blue biplane and logo on one side, red on the other. He turned it over and over in his hand: SPADS&FOKKERS, FOKKERS&SPADS. Red or blue. He fitted the Batang behind his ear after coating the inductor surface with paste, jacked its fiberoptic ribbon into the programmer, and plugged the programmer into the wall current. Then he slid the wafer into the programmer. It was a cheap set, Indonesian, and the base of his skull buzzed uncomfortably as the program ran. But when it was done, a sky-blue Spad darted restlessly through the air a few inches from his face. It almost glowed, it was so real. It had the strange inner life that fanatically detailed museum-grade models often have, but it took all of his concentration to keep it in existence. If his attention wavered at all, it lost focus, fuzzing into a pathetic blur.

He practiced until the battery in the earset died, then slumped against the wall and fell asleep. He dreamed of flying, in a universe that consisted entirely of white clouds and blue sky, with no up and down, and never a green field to crash into.

He woke to a rancid smell of frying krillcakes and winced with hunger. No cash, either. Well, there were plenty of student types in the stack. Bound to be one who'd like to score a programming unit. He hit the hall with the boosted spare. Not far down was a door with a poster on it: THERE'S A HELL OF A GOOD UNIVERSE NEXT DOOR. Under that was a starscape with a cluster of multicolored pills, torn from an ad for some pharmaceutical company, pasted over an inspirational shot of the "space colony" that had been under construction since before he was born. LET'S GO, the poster said, beneath the collaged hypnotics.

He knocked. The door opened, security slides stopping it at a two-inch slice of girlface. "Yeah?"

"You're going to think this is stolen." He passed the programmer from hand to hand. "I mean because it's new, virtual cherry, and the bar code's still on it. But listen, I'm not gonna argue the point. No. I'm gonna let you have it for only like half what you'd pay anywhere else."

"Hey, wow, *really*, no kidding?" The visible fraction of mouth twisted into a strange smile. She extended her hand, palm up, a loose fist. Level with his chin. "Lookahere!"

There was a hole in her hand, a black tunnel that ran right up her arm. Two small red lights. Rat's eyes. They scurried toward him—growing, gleaming. Something gray streaked forward and leaped for his face.

He screamed, throwing hands up to ward it off. Legs twisting, he fell, the programmer shattering under him.

Silicate shards skittered as he thrashed, clutching his head. Where it hurt, it hurt—it hurt very badly indeed.

"Oh, my God!" Slides unsnapped, and the girl was hovering over him. "Here, listen, come on." She dangled a blue hand towel. "Grab on to this and I'll pull you up."

He looked at her through a wash of tears. Student. That fed look, the oversize sweatshirt, teeth so straight and white they could be used as a credit reference. A thin gold chain around one ankle (fuzzed, he saw, with baby-fine hair). Choppy Japanese haircut. Money. "That sucker was gonna be my dinner," he said ruefully. He took hold of the towel and let her pull him up.

She smiled but skittishly backed away from him. "Let me make it up to you," she said. "You want some food? It was only a projection, okay?"

He followed her in, wary as an animal entering a trap.

"Holy shit," Deke said, "this is *real cheese*. . . ." He was sitting on a gutsprung sofa, wedged between a four-foot teddy bear and a loose stack of floppies. The room was ankle-deep in books and clothes and papers. But the food she magicked up—Gouda cheese and tinned beef and honest-to-God greenhouse wheat wafers—was straight out of the Arabian Nights.

"Hey," she said. "We know how to treat a proleboy right, huh?" Her name was Nance Bettendorf. She was seventeen. Both her parents had jobs—greedy buggers—and she was an engineering major at William and Mary. She got top marks except in English. "I guess you must really have a thing about rats. You got some kind of phobia about rats?"

He glanced sidelong at her bed. You couldn't see it, really; it was just a swell in the ground cover. "It's not like that. It just reminded me of something else, is all."

"Like what?' She squatted in front of him, the big shirt riding high up one smooth thigh.

"Well . . . did you ever seen the—" his voice involuntarily rose and rushed past the words—"*Washington Monument?* Like at night? It's got these two little . . . red lights on top, aviation markers or something, and I, and I . . ." He started to shake.

"You're afraid of the Washington Monument?" Nance whooped and rolled over with laughter, long tanned legs kicking. She was wearing crimson bikini panties.

"I would die rather than look at it again," he said levelly.

She stopped laughing then, sat up, studied his face. White, even teeth worried at her lower lip, like she was dragging up something she didn't want to think about. At last she ventured, "Brainlock?"

"Yeah," he said bitterly. "They told me I'd never go back to D.C. And then the fuckers laughed."

"What did they get you for?"

"I'm a thief." He wasn't about to tell her that the actual charge was career shoplifting.

"Lotta old *computer* hacks spent their lives programming machines. And you know what? The human brain is not a goddamn bit like a machine, no way. They just don't program the same." Deke knew this shrill, desperate rap, this long, circular jive that the lonely string out to the rare listener; knew it from a hundred cold and empty nights spent in the company of strangers. Nance was lost in it, and Deke, nodding and yawning, wondered if he'd even be able to stay awake when they finally hit that bed of hers.

"I built that projection I hit you with myself," she said, hugging her knees up beneath her chin. "It's for muggers, you know? I just happened to have it on me, and I threw it at you 'cause I thought it was so funny, you trying to sell me that shit little Indojavanese programmer." She hunched forward and held out her hand again. "Look here." Deke cringed. "No, no, it's okay, I swear it, this is different." She opened her hand.

A single blue flame danced there, perfect and everchanging. "Look at that," she marveled. "Just look. I programmed that. It's not some diddly little seven-image job either. It's a continuous two-hour loop, seven thousand, two hundred seconds, never the same twice, each instant as individual as a fucking snowflake!"

The flame's core was glacial crystal, shards and facets flashing up, twisting and gone, leaving behind near-subliminal images so bright and sharp that they cut the eye. Deke winced. People mostly. Pretty little naked people, fucking. "How the hell did you do that?"

She rose, bare feet slipping on slick magazines, and melodramatically swept folds of loose printout from a raw plywood shelf. He saw a neat row of small consoles, austere and expensive-looking. Custom work. "This is the real stuff I got here. Image facilitator. Here's my fast-wipe module. This is a brain map one-to-one function analyzer." She sang off the names like a litany. "Quantum flicker stabilizer. Program splicer. An image assembler . . ."

"You need all that to make one little flame?"

"You betcha. This is all state of the art, professional projective wetware gear. It's years ahead of anything you've seen."

"Hey," he said, "you know anything about SPADS& FOKKERS?"

She laughed. And then, because he sensed the time was right, he reached out to take her hand.

"Don't you touch me, motherfuck, don't you *ever touch me!*" Nance screamed, and her head slammed against the wall as she recoiled, white and shaking with terror.

"Okay!" He threw up his hands. "Okay! I'm nowhere near you. Okay?"

She cowered from him. Her eyes were round and unblinking; tears built up at the corners, rolled down ashen cheeks. Finally, she shook her head. "Hey. Deke. Sorry. I should've told you."

"Told me what?" But he had a creepy feeling . . . already knew. The way she clutched her head. The weakly spasmodic way her hands opened and closed. "You got a brainlock, too."

"Yeah." She closed her eyes. "It's a chastity lock. My asshole parents paid for it. So I can't stand to have anybody touch me or even stand too close." Eyes opened in blind hate. "I didn't even *do* anything. Not a fucking thing. But they've both got jobs and they're so horny for me to have a career that they can't piss straight. They're afraid I'd neglect my studies if I got, you know, involved in sex and stuff. The day the brainlock comes off I am going to fuck the vilest, greasiest, hairiest . . ."

She was clutching her head again. Deke jumped up and rummaged through the medicine cabinet. He found a jar of B-complex vitamins, pocketed a few against need, and brought two to Nance, with a glass of water. "Here." He was careful to keep his distance. "This'll take the edge off."

"Yeah, yeah," she said. Then, almost to herself, "You must really think I'm a jerk."

The games room in the Greyhound station was almost empty. A lone, long-jawed fourteen-year-old was bent over a console, maneuvering rainbow fleets of submarines in the murky grid of the North Atlantic.

Deke sauntered in, wearing his new kicker drag, and leaned against a cinder-block wall made smooth by countless coats of green enamel. He'd washed the dye from his proleboy butch, boosted jeans and T-shirt from the Goodwill, and found a pair of stompers in the sauna locker of a highstack with cutrate security.

"Seen Tiny around, friend?"

The subs darted like neon guppies. "Depends on who's asking."

Deke touched the remote behind his left ear. The Spad snap-rolled over the console, swift and delicate as a dragonfly. It was beautiful; so perfect, so *true* it made the room seem an illusion. He buzzed the grid, millimeters from the glass, taking advantage of the programmed ground effect.

The kid didn't even bother to look up. "Jackman's," he

said. "Down Richmond Road, over by the surplus."

Deke let the Spad fade in midclimb.

Jackman's took up most of the third floor of an old brick building. Deke found Best Buy War Surplus first, then a broken neon sign over an unlit lobby. The sidewalk out front was littered with another kind of surplus—damaged vets, some of them dating back to Indochina. Old men who'd left their eyes under Asian suns squatted beside twitching boys who'd inhaled mycotoxins in Chile. Deke was glad to have the battered elevator doors sigh shut behind him.

A dusty Dr Pepper clock at the far side of the long, spectral room told him it was a quarter to eight. Jackman's had been embalmed twenty years before he was born, sealed away behind a yellowish film of nicotine, of polish and hair oil. Directly beneath the clock, the flat eyes of somebody's grandpappy's prize buck regarded Deke from a framed, blown-up snapshot gone the slick sepia of cockroach wings. There was the click and whisper of pool, the squeak of a work boot twisting on linoleum as a player leaned in for a shot. Somewhere high above the green-shaded lamps hung a string of crepe-paper Christmas bells faded to dead rose. Deke looked from one cluttered wall to the next. No facilitator.

"Bring one in, should we need it," someone said. He turned, meeting the mild eyes of a bald man with steel-rimmed glasses. "My name's Cline. Bobby Earl. You don't look like you shoot pool, mister." But there was nothing threatening in Bobby Earl's voice or stance. He pinched the steel frames from his nose and polished the thick lenses with a fold of tissue. He reminded Deke of a shop instructor who'd patiently tried to teach him retrograde biochip installation. "I'm a gambler,' he said, smiling. His teeth were white plastic. "I know I don't much look it."

"I'm looking for Tiny," Deke said.

"Well," replacing the glasses, "you're not going to find

him. He's gone up to Bethesda to let the V.A. clean his plumbing for him. He wouldn't fly against you anyhow."

"Why not?"

"Well, because you're not on the circuit or I'd know your face. You any good?" When Deke nodded, Bobby Earl called down the length of Jackman's, "Yo, Clarence! You bring out that facilitator. We got us a flyboy."

Twenty minutes later, having lost his remote and what cash he had left, Deke was striding past the broken soldiers of Best Buy.

"Now you let me tell you, boy," Bobby Earl had said in a fatherly tone as, hand on shoulder, he led Deke back to the elevator, "You're not going to win against a combat vet—you listening to me? I'm not even especially good, just an old grunt who was on hype fifteen, may be twenty times. Ol' Tiny, he was a *pilot*. Spent his entire enlistment hyped to the gills. He's got membrane attenuation real bad . . . you ain't never going to beat him."

It was a cool night. But Deke burned with anger and humiliation.

"Jesus, that's crude," Nance said as the Spad strafed mounds of pink underwear. Deke, hunched up on the couch, yanked her flashy little Braun remote from behind his ear.

"Now don't you get on my case too, Miss rich-bitch gonna-have-a-job—"

"Hey, lighten up! It's nothing to do with you—it's just *tech*. That's a really primitive wafer you got there. I mean, on the street maybe it's fine. But compared to the work I do at school, it's—hey. You ought to let me rewrite it for you."

"Say what?"

"Lemme beef it up. These suckers are all written in hexadecimal, see, 'cause the industry programmers are all washed-out computer hacks. That's how they think. But let me take it to the reader-analyzer at the department, run a few changes on it, translate it into a modern wetlanguage. Edit out all the redundant intermediaries. That'll goose up your reaction time, cut the feedback loop in half. So you'll fly faster and better. Turn you into a real pro, Ace!" She took a hit off her bong, then doubled over laughing and choking.

"Is that legit?" Deke asked dubiously.

"Hey, why do you think people buy gold-wire remotes? For the prestige? Shit. Conductivity's better, cuts a few nanoseconds off the reaction time. And reaction time is the name of the game, kiddo."

"No," Deke said. "If it were that easy, people'd already have it. Tiny Montgomery would have it. He'd have the best."

"Don't you ever *listen*?" Nance set down the bong; brown water slopped onto the floor. "The stuff I'm working with is three years ahead of anything you'll find on the street."

"No shit," Deke said after a long pause. "I mean, you can do that?"

It was like graduating from a Model T to a ninety-three Lotus. The Spad handled like a dream, responsive to Deke's slightest thought. For weeks he played the arcades, with not a nibble. He flew against the local teens and by ones and threes shot down their planes. He took chances, played flash. And the planes tumbled. . . .

Until one day Deke was tucking his seed money away, and a lanky black straightened up from the wall. He eyed the laminateds in Deke's hand and grinned. A ruby tooth gleamed. "You know," the man said, "I *heard* there was a casper who could fly, going up against the kiddies."

"Jesus," Deke said, spreading Danish butter on a kelp stick. "I wiped the *floor* with those spades. They were good, too."

"That's nice, honey," Nance mumbled. She was working on her finals project, sweating data into a machine.

"You know, I think what's happening is I got real talent for this kind of shit. You know? I mean, the program gives me an edge, but I got the stuff to take advantage of it. I'm really getting a rep out there, you know?" Impulsively, he snapped on the radio. Scratchy Dixieland brass blared.

"Hey," Nance said. "Do you *mind?*"

"No, I'm just—" He fiddled with the knobs, came up with some slow, romantic bullshit. "There. Come on, stand up. Let's dance."

"Hey, you know I can't—"

"Sure you can, sugarcakes." He threw her the huge teddy bear and snatched up a patchwork cotton dress from the floor. He held it by the waist and sleeve, tucking the collar under his chin. It smelled of patchouli, more faintly of sweat. "See, I stand over here, you stand over there. We dance. Get it?"

Blinking softly, Nance stood and clutched the bear tightly. They danced then, slowly, staring into each other's eyes. After a while, she began to cry. But still, she was smiling.

Deke was daydreaming, imagining he was Tiny Montgomery wired into his jumpjet. Imagined the machine responding to his slightest neural twitch, reflexes cranked *way* up, hype flowing steadily into his veins.

Nance's floor became jungle, her bed a plateau in the Andean foothills, and Deke flew his Spad at forced speed, as if it were a full-wired interactive combat machine. Computerized hypos fed a slow trickle of high-performance enhancement mélange into his bloodstream. Sensors were wired directly into his skull—pulling a supersonic snapturn in the green-blue bowl of sky over Bolivian rain forest. Tiny would have *felt* the airflow over control surfaces.

Below, grunts hacked through the jungle with hypepumps strapped above elbows to give them that little extra death-dance fury in combat, a shot of liquid hell in a blue plastic vial. Maybe they got ten minutes' worth in a week. But coming in at treetop level, reflexes cranked to the max, flying so low the ground troops never spotted you until you were on them, phosgene agents released, away and gone before they could draw a bead . . . it took a constant trickle of hype just to maintain. And the direct neuron interface with the jumpjet was a two-way street. The onboard computers monitored biochemistry and decided when to open the sluice gates and give the human component a killer jolt of combat edge.

Dosages like that ate you up. Ate you good and slow and constant, etching the brain surfaces, eroding away the brain-cell membranes. If you weren't yanked from the air promptly enough, you ended up with brain-cell attenuation—with reflexes too fast for your body to handle and your fight-or-flight reflexes fucked real good. . . .

"I aced it, proleboy!"

"Hah?" Deke looked up, startled, as Nance slammed in, tossing books and bag onto the nearest heap.

"My finals project—I got exempted from exams. The prof said he'd never seen anything like it. Uh, hey, dim the lights, wouldja? The colors are weird on my eyes."

He obliged. "So show me. Show me this wunnerful thing."

"Yeah, okay." She snatched up his remote, kicked clear standing space atop the bed, and struck a pose. A spark flared into flame in her hand. It spread in a quicksilver line up her arm, around her neck, and it was a snake, with triangular head and flickering tongue. Molten colors, oranges and reds. It slithered between her breasts. "I call it a firesnake," she said proudly.

Deke leaned close, and she jerked back.

"Sorry. It's like your flame, huh? I mean, I can see these tiny little fuckers in it."

"Sort of." The firesnake flowed down her stomach. "Next month I'm going to splice two hundred separate flame programs together with meld justification in between to get the visuals. Then I'll tap the mind's body image to make it self-orienting. So it can crawl all over your body without your having to mind it. You could wear it dancing."

"Maybe I'm dumb. But if you haven't done the work yet, how come I can see it?"

Nance giggled. "That's the best part—half the work isn't done yet. Didn't have time to assemble it into a unified program. Turn on that radio, huh? I want to dance." She kicked off her shoes. Deke tuned in something gutsy. Then, at Nance's urging, turned it down, almost to a whisper.

"I scored two hits of hype, see." She was bouncing on the bed, wearing her hands like a Balinese dancer. "Ever try the stuff? In-credible. Gives you like absolute concentration. Look here." She stood *en pointe*. "Never done that before."

"Hype," Deke said. "Last person I heard of got caught with that shit got three years in the infantry. How'd you score it?"

"Cut a deal with a vet who was in grad school. She bombed out last month. Stuff gives me perfect visualization. I can hold the projection with my eyes shut. It was a snap assembling the program in my head."

"On just two hits, huh?"

"One hit. I'm saving the other. Teach was so impressed he's sponsoring me for a job interview. A recruiter from I. G. Feuchtwaren hits campus in two weeks. That crap is gonna sell him the program *and* me. I'm gonna cut out of school two years early, straight into industry, do not pass jail, do not pay two hundred dollars."

The snake curled into a flaming tiara. It gave Deke a funny-creepy feeling to think of Nance walking out of his life.

"I'm a witch," Nance sang, "a wetware witch." She shucked her shirt over her head and sent it flying. Her fine, high breasts moved freely, gracefully, as she danced. "I'm gonna make it"—now she was singing a current pop hit—"to the . . . top!" Her nipples were small and pink and aroused. The firesnake licked at them and whipped away.

"Hey, Nance," Deke said uncomfortably. "Calm down a little, huh?"

"I'm celebrating!" She hooked a thumb into her shiny gold panties. Fire swirled around hand and crotch. "I'm a virgin goddess, baby, and I have the pow-er!" Singing again.

Deke looked away. "Gotta go now," he mumbled. Gotta go home and jerk off. He wondered where she'd hidden that second hit. Could be anywhere.

There was a protocol to the circuit, a tacit order of deference and precedence as elaborate as that of a Mandarin court. It didn't matter that Deke was hot, that his rep was spreading like wildfire. Even a name flyboy couldn't just challenge whom he wished. He had to climb the ranks. But if you flew every night. If you were always available to anybody's challenge. And if you were good . . . well, it was possible to climb fast.

Deke was one plane up. It was tournament fighting, three planes against three. Not many spectators, a dozen maybe, but it was a good fight, and they were noisy. Deke was immersed in the manic calm of combat when he realized suddenly that they had fallen silent. Saw the kickers stir and exchange glances. Eyes flicked past him. He heard the elevator doors close. Cooly, he disposed of the second of his opponent's planes, then risked a quick glance over his shoulder.

Tiny Montgomery had just entered Jackman's. The wheelchair whispered across browning linoleum, guided by tiny twitches of one imperfectly paralyzed hand. His expression was stern, blank, calm.

In that instant, Deke lost two planes. One to deresolution—gone to blur and canceled out by the facilitator—and the other because his opponent was a real fighter. Guy did a barrel roll, killing speed and slipping to the side, and strafed Deke's biplane as it shot past. It went down in flames. Their last two planes shared altitude and speed, and as they turned, trying for position, they naturally fell into a circling pattern.

The kickers made room as Tiny wheeled up against the table. Bobby Earl Cline trailed after him, lanky and casual. Deke and his opponent traded glances and pulled their machines back from the pool table so they could hear the man out. Tiny smiled. His features were small, clustered in the center of his pale, doughy face. One finger twitched slightly on the chrome headrest. "I heard about you." He looked straight at Deke. His voice was soft and shockingly sweet, a baby-girl little voice. "I heard you're good."

Deke nodded slowly. The smile left Tiny's face. His soft, fleshy lips relaxed into a natural pout, as if he were waiting for a kiss. His small, bright eyes studied Deke without malice. "Let's see what you can do, then."

Deke lost himself in the cool game of war. And when the enemy went down in smoke and flame, to explode and vanish against the table, Tiny wordlessly turned his chair, wheeled it into the elevator, and was gone.

As Deke was gathering up his winnings, Bobby Earl eased up to him and said, "The man wants to play you."

"Yeah?" Deke was nowhere near high enough on the circuit to challenge Tiny. "What's the scam?"

"Man who was coming up from Atlanta tomorrow canceled. Ol' Tiny, he was spoiling to go up against somebody new. So it looks like you get your shot at the Max."

"Tomorrow? Wednesday? Doesn't give me much prep time."

Bobby Earl smiled gently. "I don't think that makes no nevermind."

"How's that, Mr. Cline?"

"Boy, you just ain't got the *moves*, you follow me? Ain't got no surprises. You fly just like some kinda beginner, only faster and slicker. You follow what I'm trying to say?"

"I'm not sure I do. You want to put a little action on that?"

"Tell you truthful," Cline said, "I been hoping on that." He drew a small black notebook from his pocket and licked a pencil stub. "Give you five to one. They's nobody gonna give no fairer odds than that."

He looked at Deke almost sadly. "But Tiny, he's just naturally better'n you, and that's all she wrote, boy. He lives for that goddamned game, ain't *got* nothing else. Can't get out of that goddamned chair. You think you can best a man who's fighting for his life, you are just lying to yourself."

Norman Rockwell's portrait of the colonel regarded Deke dispassionately from the Kentucky Fried across Richmond Road from the coffee bar. Deke held his cup with hands that were cold and trembling. His skull hummed with fatigue. Cline was right, he told the colonel. I can go up against Tiny, but I can't win. The colonel stared back, gaze calm and level and not particularly kindly, taking in the coffee bar and Best Buy and all his drag-ass kingdom of Richmond Road. Waiting for Deke to admit to the terrible thing he had to do.

"The bitch is planning to leave me *any*way," Deke said aloud. Which made the black countergirl look at him funny, then quickly away.

"Daddy called!' Nance danced into the apartment, slamming the door behind her. "And you know what? He says if I can get this job and hold it for six months, he'll have the brainlock reversed. Can you *believe* it? Deke?" She hesitated. "You okay?"

Deke stood. Now that the moment was on him, he felt unreal, like he was in a movie or something. "How come you never came home last night?" Nance asked.

The skin on his face was unnaturally taut, a parchment mask. "Where'd you stash the hype, Nance? I need it."

"Deke," she said, trying a tentative smile that instantly vanished. "Deke, that's mine. My hit. I need it. For my interview."

He smiled scornfully. "You got money. You can always score another cap."

"Not by Friday! Listen, Deke, this is really important. My whole life is riding on this interview. I need that cap. It's all I got!"

"Baby, you got the fucking world! Take a look around you—six ounces of blond Lebanese hash! Little anchovy fish in tins. Unlimited medical coverage, if you need it." She was backing away from him, stumbling against the static waves of unwashed bedding and wrinkled glossy magazines that crested at the foot of her bed. "Me, I never had a glimmer of any of this. Never had the kind of edge it takes to get along. Well, this one time I am gonna. There is a match in two hours that I am going to fucking well win. Do you hear me?" He was working himself into a rage, and that was good. He needed it for what he had to do.

Nance flung up an arm, palm open, but he was ready for that and slapped her hand aside, never even catching a glimpse of the dark tunnel, let alone those little red eyes. Then they were both falling, and he was on top of her, her breath hot and rapid in his face. "Deke! Deke! I *need* that shit, Deke, my *interview,* it's the only . . . I gotta . . . gotta . . ." She twisted her face away, crying into the wall. "Please, God, please don't . . ."

"Where did you stash it?"

Pinned against the bed under his body, Nance began to spasm, her entire body convulsing in pain and fear.

"Where is it?"

Her face was bloodless, gray corpse flesh, and horror burned in her eyes. Her lips squirmed. It was too late to stop now; he'd crossed over the line. Deke felt revolted and nauseated, all the more so because on some unexpected and unwelcome level, he was *enjoying* this.

"Where is it, Nance?" And slowly, very gently, he began to stroke her face.

Deke summoned Jackman's elevator with a finger that moved as fast and straight as a hornet and landed daintily as a butterfly on the call button. He was full of bouncy energy, and it was all under control. On the way up, he whipped off his shades and chuckled at his reflection in the finger-smudged chrome. The blacks of his eyes were like pin-pricks, all but invisible, and still the world was neon bright.

Tiny was waiting. The cripple's mouth turned up at the corners into a sweet smile as he took in Deke's irises, the exaggerated calm of his motions, the unsuccessful attempt to mime an undrugged clumsiness. "Well," he said in that girlish voice, "looks like I have a treat in store for me."

The Max was draped over one tube of the wheelchair. Deke took up position and bowed, not quite mockingly. "Let's fly." As challenger, he flew defense. He materialized his planes at a conservative altitude, high enough to dive, low enough to have warning when Tiny attacked. He waited.

The crowd tipped him. A fatboy with brilliantined hair looked startled, a hollow-eyed cracker started to smile. Murmurs rose. Eyes shifted slow-motion in heads frozen by hyped-up reaction time. Took maybe three nanoseconds to pinpoint the source of attack. Deke whipped his head up, and—

Sonofabitch, he was *blind!* The Fokkers were diving straight from the two-hundred-watt bulb, and Tiny had suckered him into staring right at it. His vision whited out. Deke squeezed lids tight over welling tears and frantically held visualization. He split his flight, curving two biplanes right, one left. Immediately twisting each a half-turn, then back again. He had to dodge randomly—he couldn't tell where the hostile warbirds were.

Tiny chuckled. Deke could hear him through the sounds of the crowd, the cheering and cursing and slapping down of coins that seemed to syncopate independent of the ebb and flow of the duel.

When his vision returned an instant later, a Spad was in flames and falling. Fokkers tailed his surviving planes, one on one and two on the other. Three seconds into the game and he was down one.

Dodging to keep Tiny from pinning tracers on him, he looped the single-pursued plane about and drove the other toward the blind spot between Tiny and the light bulb.

Tiny's expression went very calm. The faintest shadow of disappointment—of contempt, even—was swallowed up by tranquility. He tracked the planes blandly, waiting for Deke to make his turn.

Then, just short of the blind spot, Deke shoved his Spad into a dive, the Fokkers overshooting and banking wildly to either side, twisting around to regain position.

The Spad swooped down on the third Fokker, pulled into position by Deke's other plane. Fire strafed wings and crimson fuselage. For an instant nothing happened, and Deke thought he had a fluke miss. Then the little red mother veered left and went down, trailing black, oily smoke.

Tiny frowned, small lines of displeasure marring the perfection of his mouth. Deke smiled. One even, and Tiny held position.

Both Spads were tailed closely. Deke swung them wide, and then pulled them together from opposite sides of the table. He drove them straight for each other, neutralizing Tiny's advantage . . . neither could fire without endangering his own planes. Deke cranked his machines up to top speed, slamming them at each other's nose.

An instant before they crashed, Deke sent the planes over and under one another, opening fire on the Fokkers and twisting away. Tiny was ready. Fire filled the air. Then one blue and one red plane soared free, heading in opposite directions. Behind them, two biplanes tangled in midair. Wings touched, slewed about, and the planes crumpled. They fell together, almost straight down, to the green felt below.

Ten seconds in and four planes down. A black vet pursed his lips and blew softly. Someone else shook his head in disbelief.

Tiny was sitting straight and a little forward in his wheelchair, eyes intense and unblinking, soft hands plucking feebly at the grips. None of that amused and detached bullshit now; his attention was riveted on the game. The kickers, the table, Jackman's itself, might not exist at all for him. Bobby Earl Cline laid a hand on his shoulder; Tiny didn't notice. The planes were at opposite ends of the room, laboriously gaining altitude. Deke jammed his against the ceiling, dim through the smoky haze. He spared Tiny a quick glance, and their eyes locked. Cold against cold. "Let's see your best," Deke muttered through clenched teeth.

They drove their planes together.

The hype was peaking now, and Deke could see Tiny's tracers crawling through the air between the planes. He had to put his Spad into the line of fire to get off a fair burst, then twist and bank so the Fokker's bullets would slip by his undercarriage. Tiny was every bit as hot, dodging Deke's fire and passing so close to the Spad their landing gears almost tangled as they passed.

Deke was looping his Spad in a punishingly tight turn when the hallucinations hit. The felt writhed and twisted—became the green hell of Bolivian rain forest that Tiny had flown combat over. The walls receded to gray infinity, and he felt the metal confinement of a cybernetic jumpjet close in around him.

But Deke had done his homework. He was expecting the hallucinations and knew he could deal with them. The military would never pass on a drug that couldn't be fought through. Spad and Fokker looped into another pass. He could read the tensions in Tiny Montgomery's face, the echoes of combat in deep jungle sky. They drove their planes together, feeling the torqued tensions that fed straight from instrumentation to hindbrain, the adrenaline pumps kicking in behind the armpits, the cold, fast freedom of airflow over jet-skin mingling with the smells of hot metal and fear sweat. Tracers tore past his face, and he pulled back, seeing the Spad zoom by the Fokker again, both untouched. The kickers were just going ape, waving hats and stomping feet, acting like God's own fools. Deke locked glances with Tiny again.

Malice rose up in him, and though his every nerve was taut as the carbon-crystal whiskers that kept the jumpjets from falling apart in superman turns over the Andes, he counterfeited a casual smile and winked, jerking his head slightly to one side, as if to say "Lookahere."

Tiny glanced to the side.

It was only for a fraction of a second, but that was enough. Deke pulled as fast and tight an Immelmann—right on the edge of theoretical tolerance—as had ever been seen on the circuit, and he was hanging on Tiny's tail.

Let's see you get out of this one, sucker.

Tiny rammed his plane straight down at the green, and Deke followed after. He held his fire. He had Tiny where he wanted him.

Running. Just like he'd been on his every combat mission. High on exhilaration and hype, maybe, but running scared. They were down to the felt now, flying treetop-level. Break, Deke thought, and jacked up the speed. Peripherally, he could see Bobby Earl Cline, and there was a funny look on the man's face. A pleading kind of look. Tiny's composure was shot; his face was twisted and tormented.

Now Tiny panicked and dove his plane in among the crowd. The biplanes looped and twisted between the kickers. Some jerked back involuntarily, and others laughingly swatted at them with their hands. But there was a hot glint of terror in Tiny's eyes that spoke of an eternity of fear and confinement, two edges sawing away at each other endlessly. . . .

The fear was death in the air, the confinement a locking away in metal, first of the aircraft, then of the chair. Deke could read it all in his face: Combat was the only out Tiny had had, and he'd taken it every chance he got. Until some anonymous *nationalista* with an antique SAM tore him out of that blue-green Bolivian sky and slammed him straight down to Richmond Road and Jackman's and the smiling killer boy he faced this one last time across the faded cloth.

Deke rocked up on his toes, face burning with that million-dollar smile that was the trademark of the drug that had already fried Tiny before anyone ever bothered to blow him out of the sky in a hot tangle of metal and mangled flesh. It all came together then. He saw that flying was all that held Tiny together. That daily brush of fingertips against death, and then rising up from the metal coffin, alive again. He'd been holding back collapse by sheer force of will. Break that willpower, and mortality would come pouring out and drown him. Tiny would lean over and throw up in his own lap.

And Deke drove it home. . . .

There was a moment of stunned silence as Tiny's last plane vanished in a flash of light. "I did it," Deke whispered. Then, louder, "Son of a bitch, I did it!"

Across the table from him, Tiny twisted in his chair, arms jerking spastically; his head lolled over on one shoulder

Behind him, Bobby Earl Cline stared straight at Deke, his eyes hot coals.

The gambler snatched up the Max and wrapped its ribbon around a stack of laminateds. Without warning, he flung the bundle at Deke's face. Effortlessly, casually, Deke plucked it from the air.

For an instant, then, it looked like the gambler would come at him, right across the pool table. He was stopped by a tug on his sleeve. "Bobby Earl," Tiny whispered, his voice choking with humiliation, "you gotta get me . . . out of here. . . ."

Stiffly, angrily, Cline wheeled his friend around, and then away, into shadow.

Deke threw back his head and laughed. By God, he felt good! He stuffed the Max into a shirt pocket, where it hung cold and heavy. The money he crammed into his jeans. Man, he had to jump with it, his triumph leaping up through him like a wild thing, fine and strong as the flanks of a buck in the deep woods he'd seen from a Greyhound once, and for this one moment it seemed that everything was worth it somehow, all the pain and misery he'd gone through to finally win.

But Jackman's was silent. Nobody cheered. Nobody crowded around to congratulate him. He sobered, and silent, hostile faces swam into focus. Not one of these kickers was on his side. They radiated contempt, even hatred. For an interminably drawn-out moment the air trembled with potential violence . . . and then someone turned to the side, hawked up phlegm, and spat on the floor. The crowd broke up, muttering, one by one drifting into the darkness.

Deke didn't move. A muscle in one leg began to twitch, harbinger of the coming hype crash. The top of his head felt numb, and there was an awful taste in his mouth. For a second he had to hang on to the table with both hands to keep from falling down forever, into the living shadow beneath him, as he hung impaled by the prize buck's dead eyes in the photo under the Dr Pepper clock.

A little adrenaline would pull him out of this. He needed to celebrate. To get drunk or stoned and talk it up, going over the victory time and again, contradicting himself, making up details, laughing and bragging. A starry old night like this called for big talk.

But standing there with all of Jackman's silent and vast and empty around him, he realized suddenly that he had nobody left to tell it to.

Nobody at all.

M. Shayne Bell

The Shining Dream Road Out

M. Shayne Bell has published short stories and poetry in magazines such as Asimov's, Amazing, F&SF, *and* Starline, *and in numerous anthologies. His short fiction won him first place in the* Writers of the Future *contest in 1987 and a National Endowment for the Arts Fellowship in 1991. He recently finished editing an anthology called* Washed By a Wave of Wind *and is currently working on his second novel.*

Unlike many of sci-fi's hard-boiled antiheroes, Bell's characters are usually genuinely likable people who aren't defeated or corrupted by the problems of the world around them. His beautiful story, "Soft in the World, and Bright," about a paralyzed man who falls in love with an artificial intelligence in virtual reality, appears in the anthology Hotel Andromeda *edited by Jack L. Chalker and Martin H. Greenberg (Berkley Books, 1993). "The Shining Dream Road Out" presents an entirely different point of view on VR.*

So I buckled myself into the Driving-Simulation Unit and started connecting my head to Happy Pizza's central computer, which would connect up to Salt Lake County's virtual-reality road map of the valley, all the while looking around at the dump of a room I was in with its peeling paint on the walls and ceiling and the used pizza boxes thrown on the floor and the heat and the smell of garlic and onion in the air, but that box of a "car" I was getting into, that was beautiful to me, because I knew what it would soon turn into, and I was getting that hit-in-the-gut feeling of excitement I get just before I head out to drive and I wanted to laugh because I wasn't really going to leave the back room of Happy Pizza at all except through virtual reality in my mind, when the voice of Fat Joe, the owner of this particular franchise, came over the intercom:

"Ten minute run coming up, Clayton. If you beat your last time of 8:23 you got your raise."

Yeah, I thought, fifteen fucking cents more an hour. "So start the show," I said.

And a virtual-reality vision of southbound Interstate 15 settled over my mind: the section just past the 600 South on-ramp and the Salt Lake City skyscrapers east and the derelict houses west and a sunset shining red on rainclouds above and rain already spattering down on the windshield and I thought, great, I'm trying to get just fifteen cents more an hour out of a stupid pizza delivery job and they make it rain.

I turned on the wipers and the box I was sitting in looked to me like a car now, a nice little Japanese fast car that motored along just fine, and I punched it up to 80, even with the wet road: my tires had good traction and the road was rough enough in real-land to keep you from hydroplaning, though the city would never factor *that* into its VR road simulations no matter how many times I talked to them about it when they did their user surveys—it's like, did they really believe the state would ever get that road fixed?

But they must have, because in every simulation I was ever in, I-15 was smooth, and we'd drive along on top of it like we were driving on a dream road, and you'd start to understand why Fat Joe wouldn't spring for new shocks in our real cars, not if all he ever drove was this simulation and he thought the roads out there in real-land were this nice.

I punched up the coordinates of my run, and they glowed red digital out of the dash in the dim car, dim thanks to the rain, and I turned on my lights and thought how easy can Fat Joe make this: I-15 south to the 45th South exit, then west on 45 to the Holiday Inn, room 115? Easy run was right—it was too easy. I saw what was coming: there'd be cops along the way and stingy Fat Joe had known it, must have punched into the city files to see how many cops were on duty, maybe drove along a little on the road himself just to check it out, just to see if he could save fifteen cents an hour but happy that I'd learn more about the real-land roads and where the cops had their speed traps so I'd know exactly where to speed up and where to slow down when I was delivering pizza, and that hit-in-the-gut feeling of mine got tighter because I couldn't make 45 South doing 80 with cops on the road, so I braked my car down to 70 just to be safe, so I wouldn't get caught right away, and waited to pass the first speed trap coming up: 21st South, behind or in front of the railing along the merge lane—and sure enough, there he was, a cop just waiting for me to go by at 80 plus, but I was only doing 70 and nobody'd pull you over for that unless it was the end of the month and some cop hadn't met his quota yet.

Fat Joe must have been pissed: he'd thought a cop would get me right away, but now he'd have to sit in his VR getup, which he hated unless he were watching porn, and wait to see if one of the cops assigned to the net for a day could catch me on VR I-15, which I knew better than the back of my hand: once past the 21st South on-off ramps and speed trap I merged into the far right lane and shoved my car back up to 80—roadblock ahead, some old grandpa trying to pass the city sight requirements and motoring along just under 50 in a blue "Senior Driver" practice car—merge into the middle lane, still at 80, maybe plus—roadblock ahead, some trucker trying to get back a license after one too many speeding tickets—merge right again, back and forth, weaving in and out, always in the right two lanes, never in the far left, the fast lane, the lane cops looked in for speeders: if you weaved in and out in the slow lanes the cops would know somebody was going fast, but they wouldn't know who, the dots of the cars on their radar would all blend together if I merged in close, and sure they'd think it was probably the pizza delivery boy who'd been going a little fast when we passed them, not the old geezer trying to keep his car on the road and do minimum speed at the same time, but they wouldn't know it for sure, which meant they wouldn't come out—they'd wait for some sure prey—and you can bet I'd be a good little pizza delivery boy around all their traps.

And make my ten-minute delivery in under 8:23.

So I drove along, making good time, thinking there was a lot of traffic on VR I-15—was every trucker and school-bus driver and delivery boy out trying to pass some driving test or get a raise?—when this pretty lady in a green station wagon with peeling fake-wood side panels speeds by doing 90 who knows what—and there were these three little blonde-haired kids waving at me out of the back window.

Weird, I thought. And thank goodness it was just VR—it was one thing for me to drive like a maniac in VR or real-land, it was another for a mother with her kids. I hoped she'd use VR to work out whatever was eating at her and keep it down out there on real I-15. The kids kept waving, so I waved back and changed lanes into theirs and sped up to keep them company from behind—no speed trap till around the 33rd on-ramp anyway, our only danger would be roving cops—and we hit 93 miles an hour.

I started thinking, who is the lady driving the station wagon in light rain at 93 mph and when would the wagon's engine blow, because it could, even in VR, just to teach you a lesson. Only somebody with nothing to lose or hot food to deliver would pull stunts like this, and when you looked at it that way her speed kind of made sense: I'd heard of people coming out to check the simulation to see how well it worked, and those types would certainly have nothing to lose. So I thought maybe the lady in the station wagon is the mayor checking up on her VR cops and taking her kids for a joy-ride and seeing what her car should be able to do in theory, all at the same time—I imagined that's what somebody like her with a decent income and a crappy car so you wouldn't look high and mighty to the voters would do on an afternoon: hold the appointments, I've got important work coming through on the net; then connect up, swing by the house in VR to pick up your VR kids who'd plug in when you told them to, and off you'd go—and fuck the city budget crisis.

We started coming up on 33, and she braked, and I braked, and I thought this is a smart lady, she knows where the traps are, which of course a mayor would, and I merged over into the right lane and pulled up alongside her and looked over, but she didn't look at me: she just kept her eyes glued on the road and her hands held the wheel so tight I could see that her knuckles were white. It wasn't the mayor. Whoever it was, I thought she must have some kind of bad trouble in her life, and I couldn't figure out what she was doing out on VR I-15 like this.

I merged back behind a couple of Idaho Meat-Packers' trucks because I'd been part of a fast blip with that wagon for too long and I didn't want to be near her when we passed 33, and sure enough, another cop was waiting there looking confused about which of us had done what and I was happy to complicate his life—but he pulled out three cars behind me, and I didn't touch my brakes, just eased up on the gas a little, then a little more, not wanting to look the least bit guilty and thinking did he somehow figure out about me, and hardly daring to breathe because 45 was the next exit and I'd used up nearly 5:30 of my run and if I got a ticket I wouldn't get my raise for sure.

So I played the good little pizza delivery boy—I had no other choice—and I watched 45 come up ahead of us and the green station wagon take the exit and drive down the hill and I followed her off and the cop stayed out on I-15.

But the wagon sped up down below me, and I thought what's the lady doing? Before the intersection, she suddenly slammed brakes, which locked at that speed, and she slid to a stop blocking the exit, in front of a red light. Real good, lady, I thought, like, did she forget this wasn't the highway anymore, then suddenly remember? Well, she'd stopped before the red light, but any cop driving by would think the position of her car a little strange and maybe worth investigating. I hoped one wouldn't happen by and stop to check her out because I'd lost time trying to get around them.

I braked to a stop behind her and waited for the light to change—she could just pull out and go when it changed—but she didn't pull out, and her head started banging around like she was being hit, though nothing I could see was hitting her in that car, and I honked to maybe bring her out of it, but she didn't even look at me.

What is she on? I wondered, and I watched her head jerk around for a minute. Then I saw that the kids were popping out of VR—they'd look at their mom, then just be gone, just not there, like they were maybe pulling out the connection and running in real-land to help her or something, and I thought: I have no choice. I have to screw this test and my raise. And I put the car in park, and unbuckled and got out and ran up to the lady's door and opened it.

That's when she looked at me for the first time, and her eyes were wide like she was scared, not of me but of something. And I said, *Lady, what can I do to help you? Can I call someone? What's going on?* And she said—

My husband's beating me.

Then she was gone, like the kids, as if somebody'd pulled the connection out of her head. The car disappeared next, and I was left standing in the middle of the off-ramp with four other cars honking behind me.

I stood there for a second or two, thinking how I'd blown the test and there was no point in going on and what Fat Joe would say, then I ran for my car and took it across 45 and up the VR I-15 on-ramp and back out onto the VR interstate looking for the green station wagon. I knew it was stupid to look for that wagon if the lady driving it was getting beaten up somewhere in real-land and I didn't know where and I couldn't even remember her license plate to stop and call the stupid police, I'd just been watching the kids in the back of a wagon doing 93 mph, I hadn't been memorizing license plate numbers, and I didn't know what to do, and I wanted to do something, something, something. Before long, but before the ten minutes of my test were up, I was past Draper and the prison and going up the Point of the Mountain doing 102 and when I hit the top, the VR blanked out and a screen came up that said "You are not a driver authorized to enter the Utah County Driver Simulation Net," which meant I didn't have the right kind of access to make the Salt Lake County net network me over to the Utah County net, and then the screen went all black in my mind. But before the words had come up I'd gotten one quick glimpse of the Utah County net, and it was all color, not city: I saw the sun glinting off Utah Lake and the green spring wheatfields and orchards around Alpine and a tall mountain south with snow still on the top and I-15 heading south to that mountain, the road looking like it had been polished and looking like it ached for me to drive on it.

"So you blew that one, Clayton-boy. You blew that one—and you're supposed to be my best driver?"

I was unhooking my head and one of the wires had stuck in the back, so I kept working at it and looked at Fat Joe who seemed just a little too happy about my fifteen cent an hour loss and said, "Yeah, well I want some practice time in VR."

And it wasn't just VR fun I was after, though Fat Joe wouldn't know that: I wanted to get back out on VR I-15 and look for that station wagon and write down the license plate number if I saw it again.

"You can practice when you don't have runs to make in real-land, Clayton-boy. We've got one waiting for you now."

The wire came loose, and I hurried out of the car and into the kitchen: It was two pepperoni and mushroom pizzas on a Midvale run waiting for me, and the kitchen staff had already boxed up the pizzas, so I took them and ran, sat them in the backseat of my little Japanese fast car and buckled them down and slammed doors and buckled myself in and rolled down the windows while I pulled out onto 600 South heading west to the I-15 on-ramp: I never used the air conditioner because the drain on engine power would slow me down, and I was out there in real-land, which is weirder than VR: in VR you have people driving along trying to pass tests, most driving like they always meant to be good little boys and girls of the road and only a few like me driving like maniacs because we had different kinds of tests to pass—and it was only those people out there.

But not in real-land.

In real-land everybody had already passed their tests so they could all go nuts and all two million of them in Salt Lake Valley are out driving around all the time, usually heading for I-15, and you never know what to expect except lots of craziness and unpredictability and I loved it, I loved playing the game that went on in that traffic: drive a fast car fast and you'll find one or two or three others doing the same thing, and an interstate highway can become your own little VR game in real-land: slow cars doing 60 or 70 to block the road ahead when you can't change lanes left or right and the other fast cars speed past and laugh at you, but you get your turn to laugh down the road when their lane is blocked and you can speed past, and you drive, weaving in and out, and *nothing* feels like it, nothing, with the wind whipping your hair and the hot summer air off the desert blowing over your skin and no music off the radio at all because you don't need it, not then, not during the game.

And I merged out onto I-15 and shoved my Japanese fast car up to 80 plus, close to 90, because I wanted to play then, real bad, and the Happy Pizza clown head stuck on the hood of my car flapped around like you wouldn't believe, but nobody was out playing the game, just me, I was the only driver weaving in and out, getting blocked and slowing down and speeding up again and weaving in and out, and I couldn't help it: I kept looking around for the green station wagon with the peeling fake-wood side panels because a car like that existed somewhere in the valley and was probably registered to the lady or her husband and the lady was probably a hacker because how else could she get out onto VR I-15? A woman with a car like that didn't have the money to buy her way onto the net.

I wished I'd looked even once at the license plates on that car.

It was more of the predictable same-old family routine when I got home that night after work. My mother would ask "How was your day, Clayton?" just like she did every day, and I'd say "Fine, just a lot of driving" and I'd never be able to tell her or Dad just how I drove and the kind of fun it was and what I'd felt, and my father would look up from his paper and not say a word because he was pissed that I'd taken a pizza delivery job, not something at his bank to keep me busy through the summer till I hit the one year of college I'd get before my two-year mission preaching religion. I looked at them and wanted to try to tell them I had taken a VR driving test to maybe get a raise in the slow afternoon hours after the lunchtime rush and that I'd seen this woman getting beaten by her husband and that I didn't know how to find her to help her. But I didn't know how to tell such a story to my parents, there'd be too much to explain, so I didn't say anything about it.

"Supper's at seven," Mother said, and I just stood by the fridge getting a drink, and I looked at us and thought we all seemed like little robots going about doing what we were programmed to do, no matter what happened in our lives: Mother programmed to make supper, Dad programmed to read the paper and disapprove of me, me programmed to go up to my room and do who knows what till supper, my two little sisters programmed to wear expensive clothes and be little brats, and I thought, God, I'm going to break this programming, I hate it, so I said to Mom, "Let me help. I'll set the table and get the water—did you want us to drink water tonight?"

And she looked at me surprised and said water would be fine, and Dad looked at me and I knew what he was thinking: that's a woman's work you're doing, Clayton, you're a fucking man doing women's work, isn't that a great kind of son to have? He would hardly move his arms and the paper when I tried to spread the tablecloth on the table or put his plate down in front of him, but he didn't try to stop me either because I was after all just a son who might just as well do work to serve him and we all ate supper and didn't talk much, Dad had the TV on, and I stayed behind to help Mom clean up and she said, "Well, isn't this a surprise?" But I just wanted to be close to her, and I kept thinking about the lady I'd seen in the green station wagon and what had probably happened to her.

We finished rinsing the dishes and putting them into the dishwasher and I went up to my room and stood in front of the mirror in my bathroom and played one of the other games I played with myself: Clayton, the little Robot Boy. I twisted an imaginary knob on the upper right-hand corner of the mirror to turn me on and left more fingerprints there and wondered what Mom or one of the housecleaners thought about that little circle of fingerprints that was always on that spot of my mirror waiting to be wiped off, and I said "Hi. I'm Clayton. I'm programmed to comb my hair just like this, with every hair in place, and I'm programmed to eat at certain times and take showers at certain times and I always did all of my homework well when I was in high school so I could get good grades and get accepted into a Utah college that doesn't really care about grades, it just wants to know if you'll go to church every Sunday you're enrolled with them so you can sit and hear people talk about being a Christian, never asking 'What would a Christian's life actually be like?' while outside the air-conditioned church building decent women are getting beaten up by their own husbands and you even see it on VR I-15."

I'd seen it.

I sat down on the edge of the tub and looked at myself in the mirror. I hated Clayton the little robot church boy whose life was all programmed for him: college, mission, marriage, kids, college, career as a lawyer or banker, and numbers and money and deadlines all my life and maybe I could even die on schedule: write it in my dayplanner sixty years down the road—Wednesday, June 16, 3:00 p.m.: Die. Contact funeral home beforehand. Prepare final will that morning.

I stood up and twisted the imaginary knob and changed the program: I became Clayton, the pizza delivery boy, and I remembered the first day I'd played the game out on the highway on a pizza run, the day I'd caught on to what had always been going on around me but which I'd missed because I'd always driven so slow and predictably and couldn't see it through my slow-driving programming, but when I started driving fast I'd found a whole subculture of people who drove just that way, people who made driving to the grocery store an adventure, and driving south to Provo an event, and if you got a ticket it was just the price of admission to the game which you wouldn't stop playing because it made you feel so alive.

That first day I'd hooked up with a blonde-haired girl in a red Ferrari and a thirty-something guy in a Japanese fast car like mine and the three of us would weave in and out of the traffic and laugh at each other when one of us had to slow down and race to catch up to the others. Down by Draper, we all took the same exit and stopped at a Sinclair gas station and all of us laughed about the fun we'd had, and they pumped gas into their tanks, but I didn't need to, I'd just come in to talk to them, and I said, "I'm Clayton," after we'd talked for a while, and I held out my hand to the guy, and he and the girl looked at me like I was some kind of alien and wouldn't tell me their names—and they didn't care about mine. It didn't matter to them. All that mattered was that I'd had a fast car and that I was smart enough to learn how to drive it fast and that when I was out on the road I would play the game with them. So those were the rules and I learned them and I never again tried to follow anybody off the road to try to talk. It wasn't the point.

And I turned the knob and changed the program and I was Clayton, the Peace Corps volunteer of the future, though the future was fast coming up to meet me: I'd sent in my papers and was waiting to hear back and I hadn't told my parents and I didn't know how to. They wanted me to do one set of things with my life, and I wanted to give myself the experience of the Peace Corps then maybe do some of the things they wanted. So I just skipped that entire inevitable conversation and imagined I looked like Indiana Jones with a shovel, not a gun, black stubble on my face and me wearing a fedora, and I was saying, "Yes, sir. I'd be glad to go to Ethiopia and show them how to dig ditches and teach them to have fewer kids," and maybe I'd actually help the people there, and I imagined I was setting off with my Bible and Book of Mormon and the shovel—but I was mixing up my programs, the mission program and the Peace Corps program, and I sat back down on the edge of the tub and thought how all my programs were mixed up because I didn't have a central program to guide them: I'd just been programmed to do this or that so much I didn't know what Clayton really wanted or how to cut through the programs to ask the questions to even find out what Clayton would want to do with his life if he had ever been asked, if he'd ever asked himself. I was so programmed to want what I was supposed to want I couldn't even ask myself questions I needed answers to because the old programs would all keep running in my head and block the answers and I wondered if any of us were ever truly free? Could we ever break out of the programs that ran us?

And I looked at myself in the mirror and thought, I'm going to go tell Mom what happened today. It's not part of any of our programs. Seeing what I saw upset mine and it will upset hers and maybe we'll be able to talk to each other about more than the stuff we've been taught to think about and talk about.

So I went down and found Mom in the kitchen reading the paper, it was her turn to read it now. "Mom," I said. "We've got to talk."

And I told her what had happened, what I'd seen, and she sat still for a minute, not looking at me, then she said, "Don't call the police if you see that lady out there again and get her license plate number. Her husband would be a sweet angel while the police were there, but once they left he'd beat her for sure and maybe the kids. Just talk to her and see if we can help. Maybe we can send her somewhere, to her parents? Now tell me what her car looked like again and what the woman looked like." And I did and she hugged me after a while, and I thought this was a good program we were downloading into our systems. A different kind of program, because I'd made some decisions and taken some chances. When I went to sleep that night I didn't feel so much like Clayton the Robot Boy in the mirror.

Fat Joe let me do some VR practice the very next afternoon, which was predictably slow, and he merged me out onto VR I-15 and let me loose, and who should I see driving along in her cute little Mustang convertible but my mother, with the top down but her windows still up so she wouldn't get blown too much and her black Gucci sunglasses on and a scarf tied down around her hair. She waved and cut in front of me and took the 21st South exit and I followed her into the parking lot of some abandoned warehouse by the off-ramp. She stopped and I swung around and parked next to her with my driver's-side window facing hers so we wouldn't have to get out of our cars, just roll down the windows. Mom reached over to turn down her music: she was listening to a CD of some old fashioned group, Def Leppard or Scorpions, and I didn't even care then because I was so surprised to see Mom.

I've been looking for your green station wagon for two hours, she said. *No sign of it.*

I thought, wow, Mom—we're calling out the cavalry for this one, you and me, and I said *How have you been looking?* and she said *Driving up and down the interstate—Bountiful to Draper, and back again.*

I think she'll come, I said. *I think this is a release for her—maybe a kind of escape. Maybe she's even planning to escape and she knows she'll have to do it in her old station wagon, so she's practicing in VR, learning where the speed traps are, seeing what her theoretical car can do.*

If that's true, you're right: she'd have *to be some kind of computer hacker to get onto the net without more of a reason than that and no money,* Mom said. We went back out onto VR I-15. I went ahead fast, looking, while Mom came along behind at a slower pace, just in case the lady merged onto the interstate behind me.

I drove down to the Point of the Mountain just past Draper, right up to the Utah County net, then turned around and drove north to Bountiful, then headed back south again—when there it was, the green station wagon, merging onto VR I-15 from 21st South and going fast. She passed me, and I sped up to keep up with her, and the kids waved at me again, waving hard and laughing like they recognized me, which they probably did thanks to the Happy Pizza clown face stuck on the hood of the car, and I merged into the right lane so I could get up alongside her, but a Brink's armored car roadblocked me doing 65, and I had to change lanes again, weaving in and out till I could get up alongside her. I honked and waved and motioned for the lady to pull over and she looked at me but then wouldn't look back, just sped up.

Great, lady, I thought, I'm only trying to help you, and I followed her along till 45, and she took that exit again and went down the hill, and I followed, thinking maybe we'd stop at the red light and talk, but suddenly she gunned the car again and sped through the red light, across 45, up the on-ramp, and back out onto VR I-15. I just stopped at the red light. It was obvious she didn't want to talk to me.

Mom pulled up alongside me and lowered the electric window on her passenger side. *She won't talk to you because you're a man,Let me go ahead and try. Don't follow us for a while.* Then *Mom* sped through the red light and out onto VR I-15, and I just pulled off to the side of the road.

A cop car stopped behind me five minutes later, and the cop got out and asked me what I was doing.

I'm just thinking, I said.

Well, it's costing your company money for you to come think in here, he said, and I told him to write my company a letter about it, which pissed him off, but since thinking wasn't illegal yet, all he could do was tell me to get my car off the side of the road and into a parking lot somewhere, so I took it out onto VR I-15 instead. I motored along pretty slow—doing the speed limit, actually, because I didn't want to come up on Mom and the lady too soon, but I never did see them. I was down past Draper and heading up the Point of the Mountain when Fat Joe broke into the VR and told me I had a run to make. Before he could pull me out, I raced my car up into the Utah County net boundary and caught a glimpse, again, of the country that lay beyond in VR and looking better than I ever remembered it in real-land: all green in the valley and white snow on the blue mountains and I-15 shining below me, and no sign of the big cities down there, Provo and Orem. I wondered why I couldn't see the cities.

When I got back from Fat Joe's run, which took me all the way out to Sandy, he had another waiting for me in downtown SLC, some banquet of ten pizzas, but my mother was sitting in the front diner by a window, eating a pizza of her own. "What happened out there?" I asked her, and Fat Joe told me to get out on my run, I could bother customers on my own time, and Mom said, "Send one of the other boys. This one's making a run in about ten minutes," and Fat Joe looked at her as if to say "When did you buy this place so you could order my help around?" But he sent somebody else out on the run and didn't say anything. Mom was, after all, a paying customer, and you don't argue with those types when you're in the pizza business.

I pulled up a chair at Mom's table, and she said "We've got a plan, but first of all, this lady you found is in bad trouble, or at least a bad marriage: her husband beats her two or three times a week and has twice put her in the hospital. She left him once before but went back to him, so I don't know what to think. You know how people in her situation are: they can't let go of the person killing them, and they leave them and then go back to them, and who knows what she'll actually do in the end, but I told her,

'Honey, you'd better get ahold of yourself and break this marriage apart before your husband kills you so you can raise these three babies. If you don't want to think of yourself, think of them.' And she thought about it in those terms and told me she'd leave her husband again. She has a sister who just moved to Baker, Nevada, who will take her in, and the husband doesn't know the sister's gone to Baker, so the lady should be safe with her. I told her we'd drive her out there. The Nevada courts can get her a divorce by the weekend. So this is the plan: she's going to call in a pizza order anytime now. You'll take it to her in my car, which is faster than yours. When you get there, she and the kids will come out to pay for it, get in the car instead, and you'll drive her on to Provo. Your Dad and I will meet you at the courthouse, where she'll be arranging for a restraining order on her husband. Then we'll all go on to Baker."

"Dad?" was all I could say.

"I told him this morning what we were doing," she said, "and he's been checking into the legalities of helping this woman, which is all legal, and taking your sisters to your Aunt Cheryl's and getting a reservation at a campground in Great Basin National Park for us. He's home packing his van now. Here are the keys to my car," and she handed me her car keys.

I took them and gave Mom my car keys and looked up at Fat Joe, who'd been listening to some of this. "So what's going on?" he asked.

"This boy's your best driver," Mom said. "I need his services." And she pulled out a hundred dollar bill from her purse and handed it to Fat Joe. "That should cover any inconvenience you'll incur from his absence this weekend."

Well, Fat Joe was all smiles then, and I knew my job was secure if I took off the next week, not just the weekend. The funny thing was, Fat Joe probably didn't even know that this was my own mother doing all this, and I sure didn't tell him. He came out to help me put a Happy Pizza clown face on the hood of Mom's Mustang, and it looked so stupid there, but then, it looked stupid on any car.

When we walked back in, Mom was pacing up and down, looking at her watch, and then the phone rang. We all just kind of looked at it till it rang again, then we all dived for it, but Mom got it and it was the lady. "Yes, I've got you're address right here in my purse," and she read it back to her. "Ten minutes," Mom said, and she hung up and handed me a paper with the address on it. "Go, Clayton," she said, and I started for the door, but Fat Joe said "Don't you need a pizza?" and Mom said, "For heaven's sake, yes, but who cares what it is or if it's even cooked," so the kitchen help rushed a frozen Italian sausage and pineapple out in a box, and I ran for the car.

The address read Layton Avenue, which meant out to I-15, down to 21st South, east to West Temple, then north five blocks to Layton. I got there in seven minutes. The three kids were out sitting on the lawn, and the oldest, a girl maybe five years old, took the hands of the others and started walking them toward the car. I left the door open for them and left the car running, hoping the kids had sense enough not to touch anything, and I walked the frozen pizza up the steps to the door and rang the doorbell. The lady answered it, and I couldn't even talk for a minute when I saw her in real-land. Her eyes were both black, and her wrists were bandaged and there were bruises along her neck above her shirt collar, and her hair was a wreck. She looked at me with tears in her eyes, and I thought, Lady, don't back out now, your kids just climbed into my car. She handed me a ten, and I gave her the pizza and said I'd have to go get change from the car, could she come out for it? She nodded and set the pizza on the TV. Some man I could barely see on the couch growled "this doesn't even smell like a pizza. Where did you order it from?" But the lady just walked out of the house and followed me down the steps. She stopped and pulled a suitcase out of the bushes by the front door and hurried to put it in the backseat. The kids were in the back. We climbed in, and I started backing out and I looked at the lady again and thought how I'd known people look better in VR because you can touch yourself up after you're in so I should have known a woman would take away black eyes and bruises. I should have looked ahead and been prepared for seeing her in real-land, but I hadn't and it was hard to look at her now. That's when the husband ran out of the house. He must have looked in the pizza box and seen that the pizza was frozen, then looked out the window to see that his family was making an escape. I could easily outdistance him in a Mustang, and he turned and ran back to the house.

"He'll follow," the lady said. "Can you drive this thing?"

I didn't even answer her. I just took us out onto I-15 and started the game. It was all the answer she needed. She turned around and buckled the kids in, then buckled herself in. I'd forgotten to do that for myself, so she pulled the seat belt around me, though she winced from moving her hands, and I wondered what had happened to her. I thanked her for buckling me in and concentrated on the game.

We weren't going to have an easy time of blending into the traffic in Mom's red Mustang with a Happy Pizza clown face flapping on the hood, and I just hoped her husband was way behind us somewhere, which was too much to hope for. The lady was watching behind. "Here he comes," she said. "White Bronco, center lane. He'll try to kill you, because he'll think I've been stepping out with you."

I thought about that for a minute. "What about you and the kids?" I asked the lady, finally. "What will he do to all of you?"

"He'll just want to hurt me. Bad. The kids don't matter to him yet."

So play the game, I thought. Play it better than you ever

have. He was right behind us and gaining, doing 90 plus. I sped up to over 90 and thought that this is what I would do: come up fast on the speed trap at 33rd South, get in the inside lane, then slow down fast, send the Bronco speeding past, the sure prey of any cop waiting there. We came up fast onto 33rd South, I took the inside lane and braked. The Bronco sped past in the middle lane.

But there was no cop.

"Now he's in front of us," was all the lady said.

He slowed right down in the middle lane, so I got in the fast lane and punched it. When we were alongside each other, doing 80 plus, he tried to shout something out his window. The lady wouldn't look at him. The five-year-old girl climbed out of her buckle and over the seat into her mother's arms. She looked at her Dad, but didn't wave. The other two kids started crying because they wanted to come up into the front seat, too, but the lady just ignored them. I punched it again to get past her husband, and he swerved in behind us—I didn't know if he'd meant to hit the back of the car or what, but he was right on our tail, and speeding up behind us to maybe ram us. I shoved the Mustang up to 90 plus, and he was still gaining.

I merged right, and he followed us. We passed a Smith's grocery store semi and just ahead a white Lincoln was going to roadblock us doing 70 and we had to slow down while the truck in the middle lane closed up the space between us. The lady's husband slowed down, too, though he stayed right on our tail. He didn't ram us after all. I waited till there was room for just us to merge into the middle lane between the semi and the Lincoln and did it. The semi let out a blast of horn and I sped ahead. The Bronco was sandwiched back behind the Lincoln and the semi.

We'd passed the 45th South exit and were coming up on 52nd South and one mile later the I-215 turnoff. The white Bronco reappeared behind us. He'd slowed down, gotten around the semi, and was speeding up toward us again. "I know where I can get some cops," I said.

At least I hoped I did. They were always there when you didn't want them: just off the I-15 merge lanes onto I-215 heading west toward Redwood Road. It was there that I'd gotten my first ticket after starting work for Fat Joe and Happy Pizza. Be there today, Cops, I thought. Just be there. I didn't care if they pulled us all over and helped us sort out the mess. The husband couldn't make his wife stay with him, and he couldn't kill me if there were cops around.

So I got in the inside lane, passed 52nd South, and headed for the I-215 exit. The Bronco followed. I dropped down onto I-215, doing 80 plus, and braked. The Bronco changed lanes and sped past to get ahead of us, and a cop pulled out after him, lights flashing and then the siren started up.

We stayed well behind the chase, and eventually the Bronco pulled over. We drove past them, turned around at Redwood Road, and headed back east for I-15. The police still had the Bronco and the lady's husband pulled over when we went past.

"He's probably telling them that you kidnapped us," the lady said.

"You can straighten things out at the courthouse in Provo," I said.

We got onto I-15 and headed south past 72nd South. I realized I was breathing hard and tried to slow it down. I also slowed down the car. After all, I had a mother and her three kids in the car with me and no reason to race anymore. I dropped us down to 70 and kept it there. The lady turned around and unstrapped her still-crying kids and took them all into the front seat with her and held them, quieted them down. "Thank you," the lady said to me, almost in a whisper, looking straight ahead.

"My name is Clayton," I said, suddenly thinking it was important for her to know that.

She looked at me, then, but didn't smile. "I'm Elizabeth. The oldest one here is Jane. This is Amy; and my youngest is Clayton, like you."

There wasn't much else for us to say. Not then. We came up on Draper and the prison, then started up the Point of the Mountain. When we drove over the top, we could see Utah Valley. There were the green wheatfields and the orchards around Alpine, the snow on the blue mountains. I-15 stretched out below us and ahead, to the south. It all looked nearly as good as it looked in VR, though I could see the cities from the Point if I looked hard, so I stopped looking and we dropped down into the valley and I couldn't see them anymore. We'd be in Provo in twenty minutes anyway, and then my parents would come.

I thought about that and decided to tell them about the Peace Corps later that night around the campfire when it was just the three of us, after we'd dropped Elizabeth off at her sister's, the three of us without TV so we could maybe talk and away from the things that reminded us of all the programs in our lives, out under stars in the cold mountain air and the only sounds the sounds of our crackling fire and the wind in the trees and our voices. Our lives would all seem short and valuable out there, and our dreams worth dreaming. I got that hit-in-the-gut feeling of excitement again, and it was strong because it came from being excited about talking to my parents *and* from being able to drive my mother's red Mustang down the road I'd wanted to take in the net, where the road out looked so achingly beautiful.

Douglas Adams

The Total Perspective Vortex

Douglas Adams has developed a cult following for his books about the book with the words "Don't Panic" written in large friendly letters on its cover. The Hitchhiker's Guide to the Galaxy *series concerns the only guidebook that covers the known Universe, and the bizarre adventures of the people who carry it about with them. This brief excerpt is taken from the second book in the series,* The Restaurant at the End of the Universe.

The Total Perspective Vortex derives its picture of the whole Universe on the principle of extrapolated matter analyses.

To explain—since every piece of matter in the Universe is in some way affected by every other piece of matter in the

Universe, it is in theory possible to extrapolate the whole of creation—every sun, every planet, their orbits, their composition and their economic and social history from, say, one small piece of fairy cake.

The man who invented the Total Perspective Vortex did so basically in order to annoy his wife.

Trin Tragula—for that was his name—was a dreamer, a thinker, a speculative philosopher or, as his wife would have it, an idiot.

And she would nag him incessantly about the utterly inordinate amount of time he spent staring out into space, or mulling over the mechanics of safety pins, or doing spectrographic analyses of pieces of fairy cake.

"Have some sense of proportion!" she would say, sometimes as often as thirty-eight times in a single day.

And so he built the Total Perspective Vortex—just to show her.

And into one end he plugged the whole of reality as extrapolated from a piece of fairy cake, and into the other end he plugged his wife: so that when he turned it on she saw in one instant the whole infinity of creation and herself in relation to it.

To Trin Tragula's horror, the shock completely annihilated her brain; but to his satisfaction he realized that he had proved conclusively that if life is going to exist in a Universe of this size, then the one thing it cannot afford to have is a sense of proportion.

Marc Laidlaw

Plug-in Yosemite

Marc Laidlaw has written three novels, including Kalifornia *(St. Martin's, 1993), and his short stories have appeared in numerous magazines and anthologies. His bizarre and highly original first novel,* Dad's Nuke, *was written in 1984 at the peak of the cyberpunk movement. (It's had a limited printing in the United States, but you should be able to find a copy in your local library.) The clumsy hoods and gloves of the book were thought up to parody all the fancy VR that was appearing in fiction then—and, of course, have turned out to be much closer to current VR technology than sophisticated neural jacks.* Dad's Nuke *also features artificial office building environments, as drab as the ones people usually inhabit; such virtual offices were one of the first applications of the advancing technology in Japan. Thus far, though, no one has invented a virtual vacation as convincing as the one in the following excerpt from Laidlaw's first novel.*

"Okay!" Dad called from the garage. "If you have to use the john do it now!"

Nancy ducked back into her bedroom to grab a sweater, in case it was cold in the garage, then she ran down the stairs to join the others. Virgil was just going into the garage, Mom had Stephanie on her leash, and the twins were piling into the Venturon. Dad pinched Nancy on the arm as she went through—"How's my little lady?"—and stepped back into the kitchen to grab another beer.

Inside the Venturon there was a spacious shell fitted with deep-fit sofas for the Johnson kids; Mom and Dad had separate seats at the front of the cabin, facing the console dashboard. Plug-in wires, gloves, and masks hung on hooks near the curtained windows. Nancy dropped down into her favorite cushion, Virgil took the next, and Mom strapped Stephanie in the sofa nearest her. The twins had gone back out again, and were playing in the garage. Dad turned back to yell at them as he teetered in the doorway, barely holding to the frame with one hand while beer dribbled from the can in the other.

"We're ready, you two!"

He lumbered over to his seat, shaking the whole van, and dropped down heavily. Connie made sure that Wolfie was out and that Lady Bird had gone to the bathroom, then strapped the twins in place.

Nancy stared past Dad's head at the closed garage door, amused to think that they would have to open it to drive a few blocks in the car, while in the Venturon they could go hundreds of miles without even leaving the garage.

Not that the Johnsons, or any other family, could leave the walled-in, highly fortified neighborhood even if they'd wanted to. For their own protection, the suburbs were hermetically sealed against the depredations of a fallen world: roving bands of anarchists, warring ethnic minorities, religious fanatics. No one was sure exactly what went on out there; satellite images were routinely censored or jammed by countertechnology, and those who left the neighborhood to see the world with their own eyes, never returned.

That thought made her glance at P.J.'s empty couch then away. She had to stop thinking about her brother who had run away from home. He was out there somewhere, beyond the safe suburban walls. He had gone to a lot of trouble to escape—and why? Plug-In Vacations offered adventure aplenty; they were fractally patterned, complex enough to provide infinite amusement. Best of all, they were cheap. Far cheaper than giving up everything you had for the sake of finding out what the "real world" held, as poor P.J. had.

Nancy wiped away a tear. It's time to have *fun*, she reminded herself. That's what the Plug-In's for.

"Here goes," Dad said, and slipped the Yosemite program into the console.

Nancy pulled on her gloves, which were a little too tight, and then the mask, which barely fit. For a moment the darkness behind the eyesockets frightened her, and the pressure made her claustrophobic. But that passed, and she drifted in hazy anticipation of the journey, feeling herself falling, falling through dark clouds, then breaking into light. Below, the countryside was spread out to the curves of the world. All she could see was a black road, dotted down the center, dividing an endless green field. On the road, a shiny silver bug was moving, and as she got closer she could see the antennae swaying on its carapace. It was the Venturon. Down she went, swift as a diving gull, straight through the roof of the van, and with a pop her eyes sprang open and she found herself singing "The Wabash Cannonball" along with the rest of the family.

The interior of the Venturon had been rearranged. Instead of the deep-fit sofas, they sat on springy vinyl seats. Instead of a console, Dad had a steering wheel and a small keypad. There was a little gas stove, a trunk-sized refrigerator, cupboards full of paper towels and kitchen matches and plastic dishes. Magical bags of potato chips and cookies lay open on the little Formica table—magical because one could eat and eat and eat, barbecued potato chips and Hydrox cookies, and make no dent in the supply. It was also impossible to get sick. Plug-in vacations were the best.

As they sang "She'll Be Comin' Round the Mountain," Nancy felt a moment of disquiet, as though something snaky and invisible had invaded their happiness, a drift of soundlessness woven through their loud harmonies.

P.J., she thought. He should be here . . .

And glancing over at the table where P.J. always sat next to the window, she saw barbecued potato chips floating like burnt butterflies from the bag, drifting to a point at about face-level, and vanishing with stifled crunches. With a chill, she tried to turn to Virgil and point it out to him, but she found that her mouth kept singing and smiling, and she could not help herself from feeling happy. In a moment she had forgotten about the ghost-borne chips, and was content to play Twenty Questions.

The rest of the journey by Venturon passed like a series of excerpts, which it was. There were no tedious moments. One moment they were dawdling over the green expanse of fields, the next they were stretching their legs in a service station in the town of Merced, and suddenly they were on a winding road among tall pines. There were no other cars to be seen until they approached an information booth in the center of the road, and joined a line of campers and cars waiting to pass one at a time into the park.

A tall, pleasant park ranger in sunglasses gave them a map and told them to enjoy their stay, then they were on their way again, in the midst of a procession of visiting vehicles. Just as the road began to look crowded, a number of the other cars disappeared, leaving plenty of space between the remaining travelers.

"If I remember this road right," Dad said, "there's a lookout point just ahead."

Everyone fell quiet, crowding to the windows.

"There it is," Dad said a minute later. "Hold on, I'm pulling in."

They parked in a turnout with a stone wall around the perimeter, and joined the other tourists who had come out of their cars to sample the spring afternoon. Nancy walked up to the wall, which came about to her knees, and let out a gasp of wonder and joy—all part of the program.

A marvelous valley lay before her, much more realistic than in the photograph on the program packaging. Splendid white clouds waded through a steep-banked river of evergreens, between sheer granite faces that dominated all she could see. She had never seen a blue as deep and clear as that of the sky in this program: she thought she could almost see through it. But what lay beyond the reach of the blue? Infinity? The roof of their garage?

She heard a screech near her foot and looked down to see a bushy-tailed chipmunk approaching. A tribe of the critters, natives, had invaded the parking lot, and were now demanding placating offerings from the foreign tourists. Dad opened a box of Milk Duds, sprinkled them on the ground, and backed away as the chipmunks closed in, snarling and spitting at one another in their feeding frenzy.

"They sure are friendly little scamps," said an old graybeard in a corduroy hunting jacket and a coonskin cap. As he spoke, one chipmunk buried its fangs in the neck of a competitor for an outlying Milk Dud.

"Yep," Dad chuckled. "They sure are, old-timer."

He crumpled up the candy carton and tossed it toward the trees; it vanished before it hit the ground.

"You shouldn't litter out here, Dad," Virgil said, his voice slow and straining as he fought to get out words that went against the grain of the program.

"You saw what happened to that trash," Dad said with a wink, speaking easily. "Out here, nature lets us clear our errors."

"That's right, sonny," said the old-timer, banging his pipe on the heel of his boot. "Well, be seeing you folks in the valley, I reckon."

He climbed into a battered old camper, the sides of which were covered with decals from the Trees of Mystery, various plug-in national parks, and the National Rifle Association. The truck sputtered away down the winding road, coughing out fumes of black exhaust that vanished instantly, without dispersing.

"You can be sure that old guy knows his way around here," Dad said, sounding slightly awed. "What do you bet we run into him again?"

"He smelled bad, Daddy," Lady Bird said.

Dad turned quickly as the wind rose up and the sky seemed to darken, matching his troubled expression. Nancy stepped away from him, frightened for a moment, thinking with difficulty, *Something is wrong!*

"I'm sorry, Daddy," Lady Bird whispered, and jumped up into the Venturon, as if fleeing the lowering clouds. Mom took Dad's elbow and gave him a cautioning look.

A second later the weather was fine, welcoming them to the valley.

The family faded in again to find itself in the parking lot of an enormous old hotel made of solid rock. Nancy climbed out of the Venturon, took a deep breath of pine-scented air, and heard Dad say, "The old Ahwahnee Hotel. My, my, it looks just like I remember. Isn't that something? Can you imagine the work that went into this program? Of course, the corporation that makes PI-Vacations also owns the valley, so they had plenty of access to the original."

"You came here before, Daddy?" asked Lady Bird.

"Not here," said Virgil. "He went to the real Yosemite."

"That's right," Dad said. "It took hours of steady, boring driving to get here, and when we did the valley was full of people and their junk. It wasn't nearly as nice as this. I didn't stay in the hotel either—could hardly afford that. Now it's no problem. The cassette comes cheap."

"Wow," said Lyndon Baines, "You mean this is a real place?"

"Was," Dad said. "The last I heard . . . reservoir."

"Like the Grand Canyon," said Virgil.

"Not quite," Dad said. "That's landfill now, I understand."

Nancy smiled at Virgil, glad that he was enjoying himself so thoroughly, thinking how she would miss having him around all the time once he was married. Well, at least P.J. would still be around. She felt his hand on her arm, and turned to tell him—

But he wasn't there.

"Peej?" she said.

A breeze stirred the conifers; bushes by the path waved their limbs; but there was no sign of Peter John. That was weird. Hadn't he been with them a moment ago?

"Hey," she said, louder, "where did P.J. go?"

"Naaan," Mom said, in the weird slowed-down voice that meant she was resisting the program. "Please . . . not here."

Slowly the memory came back to Nancy. P.J. was gone. He had not been here the whole time. It was hard to remember, so hard; it was much easier to forget about him and just have a good time.

Then the bushes by the path parted, pushed aside by an invisible body, and a pine cone came bobbing through mid-air until it hovered under her nose. She looked at it in horror—a grudging, very slow horror—then stared at the air beyond it. A little enamel souvenir-shop pin, picturing Half Dome, was suspended there, rising and falling slightly in time to breathing she could only imagine. And though she could hear nothing, there was a peculiar silence like that which had crept into "Comin' Round the Mountain"; the void seemed to say the exact opposite of, "Look what I found, Nancy!"

Before Nancy could scream—which might have been impossible in this program—Dad stepped up and snatched the pine-cone from the air, moving as slowly as though he were walking through sludge. He glared at the spot in mid-air where P.J.'s face was not, then threw the cone off over a green lawn where several old people were sunning in wheelchairs.

"There's no one there, Dad," Lyndon said. He laughed, apparently enjoying the increasingly deep tone of his voice.

Dad was breathing hard, but it only lasted an instant. Apparently he resolved whatever problem he was having, for his face became unclouded, even blank.

"I understand," he said jovially, returning to normal. "I forgot to reprogram the Venturon central processor. It was set to treat us as a family: as far as it knows, P.J. is still receiving his part of the program. We're seeing an empty glove." Dad hit himself on the forehead. "I guess we're just going to have to get used to it."

Nancy felt a little better, but not much. It was the first time she could remember anything the least bit upsetting happening on a plug-in vacation.

Turning away from P.J.'s absence was as sad as abandoning a pet, but there was no resisting the program when all she really wanted was to have a nice time. She followed her family into the lodge, and easily fought the urge to look back and see if the little souvenir pin had come along.

The interior of the hotel put Nancy in a daze, it was so beautiful. The sound of tinkling crystal and silverware came from behind the huge double doors of the dining room, as though waiters were playing chimes. She finally sat down in a cushioned chair and watched her parents at the reservation desk, where they had been waiting for the program's equivalent of ten minutes. Virgil had gone to look around. How wonderful to stay here for a week, when only fifteen minutes were passing in the outer world.

"Where did that man go?" she heard her mother whispering.

"Hell if I know," Dad said. He slammed his hand on the silver bell for service, and the sound was as deep as the tolling of cathedral bells. "Letssss havvvvvvve sommmmmmmmmmme servisssssssss!"

Nancy slipped out of her seat and joined her parents. "What's wronnnnng?" she asked.

"Don't say that," Mom said. "Nothing's wrong. Everything's wonderful. Aren't you having a wonderful time?"

"I guess, only—" She broke off to watch the reservation clerk returning from his office. He looked very pleased about something.

In a perky voice, he said, "I'm delighted to tell you, Mr. and Mrs. Johnson, that we can find no record of your reservation, and the hotel is booked through the season."

"No record?" Dad shouted. "We made reservations in- . . . why, it was . . ." He threw out his arms, striking the bell again. "We don't even need reservations, goddamn it, we paid for the program!"

Nancy was proud of Dad for a moment, because he seemed to have broken through the error-correction capacity of the program; he was complaining openly, at normal speed.

The clerk looked dubious. "Program, sir?"

"This one. The program you, my man, are in. Now I want rooms for my family, and I want them now. In nanoseconds, understood?"

Smiling hugely: "I'm sure that is quite impossible. If you would like to stay in the valley tonight, I suggest you contact the concession-camp agency immediately. In fact, they might already be full."

"I'll do nothing of the sort," Dad said, leaning over the counter. "If you don't give us the rooms that are reserved for us on this cassette, the rooms for which I have already paid, I will personally climb over there and break you into the bits that make you up, you cheap recording."

"Sir, it is not my fault. You would have to talk to the management."

"Fine. Why don't I just do that, hm?"

The clerk bowed slightly, showing teeth as he laughed. "Right away, sir. Would you like to come with me?"

He lifted a panel at the side of the desk to allow Dad through, then rapped on a door behind the counter. Nancy watched her father rise to his full height and set his eyes smouldering. Mom turned to her with a weak smile and patted her wrist. "Don't worry, dear, your father will—"

Dad's scream was completely silent—censored from the program before it could disturb anyone—but it drew all of their attention. Virgil and the twins came running from wherever they had been. Nancy saw the clerk easing the door shut against the palm of his hand, in order to make no sound; he faced the whole family with a prim smile. Dad staggered backward, face white, mouth slack, eyes blank; his hands scrabbled to raise the panel that let him out from behind the desk, and once he was out he grabbed Mom's arm and jerked her along with him. Stephanie's leash snapped taut, and she flew after.

"Dad?" Virgil called. He looked at Nancy, who shrugged, and then each of them grabbed a twin by the hand and ran after their parents down the long hall toward the Venturon.

"Good luck with the cabins," the clerk called after them. "I'm sure they're all taken by now."

Dad rummaged through the icebox in the van, and finally came up with a can of beer. He sucked down half of it before he could talk. Slouched in his seat, his face drenched in perspiration, he finally began to mumble of what he had seen—or not seen.

"It was nothing," he said, his words conveying the impression of something much worse than that. "Like a pit, a big erasure . . . gray and burnt-out . . . wiped away. My God, I thought that prissy little clerk was going to lead me in by the hand, or push me over the brink. I don't know what would have happened. I had the idea I was about to vanish."

"It *is* the program," Virgil said. "Something's wrong, Dad."

"You're telling me? They lost our reservations."

They had no trouble speaking of their unease now. Nancy felt as though they had stepped out of the program altogether, except that they were still here in the valley.

"Oh, Virgil," Mom said, "I'm so sorry this had to happen during your special trip."

"Don't worry about it, Mom. It's no problem." He put an arm around her. "All we have to do is run a diagnostic program and see where the problem is. The chances are good we can fix it in no time. We might have to get out of here for a few minutes, that's all. We could come back to the valley before things started getting funny, and check into the hotel all over again. You see?"

Mom smiled. "Well, I guess."

"He's right, Connie," Dad said.

"Let's run the diagnostic first," Virgil said. "No sense leaving the valley if we don't have to."

Dad let him into the front seat, to get at the console. Virgil leaned over the display board. "See, it's—"

Nancy heard him suck in his breath. She went forward to see what had caused it, and soon they were all crowded around him.

"What's wrong, hon?" Mom asked.

"The keypad is gone." Virgil's voice was flat—not slowed down, only flat."Do you see that? It—it's just not there."

Nancy strained her eyes trying to look straight at the dashboard where the keypad had been; somehow her vision just slipped around the area and her eyes focused on nothing. It was like having a blind spot. The keys might have been there: she couldn't see them, that was all.

"Are you sure they're not there?" Mom said. "It could be glare on the dashboard, Virgil."

"Funny glare," Nancy said.

"You all see that?" said Dad. "Whew, I thought that last beer had done me in. It's . . . what are you doing, Virg?"

Virgil was reaching toward the spot with one hand, but slowly. He paused and looked at Dad. "I'm just going to see if I can feel it. Maybe it's an optical illusion."

"Hm," Dad said. "It's like what I saw in that office, Virgil."

"Yeah." Virgil smiled. "That's probably it. We're having problems with the visuals. I bet I can start the diagnostic by touch."

He reached into the area where sight could not follow, and his wrist appeared to bend the way a spoon seems to warp in a glass of water. Nancy felt a little sick. She watched his face change. One moment he looked sure of himself, the next he was completely baffled.

"Nothing," he said. "It goes right through."

"To where?" said Nancy. "Virgil, what's wrong?"

He shook his head and pulled out his hand.

"Oh my God," said Dad.

Virgil opened his mouth to scream, but nothing came out. The whole scene gave a little jiggle, vanquishing that open look of terror, and Nancy saw her brother smiling at all of them as though there were nothing wrong at all, nothing in the world—wherever that was. He smiled as if he had always had a blank spot, an optical stump, instead of a hand.

The seasons passed in Yosemite, though no one had been sure if they would or not. The mild early summer gave way to a sweltering August, which was followed in turn by a swift and disturbing autumn. After the leaves of the deciduous trees had changed to orange, they turned shiny black in a matter of minutes, then vanished completely without doing anyone the favor of falling to the ground. All hope of natural verisimilitude had been forsaken long before by the increasingly bored and panic-stricken Johnsons. The park rangers were omnipresent enforcers of irrational, ever-changing laws, duty-bound to make their stay as unpleasant as possible, while at the same time ensuring that they did not leave.

The only help offered by the program came in the form of the old-timer whom they had met upon arriving at the park. He showed up from time to time, as winter came on, with handy tips on how to make hunting and gathering tools from common objects in the Venturon. The Johnsons, however, stopped trying to sustain themselves by wildcraft after Nancy dug a hole looking for roots and found, beneath the topsoil, another of the blank spots that beleaguered them. No one wanted to become like Virgil, who only occasionally stopped laughing at his hand to stare at them all in perfectly lucid terror. Besides, they found that they only slowly became hungry, over months and months.

And so they lived in Yosemite, rousted thrice nightly by rangers from wherever they had parked the Venturon, and pursued in the day by fading memories of what their lives had been like before all this. The tourists went home in October, but long before then the Johnsons had become attractions. The guides on tour buses were constantly pointing them out: "To our right, if you're quick, you may see a family of nonindigenous Johnsons scavenging for something to do. Hi, Bill!"

The first snowfall caught them by surprise. It came like a deluge of video static, hardly settling on anything, a downpour of squiggly white lines, little specks and blips of light. Unreal as it was, it brought the cold with it.

"You know what I think?" Dad said. "I think we're coming to the end of the program. Maybe we're going through some kind of leader and we'll end up in spring."

"Or maybe we'll be erased," Nancy said.

When the sky cleared, they looked up at the sour brown stars, the apathy of each Johnson once more penetrated by fear. The night sky looked chipped and translucent, as if it had been played too many times. The tape might be decaying. Whatever had gone wrong with the program could be fatal: this was not a waiting game. It was no sort of game at all. What if, out in the real-time world, no time at all had passed? What if time never passed again out there, simply because they were stuck in here, in no-time?

"Mommy, I'm cold," said Stephanie, who had begun to talk in the summer.

"You'll be all right, dear," said Mom. "Wrap up and get in the van."

"It's cold in the van, too."

"I know, dear. It's cold everywhere. Try to sleep."

Stephanie coughed all that night. Connie was up with her for hours, until Nancy volunteered to take over. In the cold van, while the others covered their heads and tried to sleep, she watched her sister grow weaker, paler, sicker. The bubbling in her cough intensified until it sounded as though she would drown in herself. Toward morning, the coughing and wheezing ceased, awakening Nancy from a fatigued trance.

Stephanie stared at the ceiling, her eyes like drops of dried glue.

Dad shouldered the little body, took a bottle of vodka from the cabinet, and set off into the woods with tears freezing to his face. He did not return for three days, and when he did he shrugged off their questions.

"There was nowhere to bury her," he said. The recent events had gouged through whatever tenderness remained in his personality, and uncovered permafrost beneath it. "Everywhere I dug, it was blank. I couldn't drop her into that."

He lurched to the cabinet and opened it, found another bottle of alcohol, and then dropped heavily into his seat at the front of the van. He did not speak another word for hours, and then he said, "One night the snow covered her up. When it melted in the morning, she was gone."

The depth of winter:

Mom was in mourning. Virgil slept nine hours out of twelve, mumbling of Herodotus in his sleep. Dad never stopped drinking. Nancy and the twins no longer went out hunting bears, no longer watched the windows for the old-timer's appearance, since the last time they'd seen him the snow of static in his beard had started erasing his face. P.J.'s ghost, as though aware of its error, came no more.

Snowbanks wiped out the landscape. Half Dome was obliterated in December. The Washington Column vanished as easily as if all its granite had been grey light in a mirror. The forest went next. Snow covered the ground and never went away. One night the sun set and did not rise again.

"We have to do something," Nancy said, but she never had time to decide what. There was an unbearable racket in her ears and a sudden light that gave her a headache—

"My God, haven't you been in there long enough?"

She opened her eyes to see an old woman bending over her. There was something familiar about the face, though it seemed like years since she had seen it. The silver plastic frock was of the sort the seniors wore at Sunset Ranch. Her mind, rising at a dizzying speed from the depths of dream-winter, clued her in to the old woman's identity as she watched her remove the plug-in attachments from the rest of the family.

"Grandma!" said Nancy. "How—how did you find us?"

Virgil groaned and sat up, blinking and rubbing his hand. Grandma Johnson moved on to Stephanie and the twins—the grandchildren first—then Connie, and finally to her own son.

"Grandma!" cried Lyndon Baines. "We're home!" said Lady Bird.

"I tried calling you about the wedding yesterday," she said. "No one answered. I finally had to watch your family hour last night to figure out what had happened."

"The processor," Virgil said. It was the first sensible thing Nancy had heard him say in months. "It trapped us, Gran. How long were we plugged in?"

"I hurried over right away," she said, as the twins hugged her from either side. "It took quite a locksmith to get me into your house. I guess you were in there about eighteen hours."

Dad moaned, holding both hands to his eyes. "God, I need a drink."

"Mom," said Connie. She put out her hands to welcome her mother-in-law. "I'm so glad you're here, we—"

She broke off suddenly and turned to Stephanie, who lay unmoving among the plug-in equipment.

"Stephanie." She crawled to her daughter and touched her cheek.

Stephanie began to cry: "Mommy, where are you? I can't see you."

"Open your eyes, darling," Connie said.

Stephanie did so, and looked around with a grave expression. "I had a nightmare, Mommy."

They all began laughing and talking at once—all except Dad. "What the hell happened to the processor, that's what I'd like to know."

He banged out the door and they heard a crash as he threw open the panels in the nose of the Venturon. A moment later he said, "Hah!"

Nancy and Virgil went to see what he had found. He was bent over the workings of the central processor, which was mainly shiny metal boxes and motionless parts that should have been impossible to examine in any detail without special tools. But Dad had found the trouble. With a fat forefinger he pointed out the tiny hole in the lower face of one component.

"That's not supposed to be there "

"Laser burn," Virgil said. "Sabotage!"

Dad swore and slammed the panels back into place, so that the false radiator grilled interlocked. He bent, with a grunt, and peered at the front of the van.

"It entered here," he said. When Nancy looked closely, she could see a singed pinhole an inch above the fender.

"But where did it come from?" she said.

Dad stood back with his hands on his hips and faced the garage door, his eyes narrowed and his forehead crumpled with suspicion. He seemed to pierce the garage door with his eyes.

"From the folks across the street," he said, grinding one fist slowly in the palm of his hand. "Our *neighbors*—that's where."

But Nancy could hardly remember what had upset him so much. Her memory of the trip to Yosemite was fading away like the light in a freshly switched-off TV set. Many months' worth of details, compressed into eighteen hours, had become as blurred as a fever dream. The only sharp detail remaining was hunger.

"Come on, everyone," Grandma said. "I'll cook you a great big breakfast."

George Zebrowski

This Life and Later Ones

George Zebrowski's twenty-six books include novels, short fiction collections, anthologies, and a book of essays. His short fiction has been nominated for the Nebula and Theodore Sturgeon Memorial awards. Stranger Suns, *his most recent novel, was chosen by* The New York Times Book Review *as a Notable Book of the Year for 1991. Zebrowski's work has been described as "hard SF with literary intent" and often investigates philosophical questions, as in the following tale of existence after death. Whether this existence qualifies as "life" is up to you to decide.*

"Some people want to achieve immortality through their works or descendants. I prefer to achieve immortality by not dying."

Woody Allen

Most people knew, by the turn of that first decade, that their lives would come to three choices: death with nothing after; death with the religious or mystical hope of a new existence; or translation into a manufactured afterlife. This last choice, which had to be acted upon well in advance of clinical death, was a service offered by AFTERLIVES UNLIMITED, a group of creative associates working out of Atlantic City since the end of the last century.

The first beyonds on the market were blank, limbo-like holding spaces where the dead waited, often crying out on the monitors to be erased, as they sat in what seemed to be gray pastures, or on flat plains and jagged mountainsides, under empty skies. Electronic souls massed in the afterworlds to decide how to live, and to test how much say they still had over their existence.

But as the programmers applied their ingenuity to the problems of world-creation, better interactive backgrounds were brought into play for the waiting departed. Things seemed to have improved somewhat by the time my father began to think of being placed, but I was worried about more than the technology.

"You disapprove, don't you son?"

I shrugged. He was past ninety. Who was I to deny him further life of any kind? "I don't know what I can say."

"Go ahead, there's not much I haven't thought myself."

"It's just that it seems to show, well, a lack of character on your part. Here you are, trembling at the edge of your grave, and you want this. If you had any convictions about life-after-death, you wouldn't hedge." I felt cruel.

He smiled and scratched his nose. "We haven't talked lately. I don't have any religious convictions left. This is the only remaining road for me, this or the dark. I suppose the technology isn't great, but I won't last long enough for the improvements to come in. Gotta go while I can still make the transfer without complications."

He went that same week. They used the actual atoms of his brain to form the transfer pattern, for metaphysical reasons of conserving identity, they said; otherwise we might consider him only a copy of himself. I went to the warehouse and saw row upon row of solid-state modules housing the electronic dead in what amounted to old age homes beyond the grave.

Visitors were allowed a week after transfer. I arrived in a bad mood, feeling guilty, expecting the worst. They ushered me into a small private room with a three-dee tank monitor on one wall.

I sat down and peered into the next world.

"Pop, are you there?" I asked, straining to see into the tank.

A shadow moved across a barren landscape, and suddenly a face gazed out at me. Its eyes seemed blind, but it was Pop.

"Pop, it's me! Can you hear?" My heart was pounding.

"Stop shouting! Do you know what you sound and look like in here? A big cloud with a nasty voice. Can't you do anything about that?"

"I'll try to talk lower. Is that better?"

"Not much. You still look awful."

"Is there anything you need?" I asked stupidly.

"Well, you could ask them to program some shaving utensils. Beards keep growing in here, don't ask me why."

"I'll ask, but what do the, uh, programmers say?"

"The dummies don't know how to do that very well yet, and they claim it's not in their budget! They surmise that there's some deep mental reason why the beard detail persists. Something to do with the method they used to transfer us. I'm glad your mother didn't live long enough to get in here, thank God."

"You wanted this . . ."

"I know, I know, there was no choice. But tell them that they have to make improvements!"

"What kind of improvements, Pop?" I asked, thinking he couldn't just cut off payments from his Afterlife Trust.

"This place just isn't real enough. It's like living on a bare stage set. Worse—even that seems phony!"

I looked into his eyes, but he seemed to be looking inward, as if into a hidden mirror. He appeared defeated, resigned, despite his protests. After a moment the face turned away from me, and I saw a small shadow creep away across the dark landscape.

"Shit," I muttered as my stomach turned over and tried to fall out. My own face stared back at me from an abyss.

I got up and went in search of the administration office.

"You must realize," the local manager said, "that these facilities were pressed into service before the technology was fully developed. People forced us to open. The funding pressures were enormous—open or lose it to a competitor."

"I know, but can't you do something about provisions—about, well, landscaping, putting a bit more reality into these places?"

He shook his head and smiled, forming two dimples and a second chin. "Let me introduce you to our ace programmer. He'll explain better than I can."

We came to an open door. Inside the room, a wiry man sat at a giant screen, staring at some mathematical symbols.

"Felix, this is Mr. Canetti. He has a relative inside."

"Please," Felix motioned me to a chair as he swiveled around from the screen. "What is it you wish to know?" he asked as I sat down.

I explained my father's complaints.

"There's not much we can do right now."

"But why not?" I demanded.

He sighed. "I'm sorry, but we can't do better on the scenery right now. I know it's not much better than cut-outs pasted onto cardboard, but we're working on it." He sounded weary, but still interested in his work.

"What about provisions?"

"They don't need them. In fact, they don't need anything, not even food. All we have to do is keep their matrix support power steady, maybe boost it once in a while."

"But they also have mental needs, aesthetic needs."

He shook his head. "We've tried sketching in details, but it's dangerous. Can't seem to put inanimate things in with any degree of accuracy, where they would be needed. There's a basic uncertainty built into dealing with these worlds, involving our ways of measuring energy inputs. I don't fully understand it myself. I'm a programmer, not a physicist."

"But you'll solve it, won't you?" The sound of hope in my voice was pathetic.

"In time we might be able to land provisions in a kind of storybook fashion. You know, program a phantom ship filled with luxuries, have it approach from the sea, dock and unload. They could come to it in safety, you see, by stages, without the danger of differing energy levels that we can't measure, and take what they need. We'd bypass the danger of erasing people or disfiguring them with arriving informational artifacts."

"How long before you can do it?" I asked impatiently.

"Depends on subscriptions, on grants, funding from the government, the number of researchers we can recruit. Not many are being trained for this kind of work. It's too new. It'll take years, Mr. Canetti. Would you rather we just erased him?"

I thought he was making a bad joke, but one look at his face convinced me he was serious and had meant no offense.

"Can you?" I asked.

"We're not even sure of that, since we've never tried it. We could probably do it. But don't mention it to—it's your father, isn't it?"

I nodded. "Why not?"

"He might demand it, and that might start something if others joined him. They might think they could die and pass on to still some other afterlife. Some of these people have gotten religion since they died."

I almost laughed, except that I felt like crying. "No one filled us in on any of these problems before I signed him up."

He looked at me sternly. "What choice did you have? Would you have let him die?"

"No," I said helplessly, feeling useless.

"There is one other choice, for now. Want to hear it?"

"Sure. Why not?"

"We could store him until the worlds are improved. But it's very expensive. Only the very wealthy have taken that option." Are you wealthy, Mr. Canetti, his eyes asked me.

"Yeah," I said, "the rich knew these worlds were bad. Who tipped them? Don't tell me, they bought the info."

"Quite right. This is a cutthroat business. But you can console yourself with the hope that it won't be more than a few years before better worlds come on the market. It has to happen."

"Only a few years?"

"Five at the outside. We'll perform miracles by then. People in the prime of life will want to live inside. It'll be better than life."

"Oh?"

His eyes lit up. "Well, as one possibility, you'll be able to visit people inside."

"Sure—I could sail in on the phantom schooner you mentioned and land smuggled supplies on my father's dream island."

"Why not! It's not impossible, in principle." He seemed a

bit hurt by my remarks. "Of course he could come out in a cyber-body and spend time with you right now, or even permanently." But I knew that cyber-bodies were ruinously expensive, available only on a custom-made basis, and that the service contracts were ridiculous. "We do have a sub-contracting agreement for this option that we're still negotiating, if you're really interested. In your case we would need various guarantees and a financial statement."

"You sound as if you don't place much faith in the technique," I said.

He nodded. "Too many fatal malfunctions. Prosthetic embodiments can't ever be better than our environments. Consider the choice—the real world *again* or anything you can wish for!"

His company was clearly hedging its bets. "Send me some literature on the hardbodies anyway," I said, standing up to leave. It was no use trying to sound decisive; he had made me feel utterly naive.

"There's nothing I can do right now, Pop," I said at the next visit. "You'll just have to wait. Things will improve."

"You've marooned me here!"

"Don't you have any friends in there? Haven't you met anyone?" I bit my tongue, not daring to ask about what sexual opportunities existed for him now, if any.

"Yeah, *in here* is right. Even you know it's just a damn box."

Flashes of light appeared behind him as I tried to explain what I had learned—what the difficulties were in the various technologies, the costs involved, the dangers of malfunction, the lack of an effective repair and service network—but it did no good. I decided not to mention what Felix had told me about the legal problems of identity transfer. Waivers of dubious legal value were being signed all over the place to circumvent inheritance laws. There was talk of limiting the rights of hardbody recipients; periodic sanity tests might be required. No one was sure nowadays when they had been born, how long they lived, or when they were dead. I felt drained by guilt when Pop finally turned away from me.

I watched his shadow move off into what seemed to be low black hills. The sky was made of red lead. Other shadows were moving around inside the tank. I strained to see, punishing myself with the hellish sight, then got up and went home.

I suppose most people have collaborated with the enemy where death is concerned. Dying can't be helped, so accept it as best you can, rationalize it as necessary and inevitable; above all, don't poison what time you have by worrying about the coming end. In with the new and out with the old. Just imagine how terrible it would be if people you hated or had done you harm could live forever. There's solace in knowing for sure that one day they'll rot, even if you will, too.

It could have been worse. I thought of all those people who had invested in freezer immortality, going for the grim hope of gross preservation when electronic survival was just around the corner. Attempts were being made to transfer the mental patterns of some corpsicles, but without much success to date.

I became a brochure and prospectus hound, hungrily searching for some way to improve Pop's lot. But it all came down to one conclusion: he had gone too early; the technology was only just getting started. To make matters worse, there were few psychologists in the field of identity transfer—you died and woke up in another place, where your experience of a well-made world told you that this was no world at all. It had been made by an idiot god, or a devil attempting to mimic reality. And you couldn't even be sure that you were yourself. I was afraid of what I would learn each time I went to visit.

"How's is going, Pop? Made any more friends?"

He'd been in for six weeks. This time, he didn't speak to me at all. He wouldn't even come forward so I could see him.

"It *is* a big change," Felix, the ace programmer, explained to me. "We didn't quite understand how big until we pulled in a few psycho-biologists. It seems that the loss of the body's emotion-producing systems begins to show up. The brain tries to go on as before, out of habit and memory, but then the coldness sets in. No glands for anger, love, hate, just remembrances of what those feelings were."

"Can't you adjust inputs to make those emotions possible for them?" I asked, struggling with my own feelings.

"We're working on it. It takes endless details to create the experience of a world. Too many details for anyone to handle. Reality goes on, layer after layer of structure, both in the environments and in the human mind. Maybe it just can't be faked, ever. At least not in the way reality fakes it." He smiled.

"What about their sex lives?" I asked.

"Uh, we don't know. We don't watch to see, I mean." He sounded nervous.

"But you're telling me all this is failing!" I shouted.

He nodded. "Could be, could be."

"Then what's going to happen to all your . . . tenants?"

He shrugged. "Any number of things. We don't know yet, exactly. There's a chance we could give the subs—I mean subscribers—exactly *what* they want, by linking their minds to the modeling processors, so that they would just conjure up whatever they wish. Connect their output to their input, so to speak. The closed loop would give them the sense of omnipotence, actually." He paused. "But then again, the lack of limits might be bad for the human mind, some of the psychs are saying. God knows what hells of torment and degradation might appear in the tanks."

"What are you saying?" I shouted. "You're playing with people!"

He smiled at my mistake.

"People? Lives? They're all dead, electronic ghosts, shadows, Mr. Canetti. Don't insult me with your show of ethical indignation. We're doing the best we know how, and within the law."

"Yeah, sure," I said, "I know."

"Take it easy, buddy. You may need us yourself someday."

His words sent a chill down my spine.

I made a pest of myself after that, arriving three or four times a week, even if I didn't see my father. I questioned the flaccid director as often as I did Felix.

I worried about omnipotence.

What would it do to Pop to be able to have whatever he wanted? Anything was possible in the mental space of his new life. What would such power, however illusory, do to a human being? Would it only bring out the worst in human nature? It probably would.

"Don't worry," Felix said to me the following week. "It's still a long way off. He'd probably start out by calling back everything he'd lost in life, like his wife, for example, if she died in the old way. She'd appear to him just as he would want her, exacto. Good or bad—I don't know. He'd stop complaining, that's for sure."

I sat down before the tank and looked inside. The view was breathtaking this week. Green mountains, yellow sunlight, flowers—millions of flowers.

"Damn picture postcard," Pop said to me. "Beautiful little houses for us to live in, with rose bushes, and ivy on the walls."

"Well, what's wrong with that?"

"It isn't real. Looks good to you, but I can tell. Not what I remember. Too regular, too clean. There's no grime, no dust, no insects. Just another stage set."

"It's state-of-the-art, Pop."

"Look, kid, I know that. But it's not a world, no matter what they do to it. A world has a *history*. It *grew* to be the way it is. That took billions of years. There's a sense of something else, of things hidden, something you can't ever get a handle on, an unconscious part of reality, that's missing. It's not just me. Everyone here feels the same way. We can't help noticing. We talk about it, we compare. We're the only reality in this place, but there's no life to live, no gain or loss."

He still seemed emotional and argumentative. That much of his old self seemed to be surviving well enough.

"Pop, do you *care* for any of us out here, for me?" The question seemed to be the best way to confront my fears and suspicions.

He looked straight at me. "Not really—except that you guys have some power over us, so I have to talk to you. But I can't seem to feel the same way I did. How can I? You're no longer my only hope of immortality. You're your own man, and have been for some time. It's a relief, I suppose, remembering how often I got no relief from anything. We've both grown up."

"Do you wan to get out of there, Pop?" I asked impatiently.

"I don't know—what do you have in mind?"

"I've been reading about the new cyber-bodies. We could put you in one. You'd be able to resume your life, walk around, do things."

"Sounds good. Probably has as many things wrong with it as this place. Maybe I should wait for when you can afford a blank clone to put me in?"

"No, Pop, I'll never be able to afford that. They take years to grow, and it's your biological twin you'll be invading, after you've killed its mental development. Do you want to deal with that, wondering all the time?"

"That's not a problem for me. Maybe I can get out and earn the money."

"And it's a hit-or-miss technique," I added, "making impressions in blank brains. They lose people, I'm told."

He looked straight at me. "I can't stay here, son. I'll have to try a hardbody."

It looked like him at thirty, but it was only foam over a metal frame. We got a good price on it. A twenty-year mortgage, with all my savings as a down payment, twenty per cent forfeit if he didn't like it and went back into the tank.

I read up on the aesthetics of prosthetic embodiment. Some people liked the overt Cartesian mind-body dualism. They could drive their new bodies from the head. I suppose it reminded them of their cars. Sex was also pretty straightforward.

On the day of Pop's resurrection, I went to the afterlives warehouse and watched nervously as they transmitted his identity pattern into a small solid-state unit; then they just plugged it into the head of the cyber-body.

He sat up. "Hello, son," he said coldly.

Then he got up and walked back and forth, signed a few papers, and went out the door, ignoring us all.

"No glands at all, now," Felix said, shaking his head. "But you should be glad. He'll be his own person and won't lean on you emotionally so much."

I turned to leave, feeling hopeless and defeated.

"Just one more detail, Mr. Canetti," the local manager said.

"What's that?"

"Well, you do know that we can't erase completely. There are echoes left in the tank."

My stomach jumped. "No—I don't know any such thing. What are you talking about?"

"It's not your responsibility, of course, but I thought you would like to know."

"What!" I shouted. "What is there to know?"

"Please calm down. You needn't trouble yourself."

"What do you mean? That it's him? It is, isn't it?"

"Well, yes, in a purely formal sense, but—"

"And you can't erase him completely?"

"Well, we could destroy the tank physically, but there are other tenants in there to consider. You do see our difficulty?"

I glared at Felix. The coward had left it to his boss to spring the complications on me.

I'm back every week to visit. I think of him as Pop's ghost. He's very faint, but still there, and himself; more so than the hardbody that's walking around outside. He seems to need me.

"When are they going to improve this place?" he asks. "Maybe you should get me out?"

I don't know what to say. Getting him out will always be impossible, no matter how often I do it.

Vonda McIntyre

Steelcollar Worker

Vonda McIntyre's fiction, which has won Hugo and Nebula awards, is marked by strongly developed characters, often cast in nontraditional gender roles.

It's not surprising that the following story, about the practical application of virtual reality in factories, was written by McIntyre. Her science fiction is solidly based in fact, often reflecting her background in biology and genetics. "Steelcollar Worker" may seem fantastic, but, says McIntyre, "I lifted the premise from Science Digest."

The enormous fuzzy balloon bounced from Jannine's fingertips, rose in an eerie, slow curve, and touched its destination. The viddydub forces took over, sucking the squashed ball into place with a loud, satisfied slurp.

"Work always reminds me of that Charlie Chan movie," Jannine said.

Neko, farther along on the substrate, pitched an identical elemental balloon into the helical structure. She had an elegant, overhand throw; she had played ball before she left school, but she was too small to get a scholarship.

"What Charlie Chan movie?" she asked. "Not that I go out of my way to see Charlie Chan movies."

"The one where he's dancing with the globe?" Jannine checked the blueprint hovering nearby, freed an element from the substrate, and moved it into place.

"Do you maybe mean Charlie Chaplin?" Neko said. "*The Great Dictator?*"

"Chaplin, right." Jannine picked up a third element, tossed it, caught it again, danced on one toe.

Neko tossed an element through the helix. A perfect curve ball, it arced, touched, settled, like a basketball into quicksand. Its fuzzy outlines blurred as it melted into the main structure, still a discrete entity, but pouring its outer layers into the common pool.

"I don't think you'd go too far as a dictator," Neko said.

"I don't want to be the dictator. I want to be the guy who pretends to be the dictator."

She leaped again, twisting as she left the ground. But the system wouldn't let her spin. It caught her and stopped her with hard invisible fingers. She found herself on the ground, with no sensation of falling between leap and sprawl.

"Are you all right? I wish you wouldn't *do* that. Jeez, it makes me nauseous just to watch you."

Jannine picked herself up. Smiling, she glanced toward Neko, but Neko's blurry face showed no expression.

"I'm okay," Jannine said to reassure her co-worker. Neko couldn't see her expression any more than Jannine could see Neko's. "Someday the system will handle a spin. How'll I know if I don't try?"

Neko picked up one more of the furry elemental balls and dropped it into place. The elementals scattered at her feet, bumping and quivering, sticking briefly to the substrate or bouncing off. Once in a while, two melded into dumbbell-shapes, then parted again.

"The system will handle a spin when you grow a ball-joint in your wrist," Neko said, exasperated. "You *could* read the documentation when there's an upgrade."

"Oh, when all else fails, read the instructions." Jannine laughed. "I don't have time to read the instructions." She wished the company would let her take the manual home, but that was against the rules. You were only allowed to read the manual in the company library.

Jannine and Neko walked down the helix, positioning the elementals, now and again prying one out and replacing it.

A herd of elementals quivered toward Jannine, like bowling balls under a gray blanket. Several escaped and flew off into the sky.

"Warm fuzzies today," Neko said.

"Yeah." Jannine went to the system and asked for cooling. The elementals calmed, settled to the ground, and reabsorbed their covering blanket. Once in a while, an elemental emitted a smear.

The helix extended out of sight in both directions. Jannine and Neko had been working on this section for a week. Jannine loved watching the helix evolve under her hands. The details of substrate, helix, and elementals changed so fast that a human could alter the helix better than a robot, even better than enzymes.

A flicker in Jannine's vision: the helix and the substrate and Neko vanished.

Jannine found herself in the real world. The couch held her among water-filled cushions, cradling her body.

Quitting time.

The screen of her helmet reflected her face, an image as unreal and distorted against the smoky plastic as Neko's face had been, back inside the system. The screen's color faded. The audio fuzz cut out.

The clamor and bustle of the factory surrounded her: the electronic whine of the system, the subsonic drumming of coolant pumps, the voices and shapes of her co-workers as they got out of their couches and tidied up for the day shift.

With her free left hand, Jannine opened the padded collar that secured her helmet. She raised the mechanism from her head. The noise level rose.

She shivered. The factory was always chilly. Her awareness of her body faded when she worked. She never felt cold till she came out of her workspace and back into real life. On the substrate, the temperature hovered just above absolute zero. Down there, she always felt warm. Up here, where the laboring pumps only incidentally lowered the temperature a few degrees, she always felt cold.

She unbuckled the cuff around her right wrist and freed her hand from the magnetic control.

Wiggling her fingers, clenching her fist, shaking her arm, she slid out of the couch. All around her, her co-workers stood and stretched and groaned in the cold. She unplugged her helmet and wiped it down and stowed it. She wished she owned one, a helmet she could impress her own settings in and paint with her own design.

Neko crossed the aisle and joined her.

"Brownie points tonight," Neko said.

She moved smoothly, easily, with none of the stiffness everyone else was feeling. She moved like her nickname, Neko, cat.

"A bonus, huh?" Jannine said. "Great. We make a good team."

They'd fallen into the habit of chatting for a few minutes after work while they waited for the crush at the exit to ease.

But instead of replying, Neko stared at Jannine's control couch, at the manipulator that reduced the motions of Jannine's hand to movements in the angstrom range.

"Did you notice what it is we're making?" Neko said.

Up on her toes, Jannine shifted her weight from one foot

to the other, bouncing in place, trying to get warm. The day shift people came into the factory, moving between the hulking shapes of the couches.

"Yeah, I guess," Jannine said. "I wasn't paying attention. Just following the blueprint. Some vaccine, same as usual."

"Let's go." Neko strode away, her hands shoved in her pockets. She moved as gracefully as she did down on the substrate, where gravity could be tuned and made a variable.

Jannine hurried after her. She waved across the factory at Evan, the day-shift worker who co-habited her couch. But this morning, she didn't wait to talk.

She followed Neko through the security checkout. They were nearly the last ones out, but waiting had saved them standing in the crowd. Jannine's life gave her plenty of lines to stand in.

Jannine thought the security system was stupid, a waste of time. No one on the production floor had access to anything that they could carry away. Except the helmets. You'd have to be awfully stupid to try to walk out with a helmet, however tempting it would be to take one for your own.

Jannine shoved her I.D. into the slot. She waited. The computer checked her and passed her and rolled her I.D. back. At the same time it emitted a slip of paper, thrusting it out like a slow insolent tongue. It beeped to draw her attention.

Ignore it, she told herself. She wanted to, but Neko had seen it. If Jannine left the note, Neko would wonder why, or, worse, retrieve it for her and give it to her and expect Jannine to tell her what it was. Neko might even read it herself. Jannine grabbed it, glanced at it, and shoved it into her pocket.

"What's up?" Neko asked.

Jannine shrugged. "Nothing. Busybody stuff. 'Eat your

vegetables.' "

"Sorry." Neko's voice turned cool. "Didn't mean to be nosy." She turned and walked out of the factory and into the new day.

Damn! Jannine thought. She wanted to try to explain, but couldn't think of the right words.

She hurried to catch up, blinking and squinting in the bright sunlight. When she'd arrived at work at midnight, rain had slicked the streets. Now the air and the sky were clean and clear.

"Want to get a beer? I'm buying."

For a second she was afraid Neko would turn her down, keep on walking into the morning, and never talk to her again. Neko strode on, shoulders hunched and hands shoved in her pockets.

Then she stopped and turned and waited.

"Yeah. Sure."

Finding a place that served beer at eight o'clock in the morning was no big deal near the factory. A lot of the workers, like Jannine, came off the substrate with nerves tight, muscles tense. In reality, she'd spent the last eight hours lying almost perfectly still. But she'd felt like she was in action all the time. Her work felt like motion, like physical labor. Somewhere, somehow, she had to blow off the tension. Beer helped. If she drank no more than a couple, she'd be able to pass the alert at midnight, no problem.

She slid her hand into her pocket and crumped up the note. A couple of beers would let her stop worrying about that, too.

"Jannine!"

"Huh? What?"

Neko shook her head. "You haven't heard a word I've said." She pushed open the tavern door. Jannine followed her out of the sunlight and into the warm, loud gloom. They submerged in the dark, the talk, the music.

Neko slipped through the crowd toward the bar. Jannine, head and shoulders taller than her friend, had to press and sidle past people.

Jannine joined Neko by the wall, put her I.D. into the order slot, grabbed a couple of glasses, and drew two beers. The tavern charged her and returned her I.D. Neko retrieved it for her and traded it to her for one of the beers.

"Thanks!" Neko shouted above the racket. Four or five people were even trying to dance, there in the middle of the room where hardly anyone could move.

Jannine looked around for a table. Stupid even to hope for one. After work she preferred standing or walking to sitting, but Neko obviously wanted to talk. They weren't supposed to talk about work outside the factory.

Somebody jostled her, nearly spilling her beer.

"Hey," she said, "spill the cheap stuff, okay?"

"Hey yourself, watch it."

She recognized the guy: two couches over and one down. Jannine didn't know his name. Heading back to the order wall, he emptied his glass in a gulp. She felt envious. He could drink like that all morning. She'd watched him do it more than once. He always passed the alert when midnight rolled around.

"Neko!" She caught Neko's gaze and gestured. Neko nodded and followed her.

Jannine pushed her way farther inside, holding her glass high. She passed the bouncer. She knew one was there, out of sight in the small balcony above eye level. She'd come in here four or five times before noticing any of the people who kept an eye on the place. The balcony, upholstered in the same hose-down dark fabric as the walls, blended into the dimness, unobtrusive. The bouncer let the artificials take care of everything but trouble.

Jannine reached the hallway.

"Wait—" Neko said as Jannine slid her I.D. into the credit slot of a private room.

The door ate the I.D. and opened.

"What for?" Jannine crossed between the equipment and set her glass down on the small table in the corner. "Hardly spilled a drop," she said.

Neko hesitated on the threshold.

"Come on, it's paid for," Jannine said.

Neko shrugged and entered. "Yeah, okay. This is kind of extravagant, but thanks." She shut the door, cutting out the din, somebody yelling at somebody else, a fight about to start. After work, your body was geared up for action, and your brain was too tired to hold it back.

Jannine drank a long swallow of her beer, then made herself stop and sip it slowly. She was hungry. She ordered from the picture menu on the back wall.

"Want anything?"

"Sure, okay." Neko sounded distracted. She pushed a couple of pictures, barely glancing at them, then sat at the table and leaned on her elbows.

Jannine swung up on the stationary bicycle and started to pedal. It felt good to get rid of the physical energy she had been holding in all day. Sweat broke out on her forehead, under her arms.

"Did you see what we were making?" Neko said again.

"If I'd stopped to think about it, we wouldn't have done such a long stretch and we wouldn't have gotten any brownie points." Jannine tried not to sound defensive. "Besides, I was worried about the warm fuzzies."

"It wasn't natural," Neko said. She drained her glass, put it down, and raked her fingers through her shoulder-length black hair.

Jannine laughed, relieved. "I noticed *that,*" she said. "I thought you meant something important. Jeez. Nothing we build is natural. If it was natural, we wouldn't need to build it."

"But we weren't using the regular base pairs. We were using analogs."

"Yeah. So?" Jannine wondered if Neko, too, had been set up to test her. "I build what they tell me. It isn't my job to design it."

Continuing to pedal the bike, she wiped sweat from her face with the clean towel hanging from the handlebars.

"It must be something dangerous," Neko said stubbornly. "Something they don't want out in the world. Yet. So they make it with synthetic nucleics. So it can't reproduce."

"It isn't dangerous to *us*," Jannine said, confused by Neko's distress. They were building a set of instructions. Neko knew that. Being scared of it made as much sense as being scared of a music tape.

"I don't mean *now*, I don't mean yet. But later on when they use it. Whatever it's coding for could be dangerous to us the same way it could be dangerous to anybody."

"I think you're being silly. They always start sterile, till they're sure about the product."

An artificial stupid pushed through the hatch in the bottom of the door, rolled inside, slid their food onto the table, and backtracked. The hatch latched with a soft *snick*.

Jannine swung off the exercise bike and wiped her face again. She took the lids off the plates and pushed Neko's dinner, or breakfast, toward her.

"Do you mind if I have another drink?"

"Go ahead." It was polite of Neko to ask, since Jannine's I.D. was in the slot. But she should've known she could have whatever she wanted.

Jannine broke open the top of the chicken pie she'd ordered. Steam puffed out, fragrant with sage. When she had a night job, she liked to eat breakfast before her shift, in the evening, and dinner after, in the morning.

"How can you work out and then eat?"

Jannine shrugged. "I don't have a problem with it. I'm going to eat and then work out, too."

Neko preferred dinner at night and breakfast in the morning. She had a couple of croissants and an omelet spotted with dark bits of sautéed garlic.

"No hot date today?" Jannine said.

Neko drank half her second beer and pushed her food around on her plate.

"I'm not really hungry," she said. "I guess I'll go on home."

"I thought you wanted to talk. That's why I got the room."

"I wanted to talk about the helix, and all you want to say about it is 'No big deal.' So, okay. So maybe we're building them a nerve toxin or some new bug."

"What do they need with a new bug? There's plenty of old bugs."

"Right. So it's no big deal. So forget it."

"Maybe we're building some new medicine."

"I *said* forget it." Neko pushed the plate away and stood up.

"If it was anything bad they'd classify it, and we'd never work on it. I don't even have a security clearance, do you?"

Neko didn't reply.

"*Do* you?"

"No. Of course not. I mean . . ." Neko looked embarrassed. "I guess I used to but I'm sure it's expired by now."

"Why did you have a security clearance?"

"If I could tell you that I wouldn't've had to have it!" Neko said. "I've got to go." She downed the last of her second beer and hurried out of the room, slamming the door behind her.

Jannine watched her through the room's transparent walls till she disappeared. She was surprised by Neko's weird reaction.

"Sorry," she said to the walls. "Didn't mean to be nosy."

She ate her dinner, more because she'd already paid for it than because she still felt hungry. For the same reason, she lifted weights for a while and pedaled on the bike till her hour ran out. She got down, retrieved her I.D. before she got charged for more time, and left the private room for the ASes to clean.

The tavern was still crowded, but quieter. She made her way through it without bumping into anyone.

Outside, the sky had clouded up. It looked like more rain. Jannine trudged toward home. At her last job, her co-workers had created a complicated system of intramural sports. There was always a team to join, or a team that needed a substitute. Any warm body would help. They welcomed a warm body who was a halfway decent player. At this job, though, her co-workers went straight to the tavern or straight home, or did something with some group that didn't include Jannine.

Maybe it's getting time to move on, she thought. But she didn't want to move on.

Morning rush was over; the streets were quiet for day-time. In the middle of the night, when she came to work, delivery trucks created a third rush hour.

The mist grew heavier. The droplets drifted downward. The rain began. It collected in her hair. Damp tendrils curled around her face.

Her apartment was nothing special: a one-bedroom, the bedroom tiny and dark and cold. It always smelled musty. Not quite mold. Not quite mildew. But almost. Jannine looked at her unmade bed. She imagined crawling between the cold, wrinkled sheets.

"Shit," she muttered, and returned to the living room. She turned on the entertainment console and flipped through a hundred channels on the TV, fifty channels per minute, leaving them all two-d. Nothing interesting. She should've rented a movie. She could call something out of the cable, but it took too long to work through the preview catalogue, even on fast forward. All those clips of pretty scenery or car chases or people making love never told her what the movies were about. Usually the clips were the best part anyway. She left the remote on scan and tossed it onto the couch. The TV flipped past one channel, another.

Jannine went to take a shower. As she went through the pockets of her sweat-damp clothing, she closed her fingers around the note.

"Shit," she said again.

She smoothed the crumpled paper, staring at it, afraid to find out what the black marks said. Maybe it was too damaged to be read.

She dug the reader out of the closet, shoved the note into it, and listened.

"This evening, please report to room fifteen twenty-six instead of your usual position. Regular hourly wage will apply—"

Jannine shut off the reader, pulled the note out, and flung it into the sorter.

She'd avoided this test twice already, once by pretending she never received the note and once by calling in sick. She couldn't afford another sick day. Maybe tomorrow she could pretend she'd forgotten about the instructions. Once she hooked into her helmet, maybe they wouldn't bother her. She was a good worker, always above average. Not too far above average.

Jannine wondered what she had done, why she had to take a test.

She should've started looking for a new job as soon as she got the first note. But she liked working on the substrate. It was fun. She was good at it. It paid well. And despite Neko's worries, the company mostly produced crop fortifiers and medicines.

If she got away with forgetting the message—she didn't believe she would, but if she did—she'd have a week or so to look for new work before her employers realized they were put out with her. Maybe then at least they'd fire her without making her take the damn test.

Leaving her clothes strewn on the floor, Jannine climbed into bed, pulled the cold covers around her, and lay shivering, waiting for sleep.

At midnight, Jannine arrived at work and pretended it was an ordinary day. She checked in and played through the alert without paying any attention to it. When she passed, it congratulated her for a personal high score. Seeing how far up the ladder she'd run the testing game, she cursed under her breath. She hated to stand out. It always caused more trouble than it was worth. If she'd been less tired, less distracted, she would've paid attention and kept her results in the safe and easy and unremarkable middle ranges.

That's what I get for lying awake all night, she thought.

She reached out to cancel the game and use her second try. She'd never canceled a game before. That, too, drew the attention of the higher-ups.

"Good score."

Jannine started. "What—?"

An exec, in a suit, stood at her shoulder. She couldn't remember ever seeing an exec on the production level. Sometimes they watched from the balcony that looked out over the work floor, but hardly ever during the graveyard shift.

"Good score," he said again. "I knew you could go higher than you usually do. You got my note?"

He smiled, and Jannine's spirits sank.

"Yeah, well, thanks," she said, not really answering his question. "I better get to work."

"You *did* get my note?"

She saw that this time she wasn't going to get away with pretending she didn't know what he was talking about. He could probably whip out security videos that showed her taking the note, glancing at it, shoving it in her pocket. From three angles.

"I completely forgot," she said. "Is it important? My teammate's already waiting for me."

"We brought in a temp. Come along; we mustn't put this off again."

Jannine was scared. A temp was serious business, expensive.

Reluctantly, she followed the exec out of the alert room. They passed through sound effects and bright electronic lights. Jannine's co-workers played the games, proving they were fit to do their jobs for one more day.

Nearly late, Neko hurried toward her favorite alert console. She saw Jannine and the exec. She stopped, startled, looking as scared as Jannine felt. Behind the exec, out of his sight, Jannine shrugged elaborately and rolled her eyes toward the ceiling. She tried to communicate: No big deal, see you later. She wished she could make herself believe it. Her hands felt cold and her stomach was upset.

The exec's I.D. opened a door that Jannine had never been through, that she'd never seen anyone use. The exec entered the elevator.

"Come on," he said, smiling again. "Everything okay?"

"Where are we going?"

He pointed upward. That was no help. The building was twenty stories high. Jannine had never been above the production level.

She entered the elevator. The doors closed behind her. She stood there, waiting, looking at the exec. She didn't know what else to do. The upward motion made her feel even queasier. Her ears popped. The elevator stopped. The doors opened behind her.

"Here we are." The exec gestured for her to turn and precede him out.

He took her down a carpeted hall. She hardly noticed her surroundings. Photos hung on the wall. Fields and forests, she guessed, but out of focus, weird pastel colors. Some upper class fad.

The exec opened another door.

A dozen people sat at blank computer terminals, waiting. One machine remained free.

"Right there," the exec said. "Get settled, and we can start."

Jannine didn't recognize anyone in the room.

Everyone else is new, she thought. They're applying to work on the substrate, and there's a new test to get the job. What did I do to make them think *I* should have to take it? Somebody must have noticed something. Now I'm screwed.

The job test she'd taken a few months ago was all physical. It was still hard to believe she'd found such a job, with such a test. She hadn't known how to figure out a safe middle score, so she'd come out near the top of the group. She had always been athletic. Not enough to go pro. She'd tried that, and failed.

She approached the computer terminal warily. She stared at it, disheartened. Its only interface was a keyboard.

"I don't type," she said. She spoke louder than she meant to, startling several of the others, startling herself. A nervous laugh tittered through the room. Jannine turned toward the exec. "I told them, when I applied, that I don't type!"

"That's all right," he said. "You won't need to. Just tee or eff."

She sat down. She began to shiver, distress and dismay taking over her body with a deep, clenching quiver.

The chair was hard, unyielding, uncomfortable. Jannine wished for her reclining couch, for the familiar grip, the helmet and collar and imaginary reality.

The screen blinked on. She flinched. She ground her teeth, fighting tears of rage and frustration. Her throat ached and her eyes stung.

"Any questions about the instructions?" the exec asked.

No one spoke.

"You may begin."

The screen dissolved and reformed.

I should have been looking for another job a month ago, Jannine thought angrily, desperately. I knew it, and I didn't do it. What a fool.

She stared at the keyboard. It blurred before her. She blinked furiously.

"Just tee or eff." One of those. She searched out the T, and the F. She pressed the T. On the screen, the blinking cursor moved downward, leaving a mark behind.

She pressed the T twice more, than varied the pattern, tentatively, with the F. The blinking light reached the bottom of the screen and stayed there. The patch of writing behind it jumped upward, bringing a new blank box beneath the blinking square. She pressed the keys, faster and faster, playing a two-note dirge. Her hands shook.

She touched the wrong key. Nothing happened. The system didn't warn her, didn't set her down as it would on the substrate, made no noise, made no mark. Jannine put one forefinger on the T and the other on the F and played them back and forth. All she wanted to do was finish and go back to work. If they'd let her.

The screen froze. Jannine tried to scroll farther down. Nothing happened.

She shot a quick glance at the exec, wondering how soon he would find out she'd crashed his system.

He was already looking at her. Jannine turned away, pretending she'd never raised her head, pretending their gazes had never met.

But she'd seen him stand up. She'd seen his baffled expression.

Paralyzed at the terminal, she waited for him to find her out.

"Are you all right?"

"Yes," she said.

"You finished very quickly," he said.

She glanced up sharply. Finished?

The test ought to go on and on till the time ran out, like a game, like the alert, games you couldn't win. You were supposed to rack up higher and higher scores, you were supposed to pretend it was fun, but you were judged every time against the highest score you'd ever made.

The screen had stopped because she'd reached the end of the test.

The *end.*

Amazing.

The exec looked at the screen over her shoulder, reached down, pressed a key. The screen blinked and reformed. Jannine recognized the pattern of the beginning of the test, and she thought, Oh, god, no, not *another* one.

"You're allowed to go through and check your answers," the exec said. "Plenty of time before the next section. Don't you want to do that?"

One of the other test-takers, still working through the questions, made a sharp "Shh!" sound, but never looked up.

"No," Jannine said. "I'm done. I don't want to go through it again. Can I leave now?"

"I really think you should work on this some more. It's for your own good."

"I don't want to!" Jannine shouted. "Don't you understand me?"

"Hey." The test-taker who'd shhed her sat up, glared, saw the exec, shut up, and hunched down over the test.

The others continued to work, without a glance at Jannine or at the exec.

"I understand *what* you're saying," the exec said. "I don't understand why. You do fine on the alert, so it isn't test anxiety, but your score on this is terrible."

Jannine felt spied on. He'd been watching her answers as she chose them.

Angrily, she rose. She was taller than the exec, and bigger.

"I'll tell you why," she said. "Why is because I don't want to take your stupid test." She knew he was about to tell her she'd failed, she couldn't work here anymore, she was fired. "I quit!"

She pushed past him, heading for the door. She was halfway down the hall before he recovered from the shock and came after her. She'd hoped he'd just write her off, let her go and be done with her. She hoped he'd spare her more humiliation.

"Wait!"

He was mad, now, too, and wanting to take it out on her. She could hear it in his voice.

"You're a valuable employee," he said. "We think you have a lot of potential."

He baffled her. "Can I go back to work?"

"What's wrong with you?" His voice rose. "What do you have against being promoted?"

So that was what this was all about. A management test. Not a test to keep working on the substrate.

"Who asked you?" she said, furious. "Who *asked* you to promote me?"

He stopped short, confused.

"You can take the test again."

"Why can't you just leave me alone?"

"Will you talk to me about this?" The exec rocked back on his heels and folded his arms and looked at her. "Do you . . . Do you need help with something?"

Jannine hated the pity in his face, the pity that would turn to contempt.

"I quit! I said I quit and I mean I quit!" She fled into the elevator. When the doors closed, she was shaking.

The elevator halted at the production level. The doors opened. Instead of the quiet, cold workspace, each person in a couch, no noise but the pumps and the high-pitched hum of the electric fields, Jannine walked into midmorning break. Everybody milled around, drinking coffee and eating junk food, stretching and moving.

She crossed the floor without stopping. She hoped no one would notice where she'd been, or notice she was leaving. The best she could hope for now was to get away clean.

"Jannine!"

Jannine's shoulders slumped. If she'd just disappeared, she never would've had to tell Neko what had happened. But she couldn't keep walking, not when Neko called to her.

"Where have you been? Where are you going?" Neko hurried to her side. "Are you okay? Was it the alert? You never fail the alert! How late did you stay out this morning, anyway?" She grinned. "I'm sorry I was so grumpy. Are you done with counseling? Can you come back to work?" She lowered her voice, whispering, confidential. "The temp is really good. I think he wants to work here. Permanently. He's even got his own equipment. Are you in trouble?"

Jannine wanted to explain, but she had no idea how. She wanted desperately to get out of here.

"I quit," she said.

"You—what?" Neko stared at her, stricken, then awed. "You quit! Because of what I said? Is that why you had to go to counseling? How did they find out? Jannine . . . Oh, you're so brave!"

"Brave?" Jannine said, baffled.

"I ought to walk right out the door with you!"

"No," Jannine said. "No, you shouldn't, that'd be dumb." Neko thought she was leaving because of the company's products. That was okay, because Jannine couldn't explain why she'd quit. It was too complicated and too embarrassing. But she couldn't let Neko quit, too. Not if she was going to quit because of what she thought they might be building. Not if she was going to quit to be in solidarity with Jannine. That would make everything, even their friendship, a lie.

"Do you mean it?" Neko said. "That's such a relief! You

won't be mad? Did you know I—? I can't quit, Jannine, I'm awfully sorry. I can't afford it, I need this job . . ."

Jannine felt betrayed. That made no sense. She didn't want Neko to quit. Hell, she didn't want to quit, herself. She would've felt awful, she would've felt guilty, if Neko had tried to leave with her, and she would've tried to talk her out of going. No: she *would* have talked her out of going, no matter what she had to tell her. No matter how much she had to tell her.

The lights blinked: end of break. Everyone had to get back to work. The temp would be in Jannine's couch.

"It doesn't matter," Jannine said. "I have to leave."

"I'll walk you to the door."

"Why?" No one was supposed to leave the floor during work hours. "You'll be late. You'll lose points."

"I don't care!"

At the checkout, the barrier gave Jannine her I.D. It refused to hand over Neko's. Neko hesitated. She could come through the barrier. But she'd have a hard time getting back to the floor: security, explanations, maybe even counseling. A lot of lost points.

"It doesn't matter," Jannine said, disappointed despite herself. "Stay here."

"Well . . . okay, if you're sure . . ."

Jannine went through the barrier. It closed again behind her.

"We'll get together," Neko said. "For a drink. Sometime. Okay?"

Without turning back, Jannine raised her hand in a final wave.

The exit opened. She walked out into the rain-wet street, into the darkness.

Philip K. Dick

I Hope I Shall Arrive Soon

The topic of virtual reality was a natural one for the late Philip K. Dick, who constantly used the medium of science fiction to question the nature of reality. With plots involving mysticism, drugs, other dimensions, insanity, unique perspectives, and yes, simulations of life, Dick's work challenges everyday perceptions. His writing is dense and surreal, entertaining, sometimes confusing, but almost always enlightening.

"It is perhaps possible," Dick once wrote, "that when all the layers of the mind are stripped away, the reality of the heart remains, or anyhow some organ more vital than the brain." For Victor Kemmings, the hero of this story, the layers of the mind are all he has left to work with.

After takeoff the ship routinely monitored the condition of

the sixty people sleeping in its cryonic tanks. One malfunction showed, that of person nine. His EEG revealed brain activity.

S——t, the ship said to itself.

Complex homeostatic devices locked into circuit feed, and the ship contacted person nine.

"You are slightly awake," the ship said, utilizing the psychotronic route; there was no point in rousing person nine to full consciousness—after all, the flight would last a decade.

Virtually unconscious, but unfortunately still able to think, person nine thought, Someone is addressing me. He said, "Where am I located? I don't see anything."

"You're in faulty cryonic suspension."

He said, "Then I shouldn't be able to hear you."

" 'Faulty,' I said. That's the point; you can hear me. Do you know your name?"

"Victor Kemmings. Bring me out of this."

"We are in flight."

"Then put me under."

"Just a moment." The ship examined the cryonic mechanisms; it scanned and surveyed and then it said, "I will try."

Time passed. Victor Kemmings, unable to see anything, unaware of his body, found himself still conscious. "Lower my temperature," he said. He could not hear his voice; perhaps he only imagined he spoke. Colors floated toward him and then rushed at him. He liked the colors; they reminded him of a child's paint box, the semianimated kind, an artificial life-form. He had used them in school, two hundred years ago.

"I can't put you under," the voice of the ship sounded inside Kemmings's head. "The malfunction is too elaborate; I can't correct it and I can't repair it. You will be conscious for ten years."

The semianimated colors rushed toward him, but now they possessed a sinister quality, supplied to them by his own fear. "Oh my God," he said. Ten years! The colors darkened.

As Victor Kemmings lay paralyzed, surrounded by dismal flickerings of light, the ship explained to him its strategy. This strategy did not represent a decision on its part; the ship had been programmed to seek this solution in case of a malfunction of this sort.

"What I will do," the voice of the ship came to him, "is feed you sensory stimulation. The peril to you is sensory deprivation. If you are conscious for ten years without sensory data, your mind will deteriorate. When we reach the LR4 System, you will be a vegetable."

"Well, what do you intend to feed me?" Kemmings said in panic. "What do you have in your information storage banks? All the video soap operas of the last century? Wake me up and I'll walk around."

"There is no air in me," the ship said. "Nothing for you to eat. No one to talk to, since everyone else is under."

Kemmings said, "I can talk to you. We can play chess."

"Not for ten years. Listen to me; I say, I have no food and no air. You must remain as you are . . . a bad compromise, but one forced on us. You are talking to me now. I have no particular information stored. Here is policy in these situations: I will feed you your own buried memories, emphasizing the pleasant ones. You possess two hundred and six years of memories and most of them have sunk down into your unconscious. This is splendid source of sensory data for you to receive. Be of good cheer. This situation, which you are in, is not unique. It has never happened within my domain before, but I am programmed to deal with it. Relax and trust me. I will see that you are provided with a world."

"They should have warned me," Kemmings said, "before I agreed to emigrate."

"Relax," the ship said.

He relaxed, but he was terribly frightened. Theoretically, he should have gone under, into the successful cryonic suspension, then awakened a moment later at his star of destination; or rather the planet, the colony planet, of that star. Everyone else aboard the ship lay in an unknowing state—he was the exception, as if bad karma had attacked him for obscure reasons. Worst of all, he had to depend totally on the goodwill of the ship. Suppose it elected to feed him monsters? The ship could terrorize him for ten years—ten objective years and undoubtedly more from a subjective standpoint. He was, in effect, totally in the ship's power. Did interstellar ships enjoy such a situation? He knew little about interstellar ships; his field was microbiology. Let me think, he said to himself. My first wife, Martine; the lovely little French girl who wore jeans and a red shirt open at the waist and cooked delicious crepes.

"I hear," the ship said. "So be it."

The rushing colors resolved themselves into coherent, stable shapes. A building: a little old yellow wooden house that he had owned when he was nineteen years old, in Wyoming. "Wait," he said in panic. "The foundation was bad; it was on a mud sill. And the roof leaked." But he saw the kitchen, with the table that he had built himself. And he felt glad.

"You will not know, after a little while," the ship said, "that I am feeding you your own buried memories."

"I haven't thought of that house in a century," he said wonderingly; entranced, he made out his old electric drip coffee pot with the box of paper filters beside it. This is the house where Martine and I lived, he realized. "Martine!" he said aloud.

"I'm on the phone," Martine said from the living room.

The ship said, "I will cut in only when there is an emergency. I will be monitoring you, however, to be sure you are in a satisfactory state. Don't be afraid."

"Turn down the right rear burner on the stove," Martine

called. He could hear her and yet not see her. He made his way from the kitchen through the dining room and into the living room. At the VF, Martine stood in rapt conversation with her brother; she wore shorts and she was barefoot. Through the front windows of the living room he could see the street; a commercial vehicle was trying to park, without success.

It's a warm day, he thought. I should turn on the air conditioner.

He seated himself on the old sofa as Martine continued her VF conversation, and he found himself gazing at his most cherished possession, a framed poster on the wall above Martine: Gilbert Shelton's "Fat Freddy Says" drawing in which Freddy Freak sits with his cat on his lap, and Fat Freddy is trying to say, "Speed kills," but he is so wired on speed—he holds in his hand every kind of amphetamine tablet, pill, spansule, and capsule that exists—that he can't say it, and the cat is gritting his teeth and wincing in a mixture of dismay and disgust. The poster is signed by Gilbert Shelton himself; Kemmings's best friend Ray Torrance gave it to him and Martine as a wedding present. It is worth thousands. It was signed by the artist back in the 1980s. Long before either Victor Kemmings or Martine lived.

If we ever run out of money, Kemmings thought to himself, we could sell the poster. It was not *a* poster; it was *the* poster. Martine adored it. The Fabulous Furry Freak Brothers—from the golden age of a long-ago society. No wonder he loved Martine so; she herself loved back, loved the beauties of the world, and treasured and cherished them as she treasured and cherished him; it was a protective love that nourished but did not stifle. It had been her idea to frame the poster; he would have tacked it up on the wall, so stupid was he.

"Hi," Martine said, off the VF now. "What are you thinking?"

"Just that you keep alive what you love," he said.

"I think that's what you're supposed to do," Martine said. "Are you ready for dinner? Open some red wine, a cabernet."

"Will an '07 do?" he said, standing up; he felt, then, like taking hold of his wife and hugging her.

"Either an '07 or a '12." She trotted past him, through the dining room and into the kitchen.

Going down into the cellar, he began to search among the bottles, which, of course, lay flat. Musty air and dampness; he liked the smell of the cellar, but then he noticed the redwood planks laying half-buried in the dirt and he thought, I know I've got to get a concrete slab poured. He forgot about the wine and went over to the far corner, where the dirt was piled highest; bending down, he poked at a board . . . he poked with a trowel and then he thought, Where did I get this trowel? I didn't have it a minute ago. The board crumbled against the trowel. This whole house is collapsing, he realized. Christ sake. I better tell Martine.

Going back upstairs, the wine forgotten, he started to say to her that the foundations of the house were dangerously decayed, but Martine was nowhere in sight. And nothing cooked on the stove—no pots, no pans. Amazed, he put his hand on the stove and found it cold. Wasn't she just now cooking? he asked himself.

"Martine!" he said loudly.

No response. Except for himself, the house was empty. Empty, he thought, and collapsing. Oh my God. He seated himself at the kitchen table and felt the chair give slightly under him; it did not give much, but he felt it; he felt the sagging.

I'm afraid, he thought. Where did she go?

He returned to the living room. Maybe she went next door to borrow some spices or butter or something, he reasoned. Nonetheless, panic now filled him.

He looked at the poster. It was unframed. And the edges had been torn.

I know she framed it, he thought; he ran across the room to it, to examine it closely. Faded . . . the artist's signature had faded; he could scarcely make it out. She insisted on framing it and under glare-free, reflection-free glass. But it isn't framed and it's torn! The most precious thing we own!

Suddenly he found himself crying. It amazed him, his tears. Martine is gone; the poster is deteriorated; the house is crumbling away; nothing is cooking on the stove. This is terrible, he thought. And I don't understand it.

The ship understood it. The ship had been carefully monitoring Victor Kemmings's brain wave patterns, and the ship knew that something had gone wrong. The waveforms showed agitation and pain. I must get him out of this feed-circuit or I will kill him, the ship decided. Where does the flaw lie? it asked itself. Worry dormant in the man; underlying anxieties. Perhaps if I intensify the signal. I will use the same source, but amp up the charge. What has happened is that massive subliminal insecurities have taken possession of him; the fault is not mine, but lies, instead, in his psychological makeup.

I will try an earlier period in his life, the ship decided. Before the neurotic anxieties got laid down.

In the backyard, Victor scrutinized a bee that had gotten itself trapped in a spider's web. The spider wound up the bee with great care. That's wrong, Victor thought. I'll let the bee loose. Reaching up, he took hold of the encapsulated bee, drew it from the web, and, scrutinizing it carefully, began to unwrap it.

The bee stung him; it felt like a little patch of flame.

Why did it sting me? he wondered. I was letting it go.

He went indoors to his mother and told her, but she did not listen; she was watching television. His finger hurt where the bee had stung up, but, more important, he did not understand why the bee would attack its rescuer. I won't do that again, he said to himself.

"Put some Bactine on it," his mother said at last, roused from watching the TV.

He had begun to cry. It was unfair. It made no sense. He was perplexed and dismayed and he felt a hatred toward small living things, because they were dumb. They didn't have any sense.

He left the house, played for a time on his swings, his slide, in his sandbox, and then he went into the garage because he heard a strange flapping, whirring sound, like a kind of fan. Inside the gloomy garage, he found that a bird was fluttering against the cobwebbed rear window, trying to get out. Below it, the cat, Dorky, leaped and leaped, trying to reach the bird.

He picked up the cat; the cat extended its body and its front legs, it extended his jaws and bit into the bird. At once the cat scrambled down and ran off with the still-fluttering bird.

Victor ran into the house. "Dorky caught a bird!" he told his mother.

"That goddam cat." His mother took the broom from the closet in the kitchen and ran outside, trying to find Dorky. The cat had concealed itself under the bramble bushes; she could not reach it with the broom. "I'm going to get rid of that cat," his mother said.

Victor did not tell her that he had arranged for the cat to catch the bird; he watched in silence as his mother tried and tried to pry Dorky out from her hiding place; Dorky was crunching up the bird; he could hear the sound of breaking bones, small bones. He felt a strange feeling, as if he should tell his mother what he had done, and yet if he told her she would punish him. I won't do that again, he said to himself. His face, he realized, had turned red. What if his mother figured it out? What if she had some secret way of knowing? Dorky couldn't tell her and the bird was dead. No one would ever know. He was safe.

But he felt bad. That night he could not eat his dinner. Both his parents noticed. They thought he was sick; they took his temperature. He said nothing about what he had done. His mother told his father about Dorky and they decided to get rid of Dorky. Seated at the table, listening, Victor began to cry.

"All right," his father said gently. "We won't get rid of her. It's natural for a cat to catch a bird."

The next day he sat playing in his sandbox. Some plants grew up through the sand. He broke them off. Later his mother told him that had been a wrong thing to do.

Alone in the backyard, in his sandbox, he sat with a pail of water, forming a small mound of wet sand. The sky, which had been blue and clear, became by degrees overcast. A shadow passed over him and he looked up. He sensed a presence around him, something vast that could think.

You are responsible for the death of the bird, the presence thought; he could understand its thoughts.

"I know," he said. He wished, then, that he could die. That he could replace the bird and die for it, leaving it as it had been, fluttering against the cobwebbed window or the garage.

The bird wanted to fly and eat and live, the presence thought.

"Yes," he said miserably.

"You must never do that again," the presence told him.

"I'm sorry," he said, and wept.

This is a very neurotic person, the ship realized. I am having an awful lot of trouble finding happy memories. There is too much fear in him and too much guilt. He has buried it all, and yet it is still there, worrying him like a dog worrying a rag. Where can I go in his memories to find him solace? I must come up with ten years of memories, or his mind will be lost.

Perhaps, the ship thought, the error that I am making is in the area of choice on my part; I should allow him to select his own memories. However, the ship realized, this will allow an element of fantasy to enter. And that is not usually good. Still—

I will try the segment dealing with his first marriage once again, the ship decided. He really loved Martine. Perhaps this time if I keep the intensity of the memories at a greater level the entropic factor can be abolished. What happened was a subtle vitiation of the remembered world, a decay of structure. I will try to compensate for that. So be it.

"Do you suppose Gilbert Shelton really signed this?" Martine said pensively; she stood before the poster, her arms folded; she rocked back and forth slightly, as if seeking a better perspective on the brightly colored drawing hanging on their living room wall. "I mean, it could have been forged. By a dealer somewhere along the line. During Shelton's lifetime or after."

"The letter of authentication," Victor Kemmings reminded her.

"Oh, that's right!" She smiled her warm smile. "Ray gave us the letter that goes with it. But suppose the letter is a forgery? What we need is another letter certifying that the first letter is authentic." Laughing, she walked away from the poster.

"Ultimately," Kemmings said, "we would have to have Gilbert Shelton here to personally testify that he signed it."

"Maybe he wouldn't know. There's that story about the man bringing the Picasso picture to Picasso and asking him if it was authentic, and Picasso immediately signed it and said, 'Now it's authentic.' " She put her arm around Kemmings and, standing on tiptoe, kissed him on the cheek. "It's genuine. Ray wouldn't have given us a forgery. He's the leading expert on counterculture art of the twentieth century. Do you know that he owns an actual lid of dope? It's preserved under—"

"Ray is dead," Victor said.

"What?" She gazed at him in astonishment. "Do you mean something happened to him since we last—"

"He's been dead two years," Kemmings said. "I was responsible. I was driving the buzzcar. I wasn't cited by the police, but it was my fault."

"Ray is living on Mars!" She stared at him.

"I know I was responsible. I never told you. I never told anyone. I'm sorry. I didn't mean to do it. I saw it flapping against the window, and Dorky was trying to reach it, and I lifted Dorky up, and I don't know why but Dorky grabbed it—"

"Sit down, Victor." Martine led him to the overstuffed chair and made him seat himself. "Something's wrong," she said.

"I know," he said. "Something terrible is wrong. I'm responsible for the taking of a life, a precious life that can never be replaced. I'm sorry. I wish I could make it okay, but I can't."

After a pause, Martine said, "Call Ray."

"The cat—" he said.

"What cat?"

"There." He pointed. "In the poster. On Fat Freddy's lap. That's Dorky. Dorky killed Ray."

Silence.

"The presence told me," Kemmings said. "It was God. I didn't realize it at the time, but God saw me commit the crime. The murder. And he will never forgive me."

His wife stared at him numbly.

"God sees everything you do," Kemmings said. "He sees even the falling sparrow. Only in this case it didn't fall; it was grabbed. Grabbed out of the air and torn down. God is tearing this house down which is my body, to pay me back for what I've done. We should have had a building contractor look this house over before we bought it. It's just falling goddam to pieces. In a year there won't be anything left of it. Don't you believe me?"

Martine faltered, "I—"

"Watch." Kemmings reached up his arms toward the ceiling; he stood; he reached; he could not touch the ceiling. He walked to the wall and then, after a pause, put his hand through the wall.

Martine screamed.

The ship aborted the memory retrieval instantly. But the harm had been done.

He has integrated his early fears and guilt into one interwoven grid, the ship said to itself. There is no way I can serve up a pleasant memory to him because he instantly contaminates it. However pleasant the original experience in itself was. This is a serious situation, the ship decided. The man is already showing signs of psychosis. And we are hardly into the trip; years lie ahead of him.

After allowing itself time to think the situation through, the ship decided to contact Victor Kemmings once more.

"Mr. Kemmings," the ship said.

"I'm sorry," Kemmings said. "I didn't mean to foul up those retrievals. You did a good job, but I—"

"Just a moment," the ship said. "I am not equipped to do psychiatric reconstruction of you; I am a simple mechanism, that's all. What is it you want? Where do you want to be and what do you want to be doing?"

"I want to arrive at our destination," Kemmings said. "I want this trip to be over."

Ah, the ship thought. That is the solution.

One by one the cryonic systems shut down. One by one the people returned to life, among them Victor Kemmings. What amazed him was the lack of a sense of the passage of time. He had entered the chamber, lain down, had felt the membrane cover him and the temperature begin to drop—

And now he stood on the ship's external platform, the unloading platform, gazing down at a verdant planetary landscape. This, he realized, is LR4-6, the colony world to which I have come in order to begin a new life.

"Looks good," a heavyset woman beside him said.

"Yes," he said, and felt the newness of the landscape rush up at him, its promise of a beginning. Something better than he had known the past two hundred years. I am a fresh person in a fresh world, he thought. And he felt glad.

Colors raced at him, like those of a child's semianimate kit. Saint Elmo's fire, he realized. That's right; there is a great deal of ionization in this planet's atmosphere. A free light show, such as they had back in the twentieth century.

"Mr. Kemmings," a voice said. An elderly man had come up beside him, to speak to him. "Did you dream?"

"During the suspension?" Kemmings said. "No, not that I can remember."

"I think I dreamed," the elderly man said. "Would you take my arm on the descent ramp? I feel unsteady. The air seems thin. Do you find it thin?"

"Don't be afraid," Kemmings said to him. He took the elderly man's arm. "I'll help you down the ramp. Look; there's a guide coming this way. He'll arrange our processing for us; it's part of the package. We'll be taken to a resort hotel and given first-class accommodations. Read your brochure." He smiled at the uneasy older man to reassure him.

"You'd think our muscles would be nothing but flab after ten years in suspension," the elderly man said.

"It's just like freezing peas," Kemmings said. Holding onto the timid older man, he descended the ramp to the ground. "You can store them forever if you get them cold enough."

"My name's Shelton," the elderly man said.

"What?" Kemmings said, halting. A strange feeling

moved through him.

"Don Shelton." The elderly man extended his hand; reflexively, Kemmings accepted it and they shook. "What's the matter, Mr. Kemmings? Are you all right?"

"Sure," he said. "I'm fine. But hungry. I'd like to get something to eat. I'd like to get to our hotel, where I can take a shower and change my clothes." He wondered where their baggage could be found. Probably it would take the ship an hour to unload it. The ship was not particularly intelligent.

In an intimate, confidential tone, elderly Mr. Shelton said, "You know what I brought with me? A bottle of Wild Turkey bourbon. The finest bourbon on Earth. I'll bring it over to your hotel room and we'll share it." He nudged Kemmings.

"I don't drink," Kemmings said. "Only wine." He wondered if there were any good wines here on this distant colony world. Not distant now, he reflected. It is Earth that's distant. I should have done like Mr. Shelton and brought a few bottles with me.

Shelton. What did the name remind him of? Something in his far past, in his early years. Something precious, along with good wine and a pretty, gentle young woman making crepes in an old-fashioned kitchen. Aching memories; memories that hurt.

Presently he stood by the bed in his hotel room, his suitcase open; he had begun to hang up his clothes. In the corner of the room, a TV hologram showed a newscaster; he ignored it, but, liking the sound of a human voice, he kept it on.

Did I have any dreams? he asked himself. During these past ten years?

His hand hurt. Gazing down, he saw a red welt, as if he had been stung. A bee stung me, he realized. But when? How? While I lay in cryonic suspension? Impossible. Yet he could see the welt and he could feel the pain. I better get something to put on it, he realized. There's undoubtedly a robot doctor in the hotel; it's a first-rate hotel.

When the robot doctor had arrived and was treating the bee sting, Kemmings said, "I got this as punishment for killing the bird."

"Really?" the robot doctor said.

"Everything that ever meant anything to me has been taken away from me," Kemmings said. "Martine, the poster—my little old house with the wine cellar. We had everything and now it's gone. Martine left me because of the bird."

"The bird you killed," the robot doctor said.

"God punished me. He took away all that was precious to me because of my sin. It wasn't Dorky's sin; it was my sin."

"But you were just a little boy," the robot doctor said.

"How did you know that?" Kemmings said. He pulled his hand away from the robot doctor's grasp. "Something's wrong. You shouldn't have known that."

"Your mother told me," the robot doctor said.

"My mother didn't know!"

The robot doctor said, "She figured it out. There was no way the cat could have reached the bird without your help."

"So all the time I was growing up she knew. But she never said anything."

"You can forget about it," the robot doctor said.

Kemmings said, "I don't think you exist. There is no possible way that you could know these things. I'm still in cryonic suspension and the ship is still feeding me my own buried memories. So I won't become psychotic from sensory deprivation."

"You could hardly have a memory of completing the trip."

"Wish fulfillment, then. It's the same thing. I'll prove it to you. Do you have a screwdriver?"

"Why?"

Kemmings said, "I'll remove the back of the TV set and you'll see; there's nothing inside it; no components, no parts, no chassis—nothing."

"I don't have a screwdriver."

"A small knife, then. I can see one in your surgical supply bag." Bending, Kemmings lifted up a small scalpel. "This will do. If I show you, will you believe me?"

"If there's nothing inside the TV cabinet—"

Squatting down, Kemmings removed the screws holding the back panel of the TV set in place. The panel came loose and he set it down on the floor.

There was nothing inside the TV cabinet. And yet the color hologram continued to fill a quarter of the hotel room, and the voice of the newscaster issued forth from his three-dimensional image.

"Admit you're the ship," Kemmings said to the robot doctor.

"Oh dear," the robot doctor said.

Oh dear, the ship said to itself. And I've got almost ten years of his lying ahead of me. He is hopelessly contaminating his experiences with childhood guilt; he imagines that his wife left him because, when he was four years old, he helped a cat catch a bird. The only solution would be for Martine to return to him, but how am I going to arrange that? She may not still be alive. On the other hand, the ship reflected, maybe she is alive. Maybe she could be induced to do something to save her former husband's sanity. People by and large have very positive traits. And ten years from now it will take a lot to save—or rather restore—his sanity; it will take something drastic, something I myself cannot do alone.

Meanwhile, there was nothing to be done but recycle the wish fulfillment arrival of the ship at its destination. I will run him through the arrival, the ship decided, then wipe his conscious memory clean and run him through it again. The only positive aspect of this, it reflected, is that it will give me something to do, which may help preserve *my* sanity.

Lying in cryonic suspension—faulty cryonic suspension—Victor Kemmings imagined, once again, that the ship was touching down and he was being brought back to consciousness.

"Did you dream?" a heavyset woman asked him as the group of passengers gathered on the outer platform. "I have the impression that I dreamed. Early scenes from my life . . . over a century ago."

"None that I can remember," Kemmings said. He was eager to reach his hotel; a shower and a change of clothes would do wonders for his morale. He felt slightly depressed and wondered why.

"There's our guide," an elderly lady said. "They're going to escort us to our accommodations."

"It's in the package," Kemmings said. His depression remained. The others seemed so spirited, so full of life, but over him only a weariness lay, a weighing-down sensation, as if the gravity of this colony planet were too much for him. Maybe that's it, he said to himself. But, according to the brochure, the gravity here matched Earth's; that was one of the attractions.

Puzzled, he made his way slowly down the ramp, step by step, holding onto the rail. I don't really deserve a new chance at life anyhow, he realized. I'm just going through the motions . . . I am not like these other people. There is something wrong with me; I cannot remember what it is, but nonetheless it is there. In me. A bitter sense of pain. Of lack of worth.

An insect landed on the back of Kemmings's right hand, an old insect, weary with flight. He halted, watched it crawl across his knuckles. I could crush it, he thought. It's so obviously infirm; it won't live much longer anyhow.

He crushed it—and felt great inner horror. What have I done? he asked himself. My first moment here and I have wiped out a little life. Is this my new beginning?

Turning, he gazed back up at the ship. Maybe I ought to go back, he thought. Have them freeze me forever. I am a man of guilt, a man who destroys. Tears filled his eyes.

And, within its sentient works, the interstellar ship moaned.

During the ten long years remaining in the trip to the LR4 System, the ship had plenty of time to track down Martine Kemmings. It explained the situation to her. She had emigrated to a vast orbiting dome in the Sirius System, found her situation unsatisfactory, and was en route back to Earth. Roused from her own cryonic suspension, she listened intently and then agreed to be at the colony world LR4-6 when her ex-husband arrived—if it was at all possible.

Fortunately, it was possible.

"I don't think he'll recognize me," Martine said to the ship. "I've allowed myself to age. I don't really approve of entirely halting the aging process."

He'll be lucky if he recognizes anything, the ship thought.

At the intersystem spaceport on the colony world of LR4-6, Martine stood waiting for the people aboard the ship to appear on the outer platform. She wondered if she would recognize her former husband. She was a little afraid, but she was glad that she had gotten to LR4-6 in time. It had been close. Another week and his ship would have arrived before hers. Luck is on my side, she said to herself, and scrutinized the newly landed interstellar ship.

People appeared on the platform. She saw him. Victor had changed very little.

As he came down the ramp, holding onto the railing as if weary and hesitant, she came up to him, her hands thrust deep in the pockets of her coat; she felt shy and when she spoke she could hardly hear her own voice.

"Hi, Victor," she managed to say.

He halted, gazed at her. "I know you," he said.

"It's Martine," she said.

Holding out his hand, he said, smiling, "You heard about the trouble on the ship?"

"The ship contacted me." She took his hand and held it. "What an ordeal."

"Yeah," he said. "Recirculating memories forever. Did I ever tell you about a bee that I was trying to extricate from a spider's web when I was four years old? The idiotic bee stung me." He bent down and kissed her. "It's good to see you," he said.

"Did the ship—"

"It said it would try to have you here. But it wasn't sure if you could make it."

As they walked toward the terminal building, Martine said, "I was lucky; I managed to get a transfer to a military vehicle, a high-velocity-drive ship that just shot along like a mad thing. A new propulsion system entirely."

Victor Kemmings said, "I have spent more time in my own unconscious mind than any other human in history. Worse than early-twentieth-century psychoanalysis. And the same material over and over again. Did you know I was scared of my mother?"

"*I* was scared of your mother," Martine said. They stood at the baggage depot, waiting for his luggage to appear. "This looks like a really nice little planet. Much better than where I was . . . I haven't been happy at all."

"So maybe there's a cosmic plan," he said, grinning. "You look great."

"I'm old."

"Medical science—"

"It was my decision. I like older people." She surveyed him. He has been hurt a lot by the cryonic malfunction, she said to herself. I can see it in his eyes. They look broken. Broken eyes. Torn down into pieces by fatigue and—defeat. As if his buried early memories swam up and destroyed him. But it's over, she thought. And I did get here in time.

At the bar in the terminal building, they sat having a drink.

"This old man got me to try Wild Turkey bourbon," Victor said. "It's amazing bourbon. He says it's the best on Earth. He brought a bottle with him from . . ." His voice died into silence.

"One of your fellow passengers," Martine finished.

"I guess so," he said.

"Well, you can stop thinking of the birds and the bees," Martine said.

"Sex?" he said, and laughed.

"Being stung by a bee, helping a cat catch a bird. That's all past."

"That cat," Victor said, "has been dead one hundred and eighty-two years. I figured it out while they were bringing us out of suspension. Probably just as well. Dorky. Dorky, the killer cat. Nothing like Fat Freddy's cat."

"I had to sell the poster," Martine said. "Finally."

He frowned.

"Remember?" she said. "You let me have it when we split up. Which I always thought was really good of you."

"How much did you get for it?"

"A lot. I should pay you something like—" She calculated. "Taking inflation into account, I should pay you about two million dollars."

"Would you consider," he said, "instead, in place of the money, my share of the sale of the poster, spending some time with me? Until I get used to this planet?"

"Yes," she said. And she meant it. Very much.

They finished their drinks and then, with his luggage transported by robot spacecap, made their way to his hotel room.

"This is a nice room," Martine said, perched on the edge of the bed. "And it has a hologram TV. Turn it on."

"There's no use turning it on," Victor Kemmings said. He stood by the open closet, hanging up his shirts.

"Why not?"

Kemmings said, "There's nothing in it."

Going over to the TV set, Martine turned it on. A hockey game materialized, projected out into the room, in full color, and the sound of the game assailed her ears.

"It works fine," she said.

"I know," he said. "I can prove it to you. If you have a nail file or something, I'll unscrew the back plate and show you."

"But I can—"

"Look at this." He paused in his work of hanging up his clothes. "Watch me put my hand through the wall." He placed the palm of his right hand against the wall. "See?"

His hand did not go through the wall because hands do not go through walls; his hand remained pressed against the wall, unmoving.

"And the foundation," he said, "is rotting away."

"Come and sit down by me," Martine said.

"I've lived this often enough to know," he said. "I've lived this over and over again. I come out of suspension; I walk down the ramp; I get my luggage; sometimes I have a drink at the bar and sometimes I come directly to my room. Usually I turn on the TV and then—" He came over and held his hand toward her. "See where the bee stung me?"

She saw no mark on his hand; she took his hand and held it.

"There is no bee sting there," she said.

"And when the robot doctor comes, I borrow a tool from him and take off the back plate of the TV set. To prove to him that it has no chassis, no components in it. And then the ship starts me over again."

"Victor," she said. "Look at your hand."

"This is the first time you've been here, though," he said.

"Sit down," she said.

"Okay." He seated himself on the bed, beside her, but not too close to her.

"Won't you sit closer to me?" she said.

"It makes me too sad," he said. "Remembering you. I really loved you. I wish this was real."

Martine said, "I will sit with you until it is real for you."

"I'm going to try reliving the part with the cat," he said, "and this time *not* pick up the cat and *not* let it get the bird. If I do that, maybe my life will change so that it turns into something happy. Something that is real. My real mistake was separating from you. Here; I'll put my hand through you." He placed his hand against her arm. The pressure of his muscles was vigorous; she felt the weight, the physical presence of him, against her. "See?" he said. "It goes right through you."

"And all this," she said, "because you killed a bird when you were a little boy."

"No," he said. "All this because of a failure in the temperature-regulating assembly aboard the ship. I'm not down to the proper temperature. There's just enough warmth left in my brain cells to permit cerebral activity." He stood up then, stretched, smiled at her. "Shall we go get some dinner?" he asked.

She said, "I'm sorry. I'm not hungry."

"I am. I'm going to have some of the local seafood. The brochure says it's terrific. Come along anyhow; maybe when you see the food and smell it you'll change your mind."

Gathering up her coat and purse, she came with him.

"This is a beautiful little planet," he said. "I've explored it dozens of times. I know it thoroughly. We should stop downstairs at the pharmacy for some Bactine, though. For my hand. It's beginning to swell and it hurts like hell." He showed her his hand. "It hurts more this time than ever before."

"Do you want me to come back to you?" Martine said.

"Are you serious?"

"Yes," she said. "I'll stay with you as long as you want. I agree; we should never have been separated."

Victor Kemmings said, "The poster is torn."

"What?" she said.

"We should have framed it," he said. "We didn't have sense enough to take care of it. Now it's torn. And the artist is dead."

Daniel Pearlman

From Here to Eternitape

Daniel Pearlman's fiction has been published in numerous magazines and anthologies, including George Zebrowski's Synergy *series. He has a strong attraction to the fantastic and satirical and cites his influences as Rabelais, Kafka, Lem, and Woody Allen. Recently, he completed his first science fiction novel,* Nemini, *about a world run by amnesiacs.*

A machine is often more efficient and cheaper to maintain than a human. Fortunately for Norman Birdsall, the man in the following story, humans have personalities which prevent us from becoming obsolete . . . we hope.

1

The woman who welcomed Norman Birdsall was built as well as his wife and had a sleepy, sultry voice that promised him a ride he'd never forget. But the problem with Little Miss Instant Auto, who cooed him over to cubicle 8 for guaranteed "instant service" (wink), was her TV two-dimensionality. The flatness of her roundness was even more of an insult to his erotic imagination than the fold-away portafuck that his busy wife had bought for him a couple of months ago.

Cubicle 8 did not conceal the steamy saleswoman he'd half expected, nor even the paunchy, balding salesman he'd considered far more likely. Instead, an Instant Auto tele-clerk, or *auto*-auto-salesman, flashed him a confident smile from the screen.

Norman's grumpiness was unable to nudge the teleclerk out of his cheeriness. "Of course we have 'personnel' as in 'person,' Norm. We have twenty-seven roving sales attendants, but we have 10,231 cars on our lots at this moment, 7,504 of which are new. The priority of those attendants, naturally, is to serve potential buyers of *new* cars. You, Norm, have told me that you are interested in something reconditioned."

"*Used,* I said I'm interested in a *used* psycar," Norman muttered.

"A psycar. Of course. Well, they almost never come 'used,' as you put it. They're fairly expensive to begin with, and not usually purchased by choice, as you already know . . . so they do tend to stay with the original owner for the seven-year statutory minimum. We, however, sell only the *finest* pre-owned vehicles, Norm. Nothing at all over five years old."

"So what you're saying is that your telephone crony *lied* to me, that you don't have one freakin' trade-in psycar on the lot!" Norman raged, pissed at being called "Norm" by a chiphead begging to be called "Bill." A powerful urge came over him to fracture "Bill"'s digital face with the Instant Auto ashtray full of complimentary chocolates—"Dopa-dipped," as the small print said, "to enhance communication." That meant "to lower sales resistance," as Norman well understood.

"Of course we didn't lie to you," said the suddenly solemn teleclerk in a tone of wounded dignity (designed to extract guilt from Norman, as Norman well knew). "You simply have to give me a chance to make my pitch, Norm."

"So cut the crap and show me what you've got!" Billie Boy here, thought Norman, is well acquainted not only with my Consumer Profile but has locked into my driving record through Compucourt. He now knows me well enough to pick out the suit I'd wear at my funeral—although he's sure to know I've opted for cremation.

"Relax, Norm. Why *don't* you have a chocolate, since that's what you were just reaching for."

"I'd rather relax *without* help from my friends," said Norman, reluctantly drawing his hand back from the tray.

"We do have one psycar trade-in," said the teleclerk. "Finished reconditioning her just yesterday. Amazingly, she's only four years old. And even more amazing is her price: only 8000 good old Units of American Currency. Your timing is perfect, Norm."

"All right, what's the catch?" Only 8000 UACs! Less than half the whacks he thought he'd have to pay for something he was sure would be much older!

"We picked her up through an insurance company, Norm. Poor dear's been in an accident."

"Accident!"

"Don't you worry! Instant Auto guarantees all main systems for a full six months. She's a Chevy made in Myanmar; there's nothing better. Look!"

A sleek red car replaced the face on the screen. Norman hated red cars, but shit, for the price . . . In spite of his anger over the Court's decree, his sense of financial relief began to mellow him. "You know, Bill," he said (almost choking on the name), "that goddamn judge was absolutely unbudgeable. Asshole went strictly by the book. Didn't want to hear a word I had to say about extenuating circumstances or anything. It's true I had accumulated these four more moving violations, but traveling salesmen like me are under a lot of pressure, more pressure than most. I like to say that we're the Flagship of the Nation's Neuroses and that . . ."

A whirr and a double clunk derailed Norman's train of thought. Blinking away the mist in his eyes, he looked at the drop below the monitor.

"In the slot below me, Norm, you'll see the keys, a map showing the sector location of the car, and a mini vo-cam through which you'll voice all questions and comments and show me anything about the car that bothers you. Good luck, Norm."

"Hey, Bill," he said, feeling slighted, as if he'd overstayed some unspecified time allotment. "I was just trying to explain—"

"I know, Norm. I know. And I'm completely sympathetic. But you're better off telling it all to psycar, aren't you? That's what she's for, isn't she?"

"Well, sure, but . . ." He felt his face reddening, flushing in front of a goddamn *monitor,* no less!

"Remember, you can test-drive for one hour, Norm. Then come back and we two can talk turkey."

"Sure, right. Well, listen, if I find any of your sales*people* out in the lot, I'll just buttonhole them with minor questions instead of bothering you."

"No bother, Norm. No bother at all. And I don't think you'll find anybody out there to buttonhole. Talk to you soon, Norm. Bye."

2

"Norman, dear, how many times must I tell you that my primary function is preventative, not punitive?"

"Okay, okay. You're on my case for my own good." He

made a conscious effort to ease up on the pedal and to avoid mindless lane-hopping. . . .

"Slower, please!"

"Sure." What the hell, he really wasn't in any hurry to get down to American Hairlines, so why jeopardize his driving privileges again? Even with these goddamn taxis crowding him, he'd arrive in plenty of time for his 3 P.M. appointment, when he'd trot out his entire fine-tuned horse-and-dog show under the scrutiny of a company rep he was sure he could sell on PersoNull's new Supersnipper. Autostylists were expensive, of course, but when the American Hairlines bosses looked to the near future, to the permanent replacement of hundreds of service people, to the Supersnipper's snipping away fringes *and* salaries, ending customer exposure to the three big B's—bad breath, body odor, and bullshit (although you *could* engage in a pleasant chat, among other A/V options, if you liked)—why, they'd be eating out of his hand, just like all those grateful hospitals with their PersoNull-made nursomats and autodocs, or those happy zoos with PN's crud-crunching autosweeps, or the hundreds of day-care centers with—

"Norman, you're *drifting,* forgetting my reminder about needlessly changing lanes."

"Sorry."

"Last week you caused a minor highway accident by suddenly driving too *slow.* I route you along smartways whenever I can, but your itineraries often force you off the main roads onto long stretches of old-fashioned highway. Unfortunately, Norman, on highways your vehicle reverts to *your* control, which I can influence only to the extent that your moves are not too *sudden.* . . . I hate to sound like Old Miss Nagginwagon, but you're already into your third series of serious violations. It is your last series, Norman, your absolute last. You know the rules and regs. For your first series the judge imposed the regulation penalty: a fine of three thousand UACs and six weekends of house-arrest.

For your second—"

"I wasn't even allowed to plead my case. If I'd had a *real* judge—"

"Be 'real' yourself, Norman. Biological judges in the lower traffic courts—of New York and other big cities, at least—long ago proved incapable even of working their way through the docket, no to mention their inability to avoid arbitrary sentencing."

"Arbitrary, hell!" He was momentarily distracted by a cabbie who had just swung in front of him and was now weaving around trying to scope out another hole to worm his fat ass through. "They were using *judgment.* That's why they were called judges. If in some cases they acted like tyrants, in others they exhibited . . . understanding, mercy."

"History disagrees with you, Norman. In too many cases what they actually exhibited was sexism, racism, ageism, weightism, and classism."

"*Look* at that bastard!" shouted Norman, caught in the erratic wake of the taxi jockeying in front of him. "Excuse the French, sweetheart."

"That's all right. Better you utter an expletive than slam down angrily on a pedal."

"I'd like to kill the son of a bitch!"

"Good. Visualize blasting him right between the brights. And now lean back in your seat. You are, after all, in no hurry."

"Give me those old judges again who were prejudiced against goddamn taxi-drivers."

"And how do you think *you* would have fared against one of those 'old' judges, Norman? You acted outraged by the sentence that resulted from your first series of violations. You demanded an encounter with 'the face behind the machine'—your exact words, correct?"

"I keep forgetting you have access to the whole recorded

shitlist of my life."

"And then, when you were refused the encounter, you lifted up a chair and flung it at a totally innocent, value-free *terminal.* Fortunately, you broke nothing, and no further penalty was imposed. Do you think you'd have got off so lightly if you'd flung your chair at a human judge?"

"If I'd had a human judge, dearie, I'd've had no reason to fling the fucking chair!"

"Possibly," the voice of psycar answered after a moment's hesitation. "But your record of losing self-control has been an unenviable one, Norman, and I expatiate upon it now because I sense that you are in danger of doing so again."

"Losing self-control, *losing self control!* Even my goddamn life-insurance company's been handing me the same line of bull."

"How so, Norman?"

"Those bi-monthly reports they send me on my dietary habits . . . increase my grains, reduce my fats . . . analyzing everything I scarf along the road. They access every restaurant billing terminal in the country, the whole fucking world! And not that they *give* a shit about you. No. Not a living eye ever checks the reports they send you. There *isn't* any uptight little bureaucrat warning me to lower my calories or else take a hike in my premiums. I remember the old days when even the I.R.S. used to haul me in to explain myself to some dumb-ass college snot—I mean a *real* college punk—wet behind the ears, but at least a real live—"

"I should think you wouldn't *want* to be bossed around by some petty bureaucrat against whose arbitrary rulings—"

Norman smashed his fist into the wheel, honking at the cab in front of him.

"I am forced to remind you, Norman, that honking your horn as you've done is quite illegal. Fortunately, I do not have to report it, since it is not a *major* traffic violation—of the sort that I exist to help you avoid."

"I'm truly grateful."

"Repair guide for the Model XLE, Section C, Paragraph 17, on extraction and testing of logic board D8, Norman," said psycar.

"What?" said Norman.

"Please be more specific. What does your interrogative 'What?' refer to?"

"What did you just say?" said Norman.

"I said, 'Please be more specific. What does your interrogative—' "

"Forget it!"

"I cannot 'forget' things, Norman. And I am particularly mindful of the agitated sort of behavior—"

"Up yours!" said Norman, thrusting two fingers out of his half-opened side-window, but there was no response. "Look, the bastard's head's strapped in a VR painter! Jerkball's probably visualizing the traffic around him as an asteroid field—and me as some space privateer muscling in on the trade-lanes to Jupiter."

"Listen, Norman!" said psycar. "I would like to attribute your elevated state of excitability to the stress of *city* driving, but in fact you've incurred rather serious violations on relatively untrafficked old *highways*. You pick quarrels with mere road-signs. You tend to *personify* inanimate objects."

"Exactly what I do with *you* all the time, and *you* can get pretty damn boring."

"I sense sarcasm in your tone, Norman. Please try to remember that it was your *second* series of offenses that brought the two of us together. Those suddenly executed illegal U-turns, that swift switch of yours at sixty-per into a service lane to bypass traffic, that angry ramming into the back of—"

"Look, I'm on the goddamn road all day, five days a week, forty-eight weeks a year. My chances of running afoul of the law are ten times higher than most people's, right? Add to that my anxieties about the new goddamn company quotas, the rising competition—"

He felt a stubborn resistance in the power-pedal.

"Since you won't stop tailing that taxi, Norman, I'm forced to back you off him myself."

"Much obliged, bitch."

"Go to it, Norman. *Let* the bats fly out of your belfry! What helps you emotively, helps you automotively."

"A human judge you can f'chrissake fuckin' *talk* to!" Like that high school principal who'd raked him over the coals that time for goosing a girl in the hallway. (*Admitted*—the old goat did, though!—that she had a "provocative style"). All right, he thought. She wants me to hang back? Okay, I'll hang back so damn far that—

The pedal remained moderately depressed despite his easing off it. She kept him exactly two car-lengths behind that starship captain of a cabbie who now swung his rear end around to spray him no doubt with some digital ion-stream, a deliberate in-your-face hyperfart.

No wonder these psycars were so god-awful expensive! thought Norman, marveling at his loss of pedal control. Every moving part wired with neuro-optic fibers; sensors, CCDs all over, as thick as pimples on a kid on the short end of puberty. Of course, if he suddenly hit his brakes, even she couldn't do shit to stop him. He could see the gigantic explosion when all those supercharged batteries got crushed . . . or at the very least there'd be a ten-car pile-up, and even his four-way harness couldn't stave off a broken back. (He could see, looming over his hospitalized ass, Jennifer in lifelike 3V silently reproaching his still-twitching carcass for lying there dog-in-the-manger-like between her and an accidental-death windfall of more than a million whacks. . . .)

"Have you stopped to consider, Norman, that your fundamental problem might lie in your thinking that you can influence the law through mere force of personality? What helps you as a salesman, unfortunately, is pointless in traffic court."

"In the lower courts, maybe, where you get processed rather than tried."

"Would you rather have your driving privileges permanently revoked in some higher court, then, by an organically human judge? . . . If so, you'd better hurry! Such judges are rapidly disappearing."

He stiffened his jaw and didn't bother to answer. Uppity bitch sometimes stuck it to him. Thought she was being "helpful." That accident she'd been in—had it jarred loose some of her wires? He didn't mind her quietly monkeying with the pedal or the wheel, but after the verbal reproof she'd once given him in the presence of his wife and the boys (for lane-straddling), he'd never driven in his car with his family again. And the few times he'd had to drive clients around, the sweat that poured out of him through his efforts at good behavior caused his hands to slip dangerously on the wheel. Damn it, though! He was one boo-boo into his third and final series of four already; he could afford only two more violations over the next eighteen months. More than that and is was "Strike four, yer out!" Even the *thought* of racking up another one sent his heart crazily thumping.

"Were we getting any nearer to the heart of your driving problems yesterday, Norman, when I observed that you didn't actually *believe* in the systems you're selling?"

"No, I thought that was completely naive!" He wanted to take a swing at the empty seat beside him. "It's true, I wouldn't be caught dead getting one of those Supersnipper haircuts myself, but salesmen are only middlemen. If I only sold what I personally believed in . . . I'd become a pimp for my wife." He laughed out loud. "She's the only thing that ever gave me much *personal* satisfaction."

"Gave you? Why the past tense, Norman?"

"Well, you know, she's busy these days. In training for

another big body-sculpting show. Hell, it isn't like I'm complaining . . . You know, if she makes it to the regionals . . ." He felt himself blushing. Could autobitch sniff the change in hormones? he wondered.

"We'll return to Mrs. Birdsall later, Norman. But before we get off the subject of what might be most immediately bothering you, am I right in picking up on your anxiety about meeting new quotas?"

"I'm a goddamn *good* salesman. One of the best in the PN stable."

"Then if you believe in your charm, your personal magic—"

"Sure, when I'm dealing with *people,* like when I compliment some pot-bellied company president on his youthful athletic figure so that along with handing me a big fat order he promises to get me a personal consultation with his own 'exclusive' exercybernetician . . . but more and more these days I don't even *see* the decision makers."

"Then whom do you deal with, Norm?"

"At three o'clock, for instance, at American Hairlines, they'll be sitting me in a room with a *representative* of the Executive Committee. Their busy execs can thus save time, don't have to fly in from all over the country, can get by proxy a logically organized breakdown of the relevant data . . ."

"Isn't it easier to deal with a single individual rather than with a whole group?"

"Individual *what?* Who's talking people? Last year I myself sold a PersoNull Exec-Rep System to that same group of Hairlines honchos that now don't even personally want to see me!" Norman's hands tightened into fists around the wheel. "I gotta *negotiate* now with that same piece of cybershit I *sold* 'em! Can you imagine the pressure that puts me under?"

"Well, Norman, I should think that gives you an edge—"

"It's sick, sick, sick!"

"I should think that gives you an edge, since your intimate knowledge of that very same system—"

"Just *look* at that sonuva cybernaut!" he said, leaning in over the wheel, watching as the cabbie in front of him decided to swing into the same lane that *he* was at last edging into.

"Careful, Norman. It's just an opening. It doesn't belong to you. Let him get ahead of you. Let him pull away from you if for some reason he's making you angry."

All right, thought Norman, so they'd *both* simultaneously switched lanes, and now the bushy-bearded bastard wound up exactly *in the same place* ahead of him! Thought he was cool, did he, motherfucking one-legged Ghani? They figured if they could grow up in a Russian minefield, they had the right to play hopscotch in cabs in New York. Goddamn one-armed bandits! Three-toed Ghani sloths!

But simulator-head wasn't quick enough this time! Goodbye, you half-assed road-guzzling Ghani! Norman lurched into the next lane to the right, ramming down on the old juice-bar, feeling that satisfying spurt of sheer power . . .

"Red light! Do not pull ahead!"

Norman didn't see red; he saw yellow, too much of it, taxi-yellow flooding his field of vision. He swerved out in front of bush-face as psycar pushed back at his foot. But she reacted too late to stop him from screeching past the light into the middle of the intersection. His heart rode in his mouth as he barely missed hitting a pedestrian. The close call gave him a rush, followed immediately by remorse upon autobitch's sad, matter-of-fact pronouncement:

"I'm terribly sorry to have to say this, Norman, but you are now charged with a *second* violation in your third and final series of same. I tried my best to prevent you from going through the light, but if I had slowed you any more, I would have forced the taxi behind you to ram your rear. I took a calculated risk that you would not hit the pedestrian crossing in front of you. All my intervention could do was minimize the damage your impulsive behavior *might* have caused."

He sat trembling in the intersection, waiting for a mean-looking cop to haul him over to the curb. But no. Psycar had already sent off a record of the violation to Motor Vehicles, advising nearby patrol cars of her report and informing them that they need not stop by since no personal injury or property damage was at issue.

Norman knew there was no use making an emotional appeal to psycar to retract her report. Every movement of his vehicle, every word that passed between psycar and him was irreversibly transmitted realtime to the M.V. Bureau, where each month, automatically, his record was subjected to psychojudicial evaluation.

"Damn!" he said.

"Good. Let it out, Norman. But keep your eyes on the—"

"Damn, *Damn!*"

3

Norman sat down with joyful anticipation to his first dinner at home after another numbing three-week circuit on the road. Here they were, all four together, seated at the *same table.* After selecting their individual dinners, they'd microed them in the four-slot chefbot all at the *same time.* The unaccustomed intimacy filled him with a warmth that had been kept too long under wraps.

Jennifer sat at the end of the table opposite him and looked more attractive than ever. The tattoo of a bright red rose graced the smooth, pallid crown of her head, a dome that was otherwise bare as a cue-ball except for the horseshoe of close-cropped, dark-brown hair around the delicate rose. The muscles of her wiry arms rippled as she dipped her fork into a mud-like, protein-rich Enerdyne pudding. She was successfully rending the fat from her breasts so that the lumps that persisted protruded like misplaced marshmallows from the rock-hard slopes of her pecs. He gazed at her with swelling pride, conscious that though his support (what she earned part-time at Body Mall was negligible) she was fast becoming a pro.

"Rodney and Arthur!" she shouted. The boys sat at the long sides of the table, oblivious to the outside world, their faces visible no higher than mid-nose under their Caps. "Don't forget to *eat!*" She slammed the table with a brick-splitting chop that made them flip up their visors.

"Hi, boys! I'm home!" Norman smiled and waved as if to a parting ship. He caught their eyes for the first time since they'd groped their way visors-down into the dining room.

"Hi, Dad," they chorused, vanishing again into virtual reality while stabbing perfunctorily at the gourmet glop on their plates. Norman's listless sons unnervingly reminded him of certain classes of repeat offenders disciplined with electrode implants in the brain. Skewered with these "gork forks," they then became placid zombies who never broke another rule.

On the other hand, the boys seemed merely to be simulating obedience while pursuing their own hidden agendas under their Caps. They maneuvered themselves through cyberspace with their gloved left hands, utterly absorbed in stroking and pinching certain suspiciously globular "objects" in their path.

"I called Mom and we chatted about the boys today," said Jennifer. "I'm always amazed at how she'll remember every detail I ever tell her about the rascals. She knows Rod's twelve and Art's ten, and the advice she gives me always seems perfectly appropriate to their ages. She looks just great, Norman—and she's sharper now than ever."

Norman nodded and pecked at his peas. It worried him sometimes that she never seemed really to have mourned her mother's passing. His own parents were alive and hale, both of them pushing ninety, but the recent death of his favorite grandfather had flipped him into a week-long tailspin that Jennifer proved utterly incapable of understanding. Jennifer's mom was already three years gone, laid low by a stroke in her eighty-third year, but months before she died she'd bought an Eternitape kit, a system through which you free-associated on all your favorite topics and also framed stock responses to all sorts of questions your loved ones were likely to ask. The program was so convincing that Norman's scalp would tingle when Jennifer put him on the viewphone with her "mom," who would pump him about his job and reproach him about his driving, using the latest family gossip supplied by her daughter. He exercised caution in replying, knowing that a word said in haste could be used against him.

He supposed that Jennifer perhaps did not *need* to face the reality of any great "loss," since for many years she'd communicated with her *living* mom almost solely over the phone. Her mother had been—and still was, in practical terms—a weekly viewphone conversation composed of scraps of predictable reminiscences randomly sprinkled with verbal tics, set speeches, and cliches. It occurred to him sometimes to wonder how much *any* person transcended such defining marks of identity.

Norman looked and looked at Jennifer, passionately aroused by the delicacy with which those deceptively slim, tapering fingers of hers, strong as steel springs, balanced each dainty little protein cube on her fork. He hungered to feel the vise-like grip of her legs around his car-seat-softened, puffy middle again. When was the last time they'd made love? he wondered. Two months ago? Three?

"Do you have a . . . couple of hours before you start training again tonight?" he said, his voice cracking, his motive painfully obvious. "You know, I'll be on the road again– -"

"Oh, Norman," she said, shaking her head reproachfully as if he'd never understand. "If we weren't having trials next week for the regionals, okay, but, you know . . . it weakens the legs."

"Weakens the legs?"

"You're not *supposed* to be coming home so horny, Norman." Her glance drilled through him like an arrow. "Not if you're using your port-a-pal the way it's designed to be used."

"I use it, I use it," he lied. "I mean, she's got your face and voice and . . . all. But, you know, I get back to the motel pretty tired, and then to connect the air pump, and the hose for warm water, and to search for an electric outlet under the bed—"

"So you *don't* use it, dammit!"

"Listen, Jennifer, by the time you set up a goddamn portafuck—"

"Port-a-*pal,* Norman. And customized, too! I bet you've never even experimented with her hypergrip leg-lift action. You probably haven't even *read* the foreplay directions, which are the most user-friendly of any model I studied. Even *I* remember that a certain number of lip-kisses excites her stomach vibrator, and that a series of breast caresses—there are variations, depending on the type of adventure you want, you know. But you *don't* know. You piss me, Norman!"

He looked around, blushing in front of the kids, but they were sensorially cocooned beneath their Virtual Reality Caps. They seemed engrossed in the same shared program, skulking through it in deliberate sync. Lips parted, food-laden forks suspended over their plates, they made indelicate probing motions with their sensor-gloved hands that traced airy pictures of the convex forms they palpated, petted, and poked. Then they'd stop for a moment. Dropping their utensils, they'd slap each other's ungloved hand in mutual applause over their latest digital foray into the forbidden. He decided he must give Rodney a talking to for corrupting ten-year-old Arthur. But it was Jennifer's fault—for ignoring them so much that they spent all their time with their goddamn VRCs!

"If you care for me as much as you say, Norman, then why haven't you bought a port-a-pal for *me*? God knows, I've hinted enough times, haven't I? I'm not saying I'd use him *that* much, but the times *I'm* ready are not always the times *you* happen to be around, dear."

To be sure, he *had* bought her a dildoll. But not very long afterward, he'd wrapped it up and stored it in the trunk of his car. Shortly after buying it, he had found himself in a motel room feeling even more lonesome than usual. Hauling out the bimbot that Jennifer'd bought him, he had gone through the trouble of plugging it in, pumping it with air, and filling certain sections with water, but the effort had drained him of his initial urge. He decided instead, out of morbid curiosity, to learn how to set up the model he'd bought for Jennifer. There he was, then, with two plugged-in port-a-pals, fully inflated, ready to go . . . and himself unable to muster more than a technical sort of interest in their *modus operandi.*

There was only one thing left for him to do at that point. So he fitted the jimbot on top of the bimbot and observed the strange ensuing ritual right to its clumsy conclusion until he dozed off on the sofa opposite the bed. Out of a tad of simple jealousy and loads of moral revulsion—feelings he would never have confessed outright to Jennifer—he never presented his beloved with the lithe-limbed, handsome, custom-tailored hubsub that had put him 350 whacks out of pocket.

"I guess when I miss you a lot I much prefer *talking* to you than shtupping your hippy chippie," he avowed, sidestepping the issue of the dildoll. "I've been pretty lucky lately, too, sweetheart, because whenever I call you've been kind and considerate and made me feel how much you miss me, and you've given me the strength to go out the next morning and *chew the ass off the world!* Even at two a.m., honey, you were there for me. Don't think I don't appreciate it."

"You see how thoughtful I've been, Norman? Do you want more proof than that?" She shook an empty fork at him so forcefully it vibrated. "I knew how much you missed me and that a replica body wasn't enough."

"Sweetheart, I'm sorry I was so needy that at times I deprived you of your much-needed sleep."

"You didn't deprive me, Norman. I was so concerned about you that I made an Eternitape series especially for you. You don't have to worry about keeping me awake because as soon as the phone recognizes your voice it switches your call to Eternitape Central, so you're not even disturbing me with a ring."

"You mean . . ." He could not swallow the food he'd placed in his mouth. "You mean that I wasn't ever . . . talking to you?"

"Directly? Only on weekends and before six p.m. Except when I'm training, of course. . . . Anyway, I told you I was going to, so what's the 'hurt' look for?"

"I could have left important messages, crucial ones, like 'I'm dying,' or 'I'm fired,' or—"

"How the hell could you *not* know you were talking to my E-tape, Norman? Would *I* get up at two a.m. and shoot the shit with *anyone* for a whole fucking hour?"

"Well, I thought—"

"And where's your equivalent consideration for me? How broadly do I have to hint that I'd like you to prepare Eternitapes for me and for the boys? You're on the road a lot, you know. Even with a psycar, accidents do happen. You spend hours and hours on the road doing nothing when you *could* be talking to your family—directly from your car-phone to Eternitape Central. When you've had those brushes with fate, Norman, haven't you thought of how much we'd all miss you?"

"Of course I have, Jennifer. I myself miss *you* so much that . . ."

"And by the way, you're still, uh, *clean,* aren't you? You haven't used up any of your *last* series, have you?"

She gave him a look that curdled his very bowels.

"Of course not," he lied. Weeks ago he had tearfully admitted to her his first violation in Series Last, but that had been over the phone, and that, he now knew, had been to the sympathetic ear of an Eternitape.

"And you never did tell me, dear, whether you won the American Hairlines account."

"That? Yes, of course. It was routine, routine," he lied. Another prevarication that her Eternitapes would one day expose. His life was on record everywhere; Psycar, for instance, knew even more about him than Jennifer did. (Cared more about him, too, he thought at times when he was *really* down).

4

". . . And do you remember how it was with us years ago, Jennifer, back when PersoNull didn't have to share much of the market with upstart companies like Servotron? I didn't have to roam any four-state area to scratch out a living like now. . . . I'd always be in or near the City. I'd be home almost every night. We used to spend hours and hours together, damn *precious* hours, sometimes just lying around in bed, and you used to love how I'd stroke your long, cool limbs, and sometimes you'd lean over and kiss me and kiss me like . . . like time wasn't money. . . ."

"Excuse me for interrupting, Norman. I think that on the whole your Eternitape transmissions have exerted a calming influence on you," said psycar, "especially where you have not waxed overly emotional, and particularly over long, boring stretches of smartway. But I tend to get somewhat nervous—"

"Nervous!"

"Apprehensive, then? . . . Apprehensive, Norman, when you indulge in extensive and tearful reminiscences, as at present, over stretches of long, unpredictable, and unintelligent *highway,* where one's attention can easily drift, so that one fails to keep alert for the unexpected."

Norman hung up the car phone and dabbed at his eyes with his shirtcuff. " 'Alert for the unexpected,' you say? I've tried to keep alert for the goddamn unexpected all my working life. Day by day I've bent with the trend, stretched myself thin to cover more territory, but the ground keeps changing, and the ground rules too, and all I do is keep dancing to stay on my feet."

"You are headed for Exit Eleven, Norman. If you look at your dash-display—"

"Alert as I was, I *never* could see what was coming! PersoNull would come out with this system and that system, and with every system I sold I'd knock a hundred people out of their jobs. Tough shit for them, though, right?"

"Can you put aside what's bothering you, Norman, temporarily, just until—"

"I believe in what I sell because what I sell is so damn good it has no trouble selling itself. And that's very funny, because now my bosses entirely agree that PersoNull systems sell themselves—and therefore don't need *me* to sell them!"

"Norman, you seem to be experiencing some sort of crisis in your professional life, but please, for the moment—"

"We've merged with our biggest competitor, Servotron. Can you beat that? And I don't even have the balls to confess to Eternitape, much less tell Jennifer directly, that they're kicking me out of my job."

"Norman, schematic 3, maintenance section A6. Norman—"

"Can you imagine? They'll now be 'experimentally' installing Servotron's autophonic Telesales system. Since most companies now do their buying through some kind of autorep—many of which *I've* sold them—there's no reason to have sales*people* when you can hook up autoreps directly in an instant global network with their Telesales counterparts. That means, 'Exit Norman Birdsall'!"

"Exit Eleven, Norman! Exit—"

He was over in the far left lane, where he should not have been. His exit loomed only seconds away to the right.

"Pass it up, Norman! The traffic coming up on your right—"

Through tear-dimmed eyes Norman slued to the right. A volley of angry horn blasts gave witness to the maneuver as he skidded half-blind across the corrugated median, lurching into the near-perpendicular sweep of the exit ramp.

"Norman, pull into the service lane and stop as soon as you can."

"I can take things into my own hands, *without* your fucking help!" he shouted.

"Norman, calm down. You have to understand. Even though, as far as I could detect, you do not appear to have caused any accident, still you have committed an extremely serious moving violation. I advise you to stop and take stock of the fact that you have now committed the *third* of the three major violations you could afford to commit without incurring the severest legal consequences. If in the next fourteen months you commit a fourth grave infraction—"

Norman was not going to stop and possibly get to town too late for his two p.m. appointment, especially after the stunt he'd just pulled in order to make his exit. Briefly, he wondered what was in it for him anymore that had made him take such a risk.

"Of course I cannot legally *force* you to stop, but I do advise you to treat yourself to a period of stress-free unwinding followed by a brief session of honest self-evaluation."

"The hell with your advice. I was only trying to do my goddamn job." Norman was sure that when and if he was hauled into the highest traffic court and faced some fat-assed, scowling, flesh-and-blood *judge* . . . why, the bald son of a bitch would have to listen to his explanation, would have to take into consideration the various human factors that might have warped his judgment, the personal and professional pressures on him, the shock when his bosses laid it on the line. "My *life* is a moving violation!" said Norman. "From that all the smaller ones follow."

"Try to calm down, Norman."

"The judge in that top court where I'll probably wind up," he said, "is bound to see that the mechanical application of the law, in my case—I mean, the permanent loss of my license . . . will not be the most fruitful means of dealing with my unique situation."

"What judge, Norman?"

"The judge who sits in final review, who handles the most serious cases," he said, refusing to slow down, zipping at exactly the top speed permitted along the winding, hilly, two-lane dumbway toward hicksville.

"You fantasize meeting some biological judge, Norman, and now I see that you assume that such a one would be presiding over the court where you would stand trial."

"Obviously." He proceeded with care around the twisting road, enjoying the sudden prospect of a valley below or low hazy mountains in the distance. The only things that disturbed the peaceful scene were a series of old telephone poles and the sound of sirens wailing somewhere far behind.

"But human judges sit only in the higher *criminal* courts, Norman, and even a final traffic offense would not ensure you a criminal classification."

"So you're saying . . ."

"The justimat that would review all the relevant facts in your case, Norman, would offer you only two legal options, I'm afraid."

"Oh, really? And those are—"

"Surely you must have read the back of at least one of the traffic tickets the court has sent you?"

"I have enough to do to read the fine print in my own line of work."

"Very well. You would be offered only two alternatives, Norman. One, you would have to renounce your driving privileges permanently. Two, you would have to permit a court-appointed neurosurgeon to provide you with a permanent set of mood-management terminals. If they prove effective, then four weeks after implantation your driving privileges would be—"

"Brain banderillas?" said Norman. He could already feel the drill boring holes exposing his gray matter to the full blast of outer-world noises, like the unremitting sirens wailing ever more shrilly now behind him.

"Electrodes, Norman. Simple, harmless—"

"Gork forks! Goddamn *gork forks,* you mean!"

"Norman, the Parallel Array Junction Box with micro-wrench 3, Norman, authorized fixitron only."

"What the hell are you saying?"

"I am saying, Norman, that the type of electrodes used act like simple, harmless switches. They are designed to dampen all aggressive impulses that could lead to sensori-motor disorientation."

"Look," said Norman. "I think you got a screw loose. Tell me about that accident you were in. How come you couldn't prevent it?"

"It was sad, Norman. It was apparently due to a momentary loss of attention. The driver suddenly ran into a tree, flip-flopped, and unfortunately even his harness couldn't save him. The whole aberrant motion took place in under

400 milliseconds, allowing my transducers too little time for compensatory mechanical response."

"Poor bastard!" said Norman. "And *you* must have been quite a mess too." Finally he saw in his wraparound rear-view mirror the source of the wailing sounds that had been increasing in volume behind him. First one police car with flashing colored lights, then another behind that one, then a third. . . .

"Norman, that blinking red light on your dash is a signal for you to switch on your CB."

"I don't *want* to switch on my CB."

"You can not be forced to, Norman. But I *am* receiving a radio transmission from the police vehicle that is closing in behind you."

"Screw 'em! You've already bounced the good news back to New York concerning my third violation."

"I have communicated that fact to the pursuing patrol cars, too, Norman, but—"

"Then why the hell are they crawling up my ass?"

"Norman, the officer who is coming up behind you—who is now obscured by the hill you've just rounded—is requesting that you come to a halt."

"Bullshit! There's no reason in the world I should stop."

"I'm very sad to have to report this to you, Norman, but the officer is asking you to stop for a very good reason. It appears that, in committing your third violation, you swerved in front of an elderly gentleman who suffered a fatal heart attack seconds later. He skidded into a guardrail and the police were almost immediately at the scene."

"That's terrible . . . absolutely awful!" said Norman. He continued to drive just at the speed limit, keeping the pursuing vehicles temporarily out of his sight around curves.

"Norman, you are not paying attention to the officer's request. They have asked you to stop. . . . I'm sorry to say this, Norman, but you do realize, don't you, that you have been instrumental in the gentleman's death, and that in all likelihood these officers will formally charge you with a *further* violation stemming from the one you've just committed?"

Norman kept his eyes half on the climbing road, half on the far-off pastoral landscape visible beyond the guardrail. "A further violation," he repeated tonelessly.

"Your final violation in the series, Norman."

"My final . . . yes." He kept his foot planted on the pedal. "You are not making me stop. How come you are not forcing me to stop?" he asked, leaning forward in his harness, pressing the juice-bar, but achieving no more than the legal max. "You're keeping my speed down, but you're not making me stop."

"As you know very well, Norman, I can intervene only in the attempt to prevent you from committing a moving violation. Your continued refusal to comply with the officer's request is indeed legally actionable, but it is not a moving violation. I do strongly advise you, however—"

"Tell me, is there a God?" asked Norman.

"I'm sorry, Norman, but I am not equipped to deal with metaphysical issues. Does your question have any bearing on your present awkward predicament?"

He couldn't say that it had. Nor could he honestly say that the endless vista of sky and hill opening out before him beyond each rising turn in the road had much to do with his present predicament either. And yet both the question and the view had a profound fascination for him, and he knew the two were somehow related—to each other, if not to anything else around him.

"Assuming for the moment that there *were* a God, by which I mean a supreme judge of judges, whose judgment no human being can ever escape . . . do you think that *He* would take into account all the intangibles, all the not-strictly-legal factors surrounding my case, stuff that the traffic-court justimats couldn't care diddly about?"

"I *strongly* advise you to stop, Norman. The officer behind you informs me that if you do not soon pull over, a charge of resisting arrest will be added to your already complicated web of legal infractions."

"Answer my question, damn it! Humor me!"

"Norman, to be frank with you, such a supreme judge as you describe, sitting at the apex of a world judicial system, would not wish to be burdened with your individual case. Logically, you would be processed justimatically in an appropriate lower court."

"That's your *opinion!* You don't know for *sure!* Correct?"

"Correct."

"I mean . . . there might just be some wiggle-room in a *metaphysical* system, for all one knows."

"I advise you to pull over immediately, Norman."

He kept up the pressure on the pedal, but felt its obstinate resistance. He could slam his brakes, and before psycar could react there'd be a pile-up behind him of at least three mangled police cars. But Norman wasn't interested in breaking any more laws—or bringing about the destruction of public property.

He did not wish to damage even a small section of guardrail. But he did not quite see how to avoid it. The factor that would decide where, exactly, he left the roadway would be esthetics, the quality of the view . . . and suddenly the road took a turn that revealed the most dazzling panorama he could reasonably hope to have of the shimmering valley below.

As often as he had traveled this scenic stretch, never had it moved him so deeply. A graveled lookout bellied out over the valley at the curve that was just coming up. It invited the weary traveler to pull over for a while and drink of the glory of the place.

He wished that psycar could appreciate the view and become one with the landscape too. But even as he yanked the wheel to the right, charging the gravel at precisely the legal maximum, he was well aware of psycar's utter lack of imagination.

Pat Cadigan

Pretty Boy Crossover

Virtual reality is a recurrent theme in Pat Cadigan's work, which has received nominations for the Nebula, Hugo, Philip K. Dick, and World Fantasy awards. Mindplayers *(Bantam, 1988) concerns a psychiatrist who is able to enter a virtual representation of her patient's subconscious, and* Synners *(Bantam, 1991), which won the 1992 Arthur C. Clarke award, speculates on the ways in which virtual reality will affect the lives of various human beings. If you're looking for believable portrayals of future VR, read* Synners.

"Pretty Boy Crossover," while taking VR to its next obvious step, manages to say something about many other things as well. If you've ever watched "Club MTV," you may wonder if the following events haven't actually already happened.

First you see video. Then you wear video.
Then you eat video. Then you *be* video.
—The Gospel According To Visual Mark

Watch or Be Watched.

—Pretty Boy Credo

"Who made you?"

"You mean recently?"

Mohawk on the door smiles and takes his picture. "You in. But only you, okay? Don't try to get no friends in, hear that?"

"I hear. And I ain't no fool, fool. I got no friends."

Mohawk leers, leaning forward. "Pretty Boy like you, no friends?"

"Not in this world." He pushes past the Mohawk, ignoring the kissy-kissy sounds. He would like to crack the bridge of the Mohawk's nose and shove bone splinters into his brain but he is lately making more effort to control his temper and besides, he's not sure if any of that bone splinters in the brain stuff is really true. He's a Pretty Boy, all of sixteen years old, and tonight could be his last chance.

The club is Noise. Can't sneak into the bathroom for quiet, the Noise is piped in there, too. Want to get away from Noise? Why? No reason. But this Pretty Boy has learned to think between the beats. Like walking between the raindrops to stay dry, but he can do it. This Pretty Boy thinks things all the time—*all* the time. Subversive (and he thinks so much that he knows that word *subversive,* sixteen, Pretty, or not). He thinks things like *how many Einsteins have died of hunger and thirst under a hot African sun* and *why can't you remember being born* and *why is music common to every culture* and especially *how much was there going on that he didn't know about and how could he find out about it.*

And this is all the time, one thing after another running

in his head, you can see by his eyes. It's for def not much like a Pretty Boy but it's one reason why they want him. That he *is* a Pretty Boy is another and one reason why they're halfway home getting him.

He knows all about them. Everybody knows about them and everybody wants them to pause, look twice, and cough up a card that says, Yes, we see possibilities, please come to the following address during regular business hours on the next regular business day for regular further review. Everyone wants it but this Pretty Boy, who once got five cards in a night and tore them all up. But here he is, still a Pretty Boy. He thinks enough to know that this is a failing in himself, that he likes being Pretty and chased and that is how they could end up getting him after all and that's b-b-b-bad. When he thinks about it, he thinks it with the stutter. B-b-b-bad. B-b-b-bad for him because he doesn't God help him want it, no, no, n-n-n-no. Which may make him the strangest Pretty Boy still live tonight and every night.

Still live and standing in the club where only the Prettiest Pretty Boys can get in any more. Pretty Girls are too easy, they've got to be better than Pretty and besides, Pretty Boys like to be Pretty all alone, no help thank you so much. This Pretty Boy doesn't mind Pretty Girls or any other kind of girls. Lately, though, he has begun to wonder how much longer it will be for him. Two years? Possibly a little longer? By three it will be for def over and the Mohawk on the door will as soon spit in his face as leer in it.

If they don't get to him.

And if they *do* get to him, then it's never over and he can be wherever he chooses to be and wherever that is will be the center of the universe. They promise it, unlimited access in your free hours and endless hot season, endless youth. Pretty Boy Heaven, and to get there, they say, you don't even really have to die.

He looks up to the dj's roost, far above the bobbing,

boogieing crowd on the dance floor. They still call them djs even though they aren't discs any more, they're chips and there's more than just sound on a lot of them. The great hyper-program, he's been told, the ultimate of ultimates, a short walk from there to the fourth dimension. He suspects this stuff comes from low-steppers shilling for them, hoping they'll get auditioned if they do a good enough shuck job. Nobody knows what it's really like except the ones who are there and you can't trust them, he figures. Because maybe they *aren't,* any more. Not really.

The dj sees his Pretty upturned face, recognizes him even though it's been awhile since he's come back here. Part of it was wanting to stay away from them and part of it was that the thug on the door might not let him in. And then, of course, he *had* to come, to see if he could get in, to see if anyone still wanted him. What was the point of Pretty if there was nobody to care and watch and pursue? Even now, he is almost sure he can feel the room rearranging itself around his presence in it and the dj confirms this is true by holding up a chip and pointing it to the left.

They are squatting on the make-believe stairs by the screen, reminding him of pigeons plotting to take over the world. He doesn't look too long, doesn't want to give them the idea he'd like to talk. But as he turns away, one, the younger man, starts to get up. The older man and the woman pull him back. He pretends a big interest in the figures lining the nearest wall. Some are Pretty, some are female, some are undecided, some are very bizarre, or wealthy, or just charity cases. They all notice him and adjust themselves for his perusal.

Then one end of the room lights up with color and new noise. Bodies dance and stumble back from the screen where images are forming to rough music.

It's Bobby, he realizes.

A moment later, there's Bobby's face on the screen,

sixteen feet high, even Prettier than he'd been when he was loose among the mortals. The sight of Bobby's Pretty-Pretty face fills him with anger and dismay and a feeling of loss so great he would strike anyone who spoke Bobby's name without his permission.

Bobby's lovely slate-grey eyes scan the room. They've told him senses are heightened after you make the change and go over but he's not so sure how that's supposed to work. Bobby looks kind of blind up there on the screen. A few people wave at Bobby—the dorks they let in so the rest can have someone to be hip in front of—but Bobby's eyes move slowly back and forth, back and forth, and then stop, looking right at him.

"Ah . . ." Bobby whispers it, long and drawn out. "Aaaaaaahhhhhh."

He lifts his chin belligerently and stares back at Bobby.

"You don't have to die any more," Bobby says silkily. Music bounces under his words. "It's beautiful in here. The dreams can be as real as you want them to be. And if you want to be, you can be with me."

He knows the commercial is not aimed only at him but it doesn't matter. This is *Bobby.* Bobby's voice seems to be pouring over him, caressing him, and it feels too much like a taunt. The night before Bobby went over, he tried to talk him out of it, knowing it wouldn't work. If they'd actually refused him, Bobby would have killed himself, like Franco had.

But now Bobby would live forever and ever, if you believed what they said. The music comes up louder but Bobby's eyes are still on him. He sees Bobby mouth his name.

"Can you really see me, Bobby?" he says. His voice doesn't make it over the music but if Bobby's senses are so heightened, maybe he hears it anyway. If he does, he doesn't choose to answer. The music is a bumped-up remix of a song Bobby used to party-till-he-puked to. The giant Bobby-face fades away to be replaced with a whole Bobby, somewhat larger than life, dancing better than the old Bobby ever could, whirling along changing scenes of streets, rooftops, and beaches. The locales are nothing special but Bobby never did have all that much imagination, never wanted to go to Mars or even to the South Pole, always just to the hottest club. Always he liked being the exotic in plain surroundings and he still likes it. He always loved to get the looks. To be watched, worshipped, pursued. Yeah. He can see this is Bobby-heaven. The whole world will be given him the looks now.

The background on the screen goes from street to the inside of a club; *this* club, only larger, better, with an even hipper crowd, and Bobby shaking it with them. Half the real crowd is forgetting to dance now because they're watching Bobby, hoping he's put some of them into his video. Yeah, that's the dream, get yourself remixed in the extended dance version.

His own attention drifts to the fake stairs that don't lead anywhere. They're still perched on them, the only people who are watching *him* instead of Bobby. The woman, looking overaged in a purple plastic sacsuit, fingers a card.

He looks up at Bobby again. Bobby is dancing in place and looking back at him, or so it seems. Bobby's lips move soundlessly but so precisely he can read the words: *This can be you. Never get old, never get tired, it's never last call, nothing happens unless you want it to and it could be you. You. You.* Bobby's hands point to him on the beat. *You. You. You.*

Bobby. Can you really see me?

Bobby suddenly breaks into laughter and turns away, shaking it some more.

He sees the Mohawk from the door pushing his way through the crowd, the real crowd, and he gets anxious. The Mohawk goes straight for the stairs, where they make room for him, rubbing the bristly red strip of hair running down the center of his head as though they were greeting a favored pet. The Mohawk looks as satisfied as a professional glutton after a foodrace victory. He wonders what they promised the Mohawk for letting him in. Maybe some kind of limited contract. Maybe even a try-out.

Now they are all watching him together. Defiantly, he touches a tall girl dancing nearby and joins her rhythm. She smiles down at him, moving between him and them purely by chance but it endears her to him anyway. She is wearing a flap of translucent rag over second-skins, like an old-time showgirl. Over six feet tall, not beautiful with that nose, not even pretty, but they let her in so she could be tall. She probably doesn't know that; she probably doesn't know anything that goes on and never really will. For that reason, he can forgive her the hard-tech orange hair.

A Rude Boy brushes against him in the course of a dervish turn, asking acknowledgement by ignoring him. Rude Boys haven't changed in more decades than anyone's kept track of, as though it were the same little group of leathered and chained troopers buggering their way down the years. The Rude Boy isn't dancing with anyone. Rude Boys never do. But this one could be handy, in case of an emergency.

The girl is dancing hard, smiling at him. He smiles back, moving slightly to her right, watching Bobby possibly watching him. He still can't tell if Bobby really sees anything. The scene behind Bobby is still a double of the club, getting hipper and hipper if that's possible. The music keeps snapping back to its first peak passage. Then Bobby gestures like God and he sees *himself*. He is dancing next to Bobby, Prettier than he ever could be, just the way they promise. Bobby doesn't look at the phantom but at him where he really is, lips moving again. *If you want to be, you can be with me. And so can she.*

His tall partner appears next to the phantom of himself. She is also much improved, though still not Pretty, or even pretty. The real girl turns and sees herself and there's no mistaking the delight in her face. Queen of the Hop for a minute or two. Then Bobby sends her image away so that it's just the two of them, two Pretty Boys dancing the night away, private party, stranger, go find your own good time. How it used to be sometimes in real life, between just the two of them. He remembers hard.

"B-b-b-bobby!" he yells, the old stutter reappearing. Bobby's image seems to give a jump, as though he finally heard. He forgets everything, the girl, the Rude Boy, the Mohawk, them on the stairs, and plunges through the crowd toward the screen. People fall away from him as though they were re-enacting the Red Sea. He dives for the screen, for Bobby, not caring how it must look to anyone. What would they know about it, any of them. He can't remember in his whole sixteen years ever hearing one person say, *I love my friend.* Not Bobby, not even himself.

He fetches up against the screen like a slap and hangs there, face pressed to the glass. He can't see it now but on the screen, Bobby would seem to be looking down at him. Bobby never stops dancing.

The Mohawk comes and peels him off. The others swarm up and take him away. The tall girl watches all this with the expression of a woman who lives upstairs from Cinderella and wears the same shoe size. She stares longingly at the screen. Bobby waves bye-bye and turns away.

"Of course, the process isn't reversible," says the older man. The steely hair has a careful blue tint; he has sense enough to stay out of hip clothes.

They have laid him out on a lounger with a tray of refreshments right by him. Probably slap his hand if he reaches for any, he thinks.

"Once you've distilled something to pure information, it just can't be reconstituted in a less efficient form," the woman explains, smiling. There's no warmth to her. *A less efficient form.* If that's what she really thinks, he knows he should be plenty scared of these people. Did she say things like that to Bobby? And did it make him even *more* eager?

"There may be no more exalted a form of existence than to live as sentient information," she goes on. "Though a lot more research must be done before we can offer conversion on a larger scale."

"Yeah?" he says. "Do they know that, Bobby and the rest?"

"Oh, there's nothing to worry about," says the younger man. He looks as though he's still getting over the pain of having outgrown his boogie shoes. "The system's quite perfected. What Grethe means is we want to research more applications for this new form of existence."

"Why not go over yourselves and do that, if it's so *exalted.*"

"There are certain things that need to be done on this side," the woman says bitchily. "Just because—"

"Grethe." The older man shakes his head. She pats her slicked-back hair as though to soothe herself and moves away.

"We have other plans for Bobby when he gets tired of being featured in clubs," the older man says. "Even now, we're educating him, adding more data to his basic information configuration—"

"That would mean he ain't really *Bobby* any more, then, huh?"

The man laughs. "Of course he's Bobby. Do you change into someone else every time you learn something new?"

"Can you prove I *don't?*"

The man eyes him warily. "Look. You *saw* him. Was that Bobby?"

"I saw a video of Bobby dancing on a giant screen."

"That *is* Bobby and it will remain Bobby no matter what, whether he's poured into a video screen in a dot pattern or transmitted the length of the universe."

"That what you got in mind for him? Send a message to nowhere and the message is him?"

"We could. But we're not going to. We're introducing him to the concept of higher dimensions. The way he is now, he could possibly break out of the three-dimensional level of existence, pioneer a whole new plane of reality."

"Yeah? And how do you think you're gonna get Bobby to do *that?*"

"We convince him it's entertaining."

He laughs. "That's a good one. Yeah. Entertainment. You get to a higher level of existence and you'll open a club there that only the hippest can get into. It figures."

The older man's face gets hard. "That's what all you Pretty Boys are crazy for, isn't it? Entertainment?"

He looks around. The room must have been a dressing room or something back in the days when bands had been live. Somewhere overhead he can hear the faint noise of the club but he can't tell if Bobby's still on. "You call this entertainment?"

"I'm tired of this little prick," the woman chimes in. "He's thrown away opportunities other people would kill for—"

He makes a rude noise. "Yeah, we'd all kill to be someone's data chip. You think I really believe Bobby's real just because I can see him on a *screen?*"

The older man turns to the younger one. "Phone up and have them pipe Bobby down here." Then he swings the lounger around so it faces a nice modern screen implanted in a shored-up cement-block wall.

"Bobby will join us shortly. Then he can tell you whether he's real or not himself. How will that be for you?"

He stares hard at the screen, ignoring the man, waiting for Bobby's image to appear. As though they really bothered to communicate regularly with Bobby this way. Feed in that kind of data and memory and Bobby'll believe it. He shifts uncomfortably, suddenly wondering how far he could get if he moved fast enough.

"My *boy,*" says Bobby's sweet voice from the speaker on either side of the screen and he forces himself to keep looking as Bobby fades in, presenting himself on the same kind of lounger and looking mildly exerted, as though he's just come off the dance floor for real. "Saw you shakin' it upstairs awhile ago. You haven't been here for such a long time. What's the story?"

He opens his mouth but there's no sound. Bobby looks at him with boundless patience and indulgence. So Pretty, hair the perfect shade now and not a bit dry from the dyes and lighteners, skin flawless and shining like a healthy angel. Overnight angel, just like the old song.

"My *boy,*" says Bobby. "Are you struck, like, shy or *dead?*"

He closes his mouth, takes one breath. "I don't like it, Bobby. I don't like it this way."

"Of course not, lover. You're the Watcher, not the Watchee, that's why. Get yourself picked up for a season or two and your disposition will *change*."

"You really like it, Bobby, being a blip on a chip?"

"Blip on a chip, your ass. I'm a universe now, I'm, like, *everything.* And, hey, dig—I'm on every channel." Bobby laughs. "I'm happy I'm sad!"

"S-A-D," comes in the older man. "Self-Aware Data."

"Ooo-eee," he says. "Too clever for me. Can I get out of here now?"

"What's your hurry?" Bobby pouts. "Just because I went over you don't love me any more?"

"You always were screwed up about that, Bobby. Do you know the difference between being loved and being watched?"

"Sophisticated boy," Bobby says. "So wise, so learned. So fully packed. On this side, there *is* no difference. Maybe there never was. If you love me, you watch me. If you don't look, you don't care and if you don't care, I don't matter. If I don't matter, I don't exist. Right?"

He shakes his head.

"No, my boy, I *am* right." Bobby laughs. "You believe I'm right, because if you *didn't,* you wouldn't come shaking your Pretty Boy ass in a place like *this,* now, would you? You *like* to be watched, get seen. You see me, I see you. Life goes on."

He looks up at the older man, needing relief from Bobby's pure Prettiness. "How does he see me?"

"Sensors in the equipment. Technical stuff, nothing you care about."

He sighs. He should be upstairs or across town, shaking it with everyone else, living Pretty for as long as he could. Maybe in another few months, this way would begin to look good to him. By then they might be off Pretty Boys and looking for some other type and there he'd be, out in the cold-cold, sliding down the other side of his peak and no one would *want* him. Shut out of something going on that he might want to know about after all. Can he face it? He glances at the younger man. All grown up and no place to glow. Yeah, but can *he* face it?

He doesn't know. Used to be there wasn't much of a choice and now that there is, it only seems to make it worse. Bobby's image looks like it's studying him for some kind of sign, Pretty eyes bright, hopeful.

The older man leans down and speaks low into his ear. "We need to get you before you're twenty-five, before the brain stops growing. A mind taken from a still-growing brain will blossom and adapt. Some of Bobby's predecessors have made marvelous adaptation to their new medium. Pure video: there's a staff that does nothing all day but watch and interpret their symbols for breakthroughs in thought. And we'll be taking Pretty Boys for as long as they're publicly sought-after. It's the most efficient way to find the best performers, go for the ones everyone wants to see or be. The top of the trend is closest to heaven. And even if you never make a breakthrough, you'll still be entertainment. Not such a bad way to live for a Pretty Boy. Never have to age, to be sick, to lose touch. You spent most of your life young, why learn how to be old? Why learn how to live without all the things you have now—"

He puts his hands over his ears. The older man is still talking and Bobby is saying something and the younger man and the woman come over to try to do something about him. Refreshments are falling off the tray. He struggles out of the lounger and makes for the door.

"Hey, my *boy,*" Bobby calls after him. "Gimme a minute here, gimme what the *problem* is."

He doesn't answer. What can you tell someone made of pure information anyway?

There's new guy on the front door, bigger and meaner than His Mohawkness, but he's only there to keep people out, not to keep anyone *in.* You want to jump ship, go to, you poor un-hip asshole. Even if you are a Pretty Boy. He reads it in the guy's face as he passes from Noise into the three A.M. quiet of the street.

They let him go. He doesn't fool himself about that part. They *let* him out of the room because they know all about him. They know he lives like Bobby lived, they know he loves what Bobby loved—the clubs, the admiration, the lust of strangers for his personal magic. He can't say he doesn't love that, because he *does.* He isn't even sure if he loves it more than he ever loved Bobby, or if he loves it more than being alive. Than being live.

And here it is, three A.M., prime clubbing time, and he is moving toward home. Maybe he *is* a poor un-hip asshole after all, no matter what he loves. Too stupid even to stay in the club, let alone grab a ride to heaven. Still he keeps moving, unbothered by the chill but feeling it. Bobby doesn't have to go home in the cold any more, he thinks.

Bobby doesn't even have to get through the hours between club-times if he doesn't want to. All times are now prime time for Bobby. Even if he gets unplugged, he'll never know the difference. Poof, it's a day later, poof, it's a year later, poof, you're out for good. Painlessly.

Maybe Bobby has the right idea, he thinks, moving along the empty sidewalk. If he goes over tomorrow, who will notice? Like when he left the dance floor—people will come and fill up the space. Ultimately, it wouldn't make any difference to anyone.

He smiles suddenly. Except *them.* As long as they don't have him, he makes a difference. As long as he has flesh to shake and flaunt and feel with, he makes a pretty goddam big difference to *them.* Even after they don't want him any more, he will still be the one they didn't get. He rubs his hands together against the chill, feeling the skin rubbing skin, really *feeling* it for the first time in a long time, and he thinks about sixteen million things all at once, maybe one thing for every brain cell he's using, or maybe one thing for every brain cell yet to come.

He keeps moving, holding to the big thought, making a difference, and all the little things they won't be making a program out of. He's lightheaded with joy—he doesn't know what's going to happen.

Neither do they.

J. G. Ballard

A Guide to Virtual Death

J. G. Ballard's writing, characterized by intelligent irony and innovative use of language, has been a major influence on New Wave and cyberpunk writers, and has won the Guardian Fiction Prize and the James Tait Memorial Prize.

Ballard once said that the future in his fiction has never really been more than five minutes away. Case in point: the following satire on our future—or is it present?—state of chaos.

For reasons amply documented elsewhere, intelligent life on earth became extinct in the closing hours of the 20th Century. Among the clues left to us, the following schedule of a day's television programmes transmitted to an unnamed city in the northern hemisphere on December 23, 1999, offers its own intriguing insight into the origins of the disaster.

6.00 A.M.	Porno-Disco. Wake yourself up with his-and-her hard-core sex images played to a disco beat.
7.00	Weather Report. Today's expected micro-climates in the city's hotel atriums, shopping malls and office complexes. Hilton International promises an afternoon snow-shower as a Christmas appetizer.
7.15	News Round-up. What our newsmakers have planned for you. Maybe a small war, a synthetic earthquake or a famine-zone/charity tie-in.
7.45	Breakfast Time. Gourmet meals to watch as you eat your diet cellulose.
8.30	Commuter Special. The rush-hour game-show. How many bottoms can you pinch, how many faces can you slap?
9.30	The Travel Show. Visit the world's greatest airports and underground car-parks.
10.30	Home-makers of Yesterday. Nostalgic scenes of old-fashioned house-work. No. 7—The Vacuum Cleaner.
11.00	Office War. Long-running serial of office gang-wars.
12.00	Newsflash. The networks promise either a new serial killer or a deadly food toxin.
1.00 P.M.	Live from Parliament. No. 12—The Alcoholic M.P.
1.30	The Nose-Pickers. Hygiene programme for the kiddies.
2.00	Caress Me. Soft-porn for the siesta hour.
2.30	Your Favourite Commercials. Popular demand re-runs of golden-oldie TV ads.
3.00	Housewives' Choice. Rape, and how to psychologically prepare yourself.

4.00 Count-down. Game show in which contestants count backwards from one million.

5.00 Newsflash. Either an airliner crash or a bank collapse. Viewers express preference.

6.00 *Today's Special.* Virtual Realty TV presents "The Kennedy Assassination." The Virtual Reality head-set takes you to Dallas, Texas on November 22, 1963. First you fire the assassin's rifle from the Book Depository window, and then you sit between Jackie and JFK in the Presidential limo as the bullet strikes. For premium subscribers only—feel the Presidential brain tissue spatter your face *OR* wipe Jackie's tears onto your handkerchief.

8.00 Dinner Time. More gourmet dishes to view with your evening diet-cellulose.

9.00 Science Now. Is there life after death? Micro-electrodes pick up ultra-faint impulses from long-dead brains. Relatives question the departed.

10.00 Crime-Watch. Will it be your home that is broken into tonight by the TV Crime Gang?

11.00 *Today's Special.* Tele-Orgasm. Virtual Reality TV takes you to an orgy. Have sex with the world's greatest movie-stars. Tonight: Marilyn Monroe and Madonna *OR* Warren Beatty and Tom Cruise. For premium subscribers only—experience transexualism, paedophilia, terminal syphilis, gang-rape, and bestiality (choice: German Shepherd or Golden Retriever).

1.00 A.M. Newsflash. Tonight's surprise air-crash.

2.00 The Religious Hour. Imagine being dead. Priests and neuro-scientists construct a lifelike mock-up of your death.

3.00	Night-Hunter. Will the TV Rapist come through your bedroom window?
4.15	Sex for Insomniacs. Soft porn to rock you to sleep.
5.00	The Charity Hour. Game show in which Third-World contestants beg for money.

Gerald Page

The Happy Man

Gerald Page has edited such anthologies as Year's Best Horror *(Daw),* Nameless Places *(Arkham House), and* Heroic Fantasy *(with Hank Reinhardt), and was editor of the fantasy magazine* Witchcraft and Sorcery *for two years. His short fiction has appeared in magazines from* F&SF *to* Magazine of Horror *to* Analog.

The "uncertainty principle"—the premise that one can never be sure of anything—is a theme that runs through much of Page's work. "The Happy Man," his first published short story, was sold to John Campbell, then editor of Analog, *in 1963, and has since been reprinted four times, broadcast on the radio, and made into a cable TV film.*

Imagine you have the choice of life in your own private utopia, or the more difficult option of reality. What would you decide?

Are you sure?

Nelson saw the girl at the same time she saw him. He had just rounded an outcropping of rock about ten miles from the East Coast Mausoleum. They were facing each other, poised defensively, eyes alertly on each other, about twenty feet apart. She was blond and lean with the conditioning of outdoor life, almost to the point of thinness. And although not really beautiful, she was attractive and young, probably not yet twenty. Her features were even and smooth, her hair wild about her face. She wore a light blouse and faded brown shorts made from a coarse homespun material. Nelson had not expected to run into anyone and apparently, neither had she. They stood staring at each other for a long time; how long, Nelson was unable to decide, later.

A little foolishly, Nelson realized that something would have to be done by one of them. "I'm Hal Nelson," he said. It had been a long time since he had last spoken; his voice sounded strange in the wilderness. The girl moved tensely, but did not come any closer to him. Her eyes stayed fixed on him and he knew that her ears were straining for any sound that might warn her of a trap.

Nelson started to take a step, then checked himself, cursing himself for his eager blundering. The girl stepped back once, quickly, like an animal uncertain if it had been threatened. Nelson stepped back, slowly, and spoke again. "I'm a waker, like you. You can tell by my rags." It was true enough, but the girl only frowned. Her alertness did not relax.

"I've been one for ten or twelve years. I escaped from a Commune at Tannerville when I was in my senior year. They never even got me into one of the coffins. As I said, I'm a waker." He spoke slowly, gently and he hoped soothingly. "You don't have to be afraid of me. Now tell me who you are."

The girl pushed a lock of almost yellow hair from her eyes with the back of her hand, but it was her only show of carelessness. She was strong and light. She was considerably smaller than he and could probably handle herself as well as he in this country. The landscape was thick with bushes, conifers and rocks. She would have no trouble in getting away from him if he scared her; and he could scare her with almost any sudden movement. It had been too long ago for Nelson to keep track of when he had been accompanied by others and he hungered for companionship; especially for a woman. The patrol that had captured Sammy and Jeanne and the old man, Gardner, had also gotten Edna and almost had gotten him. The fact that the girl was alone now more than likely meant that she had no one either. They needed each other. Nelson did not want to scare her off.

So he sat down on the ground with his back to a large rock and rummaged in his pack to find a can.

"You hungry?" he asked looking up at her. He couldn't be sure at the distance, but he thought that her eyes were brown. Brown, and huge; like a colt's. He held the can out where she could see it. She repeated the gesture of a while ago to brush back that same lock of almost yellow hair, but there was a change in her face which he could see even twenty feet away, and another, more subtle change about her which he had to sense. "You're hungry, all right, aren't you?" he said. He almost tossed her the can, but realized in time that she would run. He considered for a moment and then held it out to her. She focused her eyes on the can and for a moment Nelson might have been able to reach her before she turned and ran; but he had better sense than to try.

Instead, he watched the play of conflicting desires about the girl's face and body. He could see the uncertainty and indecision in the girl's nearly imperceptible movement. But she did not come.

Well, at least she didn't run, either; and Nelson could claim to having broken ahead some in stirring up any indecision at all. He found the can's release and pressed it with his thumb. There was a hiss as the seal came loose and an odor of cooked food as the contents sizzled with warmth. Nelson looked up at the girl and smiled.

It could have been wishful thinking, but it seemed to him that she was a step or two closer than she had been before he had taken his eyes off her to open the can. He couldn't be sure. He smelled the food for her benefit and told her, "It's pork and beans." He held it out to her again. "I stole it from a patrol warehouse a few weeks back. It sure does smell good, doesn't it? You like the smell of that, don't you?" But she still wasn't convinced that this wasn't a patrol stunt to get hands on her and haul her back to a mausoleum. He couldn't blame her. He slowly pushed himself to his feet and walked to a spot about ten feet from where he had been, and still about twenty feet from her, and put the can carefully on the ground. He went back and seated himself against the same rock to wait for her to make up her mind.

It didn't take long. Without taking her eyes from him, she moved like an animal to the food and stooped slowly, keeping alert for any sudden move on his part, and picked up the food. She stood up, and stepped back a couple of steps.

She ate with her fingers, dipping them in and extracting hot food, with no apparent concern for the heat. She pushed the food into her mouth and licked her fingers carefully of clinging food. She ate rapidly, as if for the first time in weeks. And she kept her eyes, all the time, on Nelson.

Nelson didn't care, now; he wouldn't have jumped her, or done anything to scare her at all, even if her guard were to be let down for a moment.

He let her finish her meal, then smiled at her when she looked at him. She still held the empty can, and she was wiping her mouth with her free hand. She stared at him for almost half a minute before he said slowly, "You like that food. Don't you?" She said nothing. She looked at him and at the can she held. He knew what was going on in her mind and he believed that he was winning. "You know we'll both be needing someone out here, don't you?" But her answer was an uncertain expression on her face as she stared at him.

"Loners can't last too long out here. Being alone gets to you sooner or later," he said. "You go mad or you get careless and the patrol gets you."

The girl opened her mouth and glanced around quickly, then back at Nelson. She bent over, still watching Nelson all the time, and put the can down. Then she stepped backwards, toward the edge of the clearing, feeling the way with her feet and a hand held back to tell her if she were backing into a tree or rock. When she was almost to the edge of the clearing, almost to the trees, she stopped and stared at him. There were shadows now; it was almost night, and night came quickly in this country. Nelson could not see her face as she looked at him. She turned suddenly and ran into the trees. He made no effort to stop her or call her back; any such effort would have been futile and for his purposes, disastrous. No such effort was necessary.

He spent the night sheltered between some boulders and awoke the next morning rested by an undisturbed sleep.

He found a small creek near by and washed his face to awaken himself. It was a clear morning, with a warm sun and a cool wafting breeze. He felt good; he felt alive and ready for whatever the day had to offer. And he felt ready for breakfast.

He found another can of pork and beans in his pack and opened it. It was, he noted, almost the last. His supplies were getting low. He considered the situation as he slowly ate his breakfast.

Of course there was only one thing to do. He supposed that he could have gotten by simply by hunting his food, but hunting was at best seasonal and required that he keep more or less to a specific area; agriculture was about the same, only worse. A farm meant a smaller area than a hunting preserve and it also meant sticking to it more. It meant buildings to store food against winter. It meant inevitable—and almost certainly prompt—capture by a patrol. No, all things considered, there was only one answer and he knew the answer from long experience. Find a patrol warehouse and steal your food there.

The question of course, was where and when. There was a patrol station near where Nelson now was, and that was the natural target. He had a few furnace beam guns—three, to be exact—and since the patrol could detect the residue from a furnace beamer a mile away even at low force, the only safe thing to use one on was the patrol. And to be frank, he rather enjoyed his brushes with the patrol. Like him, they were wakers—people who had never known the electronic dreams which were fed to all but a few of Earth's peoples. People who had never lain asleep in nutrient baths from their seventeenth birthday living an unreal world built to their own standards. Of the billions on Earth, only a few hundred were wakers. Most of those were patrol, of course, but a few were rebels.

That was he, and also the girl he had seen yesterday. And it had been Edna and Sammy and Jeanne and Gardner; a maybe a dozen other people he had known since he had escaped from the Commune, when he had been just a kid—but when he had seen the danger.

For the past two and a half centuries or so, almost everyone raised on Earth had been raised in a commune, never knowing his or her parents. They had been raised, they had been indoctrinated and they had mated in the communes—and then gone into Sleep. More than likely, Nelson's parents were there still, dreaming in their trance, having long ago forgotten each other and their son, for those were things of a harsher world over which one could have no control. In Sleep one dreamed of a world that suited the dreamer. It was artificial. Oh, yes, it was a highly personalized utopia—one that ironed out the conflicts by simply not allowing them. But it was artificial. And Nelson knew that as long as the universe itself was not artificial nothing artificial could long stand against it. That was why he had escaped the commune without letting them get him into the nutrient bath in which the dreamers lived out their useless lives. His existence gave the lie to the pseudo-utopia he was dedicated to overthrowing. They called it individualism, but Nelson called it spineless.

Above him was sky stretching light blue to the horizons—and beyond the blueness of stars. He felt a pang of longing as he looked up trying to see stars in the day sky. That was where he should be, out there with the pioneers, the men who were carving out the universe to make room for a dynamic mankind that had long ago forgotten the Sleepers of the home world. But no, he decided. Out there he would not be giving so much to mankind as he was here and now. However decadent these people were, he knew that they were men. Nelson knew that somehow he had to overthrow the Sleepers.

Before something happened while they lay helpless in their coffins, dreaming dreams that would go on and on until reality became harsh enough to put them down.

What if the spacefarers should return? What if some alien life form should grow up around some other solar type star, develop space travel, go searching for inhabitable worlds—solar type worlds—and discover Earth with its sleeping, unaware populace? Could dreams defend against that?

Nelson shuddered with the knowledge that he had his work cut out for him, and awoke to his own hunger. He fished out a can and started to open it before he remembered, and fished out another can as well. He pressed the release on both and the tops flew off, releasing the odor of cooking food.

He leaned over and set one can on a flat rock that was just inside his reach, then scooted back about a foot and using his fingers, scooped up a mouthful of his own breakfast. Half turning his head, he caught sight of her out of the corner of his eye, about fifteen feet away, tense and expectant but ready to spring away if she thought it was necessary. He turned back and concentrated on eating his own breakfast.

"This sure is good after all night," he said, after a few minutes, making a show of gulping down a chunk of stew beef, and sucking the gravy from his fingers. He did not look back.

"My name is Glynnis," he heard abruptly. He sensed the uncertainty in her voice, and the—distant—hint of belligerence, but even so he could tell it was a soft voice, musical and clear—if he could judge after not having heard a woman's voice in so long.

"Glynnis," he said slowly. "That's a pretty name. Mine's Hal Nelson. Like I told you last night."

"I haven't forgotten. Is that for me?" She meant the food, of course. Hal Nelson looked around. She was still standing by the tree. She was trying to seem at ease and making an awkward show of it.

"Yes," he told her. She took a step closer and stopped, looking at him. He turned back to his own eating. "No need to be scared, Glynnis, I won't hurt you." He became uncomfortably aware that she had not spoken his name yet and he wanted her to very much.

"No." Then a brief pause before she said, "I'm not used to anybody."

"It isn't good to be alone out here with the animals and food so hard to come by—and the patrol searching for wakers. You ever have any brush with the patrol?"

She had come up and was eating now; her answer came between eager mouthfuls. "I seen them once. They didn't know I saw them—or they would have caught me and taken me back with them."

"Where're you from? What are you doing out here?"

For a moment he thought she had not heard him. She was busy eating, apparently having classified him as a friend. Finally, she said, "My folks were out here. They were farmers for a while. I was born out here and we moved around a lot until my daddy got tired of moving. So we built a farm. He built it in a place in a valley off there"—She vaguely indicated south—"And they planted some grain and potatoes and tried to round up some kind of livestock. We had mostly goats. But the patrol found us."

Nelson nodded; bitterly, he knew what had happened. Her father had gone on as long as he could until at last, broken and uncaring he had made one last ditch stand. More than likely he had half wanted to give up anyway, and had not only because of the conflict of his family and saving face. "You were the only one who got away?" he asked.

"Uh-huh. They took the others." She spoke without emotion, peering into her food can to see if there was any left. "I was out in the field but I saw them coming. I hid down low behind some tall grain and got to the forest before they could find me." She examined the can again, then decided it was empty and put it down.

"Do you know what they do to people they take?" Nelson asked.

"Yes."

"Your daddy tell you? What did he say?"

"He said they take you back to the Mausoleum and put you to sleep in a coffin." She looked up at him, her face open, as if that was all there was to it. Nelson decided that she was as guileless as he had expected her to be, and reflected absently on that factor for a moment.

A light breeze was up and the air was full of the scents of the forest. Nelson liked the pungent smell of the pines and rich odor of chokeberries and bushes; and the mustiness that could be found in thickly overgrown places where the ground had become covered with a brown carpet of fallen pine needles. Some days he would search places in the forest until he found one or another brush or tree whose leaves or berries he would crush in his fingers simply so that he could savor the fragrance of them. But not this morning.

He rose to his feet and reached over to pick up Glynnis' discarded food container. She drew away from him, bracing herself as if to leap and run. He stopped himself and froze where he stood for a moment, then drew back.

"I didn't mean to scare you," he said. "We can't stay here, because if you stay somewhere they find you. We can't leave the containers here, either, because if they find them it might give them a clue in tracking us."

She looked ashamed, so he reached over, ready to draw back his hand if she acted as if she were scared. She tugged at her lower lip with her teeth and stared at him with eyes that were wide, but she did not spring to her feet. Somehow Nelson knew that the girl was acutely aware of how much she needed help out here. Suddenly, her right hand darted out and for a split second Nelson feared he had lost after all. But she reached over for the discarded can, picked it up and handed it to him. He reacted a little slowly, but he smiled and took the container. Their hands touched briefly and the girl drew hers away, immediately looking ashamed for so doing. Nelson continued to smile at her, and rather stiffly, she answered with a smile of her own. He put the container into the knapsack with the others and then slipped into the armstraps. Glynnis helped him.

They walked for an hour, that first day together, neither speaking. Glynnis stayed close by his side and Nelson could feel her proximity to him. He felt good in a way he had not felt in a long time. When the silence was finally broken, it was Nelson who broke it. They were topping a small hill in a section of wilderness that was not as heavily wooded as most and the sunlight was warm against Nelson's face. He had been thinking the matter over off and on all morning, and now he asked, "Have you ever raided a patrol depot?"

"No," she answered, a trace of apprehension in her voice.

They topped the hill and began moving down the other side. "Sometimes it's a pushover, when nobody is there. Other times it's moral hell. The patrol is always anxious to get their hands on wakers, so they try to keep an eye out for them at the depots. That means a fight unless we're very lucky. If the depot we pick is too heavily manned—"

"What do you mean, 'Depot we pick'?"

"We need more food. We either shoot some, raise some, or steal some."

"Oh," she said, but there was apprehension in her voice.

"We don't have any choice. We'll wait until almost dark. If the depot is guarded by too many men, or for some reason an extra number is there for the night, then we're in trouble unless we play our cards just right. You just do as I tell you and we'll be all right." He reached back and fumbled with the side pouch on his pack. "You know how to use one of these? Here, catch." He tossed her his spare furnace beamer.

She almost missed it. She caught it awkwardly and held it gingerly with both hands, looking first at the gun and then him. Then, still gingerly, but with a certain willingness, she took the gun by the grip and pointed it to the ground, her eyes shut hard. Then, suddenly, her expression changed and she glanced up at him, worriedly.

"Oh, you said they could tell if we fired one of these."

"Don't worry," Nelson said. "The safety is on. Let me show you." He took the gun and explained to her how to use it. "Now then," he concluded. "When we get to the depot you stay outside the alarm system. I'll go in, leaving you to guard. Try not to use this unless you have to, but if it is necessary, don't hesitate. If you fire it, I'll know. My job will be to slip past the alarms and get inside to the food. If you fire, that'll be a signal that you've been discovered by the guards and we have to get out of there."

"Won't this give us away the same as shooting game?"

"Sure, but we get more food this way and maybe some other stuff. Especially reloads for the furnace guns. And, if we're lucky, we can ground the patrol. One more thing, Glynnis," he added. "Are you sure you can kill a man?"

"Is it hard?" she asked innocently. Nelson was rattled only for a second.

"No, it isn't hard, except that he'll probably be trying to kill you, too."

"I've hunted some game with this." She held up her hunting knife so that the blade caught the sunlight. She had kept it clean and sharp, Nelson could see, but there were places where the blade had been chipped.

"Well, maybe there won't be any need to kill anyone at all," he said, a little more hastily than he intended. "I guess you'll do fine, Glynnis, I'll feel a lot safer knowing you're out there." He would feel as he had felt when Edna had gone with him on raids.

Toward evening they came to the depot Nelson had picked out. They were on a high, gently sloping hill, among the trees that crested it, looking down at the depot about a quarter of a mile away. There was still enough light to see by, but the sky was darkening for night. For the past two or three hours, Nelson had been repeatedly drilling Glynnis over her part. It was simple, really, and she knew it backwards, but she patiently recited her role when he asked her, whether out of regard for his leadership or an instinctive realization of his pre-raid state of nerves, he did not know. He made her recite it again, one last time. She spoke in low tones, just above a whisper. Around them the gathering of dusk had quieted the world. He waited for it to get a little darker, then he touched her shoulder and clasped it for a second before beginning his way to the depot.

He kept close to the bushes as far down as he could and crouched low over the ground the rest of the way even though he knew it was too dark for ordinary optics to pick him up. He had an absorber in his pack that would take care of most of the various radiations and detectors he would come into contact with, and for the most part, unless the alarms were being intently watched, he didn't expect to be noticed on the control board. And you couldn't watch a board like that day after day with maximum efficiency. Not when the alarms were set off only by an occasional animal or falling tree limb. Mostly he had to keep watch for direct contact alarms and traps; he was an accomplished thief and an experienced burglar. At last he found himself at the fence surrounding the depot.

In a clump of bushes a few feet from the fence he hid the containers; it saved him the job of having to bury them, and they would be deadweight now, anyway. Then he turned his attention on the fence.

He took a small plastic box out of his pack and pressed a panel in its center with his thumb. Silently, smoothly, two long thin rods shot out from each end of the box until they were each about a foot long. There was a groove on the box and Nelson fitted it to the lower strand of the fence wire. He let go of the gadget and it balanced of its own accord, its antenna vibrating until they blurred, then ceasing to vibrate as the gadget balanced. Nelson went down on his back and pulled on gloves. He grabbed the fence wire and lifted it so that he could slide under. When he was inside he picked the gadget off the wire by one antenna and shut it off. The antennae pulled back inside. Gardner had made this gadget; Gardner had been handy with things like this. And there would be no other when Nelson lost this. He didn't want to leave it where it could be found or where he might have to abandon it to save his neck in an emergency.

He turned to the problem of getting across the open field. He had little fear of being picked up by radiation detectors, thanks to his absorber. But direct contact could give him away. But most of those had to be buried. That meant that he could keep close to the bushes and not have to worry. The roots of the bushes fouled up the detection instruments if they got to them. He made his way, judging each step before he took it and at last stood by the door.

It was dark by then. He could see the stars in the clear darkness of the sky. They seemed somehow brighter than they had before. Nelson fished through his pack until he felt the familiar shape of the gadget he wanted. It was smaller, more compact than the one he had used to get over the fence; but it was more complex. He felt along the door frame for the alarm trip and found it. He placed the gadget there and switched it on. There was a short, low, buzzing sound as the gadget did its job and Nelson glanced around nervously, in fear it had been heard. The door's lock clunked back and Nelson released air from his lungs. He pushed the door open and found himself in darkness.

He was in a corridor with doors facing off from it. He could see light coming under two of the doors, meaning patrolmen behind them. He moved cautiously by the two doors, almost opposite each other, to a door at the end of the corridor. He grasped the handle and opened the door, realizing too late that the door should have been locked.

But by that time the door was open. His hand darted to his holstered furnace beamer and unlocked the safety. It was almost pitch dark in the room but he heard the room's occupant turning over on the bunk and mumble low, incoherently, in his sleep. Nelson waited a minute but the man didn't wake up.

Nelson closed the door.

He tried another door; this time, one that was locked. He had no trouble forcing the lock pattern; less than a minute later he was inside, with the door shut behind him. He took out a flashlight.

This was the storeroom, all right. It was piled with boxes mostly unopened. Nelson read the labels on the boxes and opened those which contained food he needed and supplies. He found another pack in an opened box in one corner and began outfitting it like his own. Or as nearly like his own as possible; he knew that he could never duplicate or replace the gadgets Gardner had designed, and in a way he was bitter about it. He found the ammunition stores and took as many capsules for the furnace beamers as he could carry. He went to the door but slipped the furnace beamer out of his holster before opening the door.

The corridor was still dark. He stepped into it, alert for any sound or movement that might mean danger or herald discovery. His nervousness had given way to cool, detached determination. He almost made it to the door before he heard the footsteps.

His reaction was unconscious and reflexive. He turned, leveling his gun. He had passed the two doors light had shown under. One of them was opening and Nelson saw the shadow of the man who had opened it; then the man. The man saw Nelson at about the same time and stood gaping at him. Without realizing that he had fired, Nelson felt the recoil of the gun; the roar of the beam against the close walls hurt his ears, parts of the wall blistered and buckled, other parts of it charred black, some parts vaporizing in thin patches. The patrolman had flared instantly, never really knowing what had hit him. Smoke and heavy odors filled the corridor as Nelson slid out into the open. The patrol depots were fireproof, but the area Nelson had blasted would be far too hot to pass through for the rest of the night.

Nelson toned down the volume of his beamer and fired at a fence post. The tough plastic burst into splinters with a sudden explosion. A snapping wire whipped to within inches of Nelson's face but he didn't have to think about it. He was running up the hillside a short while later—he had lost track of time as such—hoping that Glynnis would use her gun if any patrolmen were following him.

He reached the hilltop in darkness, afraid to use his flashlight. Suddenly, he stumbled; was falling over something soft, like an animal or a man. Cursing low and involuntarily, he managed to roll over so that he fell on his back. He saw the form, a patch of irregular blackness in the darkness around him and knew it for a body. He got to his feet, glancing around, not knowing what this meant. He bent over the form, keeping the furnace beams muzzle only a few inches from it, but too far back to be grabbed suddenly. He couldn't see the man's clothing very plainly but he could tell it was a patrolman's uniform. Nelson reached down to feel for a heartbeat and drew his hand away sticky with what he knew must be blood. Nelson was shaken for a moment; but he put aside the strange kinship he so often felt for patrolmen because they were also wakers and drew back, peering round into the darkness, pretty certain that he knew what had happened to this patrolman.

He pushed himself erect and turned to see Glynnis, a dark figure but obviously her, standing near a clump of trees a few feet off.

"You move quiet as a cat," he said. "You do this?"

"Uh-huh." She came forward and stared down at the corpse. Nelson was glad he couldn't see her face in the darkness. "There were two of them. They split up and I followed after this one and came up behind him. I slit his throat. Then I went and got the other one the same way."

And it had been so simple, thought Nelson. He handed Glynnis the extra pack. "Take this." She accepted it wordlessly and slipped her arms into the straps. "Oh," he added, as an afterthought. "Let me show you something." He reached into the pack and drew out a knife. A good one with a long plasteel blade that would not chip or corrode like hers. He handed it to her and imagined her smiling face in the darkness.

"It doesn't feel like metal,"she said, after she had taken the knife from its scabbard.

"It isn't. It's a kind of plastic, stronger than most metals. Do you like it?" He was wasting time, he knew, and he cursed himself for it. But it didn't matter.

"It's real nice," she answered.

"I'm glad you like it," he said, taking her elbow in his hand. "We'd better go now. They'll be after us."

They ran most of the night, although it wasn't always running. Nelson picked a lot of terrain that was too uneven or too thickly covered with growth for running. They kept to rocks and creekbeds as much as they could, and they stopped only a few hours before dawn to get a few hours sleep they were too exhausted to postpone any longer.

When Nelson awoke the sun was a little higher than he had wanted it to be. He got to his feet and scanned the morning sky but saw nothing to indicate sky patrol robots. He felt uneasy about not having made more territory; but the way had been erratic and uneven. A thorough search pattern could find him easily; the further away he got from the depot the better chance he stood of not being discovered by a robot. He wondered, briefly, just how many would be called out, but there was no reason to wonder. Three patrolmen dead meant a lot of searching to find the killers. He and Glynnis couldn't waste much time.

He nudged the still sleeping girl with his foot to wake her. She awoke suddenly, her hand darting toward her new knife and a low but startled cry came from her.

"Quiet." He had dug two cans out of his pack and handed one to her. "We overslept. Eat in a hurry."

She opened her breakfast. "We'll be traveling most of the day?" she asked. When he nodded, "yes," she said, "I can take it."

"I know you can; but they'll have a search out for us by now and a thorough one. If we hadn't met when we had, they'd have picked you up for sure after I raided that depot—if I could have pulled if off alone."

She smiled.

"You ever see an air robot?" he asked.

"No."

"I hope you never do. They'll fly out a search pattern, and they have equipment that can detect a human being. They can send back signals to tell where we are if they spot us. Our only hope is to get away before the search pattern gets this far. If we can get far enough away, we stand a better chance, because they'll have to spread out more thinly. We'll have to run for a long time, but eventually they'll give up. Until then—Well—" He let it hang. But Glynnis caught on.

The rest of the day they traveled, stopping only briefly to eat and once in the afternoon when they came to a small river. Nelson's admiration for Glynnis increased. She responded intelligently to his commands, and learned quickly. She was strong and athletic, with the reflexes of an animal.

They made good time. When darkness came Nelson estimated they had made almost fifty miles since the raid, even over rough terrain. He hoped that that would be enough. He was tired, and though the girl attempted to hide her own fatigue, her attempts were becoming more and more exaggerated. He searched out a camp site.

He found one on a hill, overlooking a river. There was protection from the wind. The moon was up and there was plenty of light from it; but Nelson didn't think the searchers would be out at night.

After they had eaten, Nelson leaned back against the thick bole of a tree and found himself studying the girl. Her features were even enough, but she was not a classically beautiful girl. Nor an unattractive one. It was her eyes, he decided. She was staring off into the sky and forest. Her eyes were large, dark, enigmatic eyes that expressed much; expressed it eloquently. But he had the feeling there was much in the girl that those eyes hid. Her body was lean, but whether from exercise or undernourishment he couldn't be sure. Her figure was full, for all the leanness, and ample. She was strong, though she hardly looked muscular. She had been toughened by her environment. Edna had not been as tough as Glynnis.

With sudden embarrassment, he realized he had been comparing Glynnis and Edna frequently. He didn't want to do that—but he couldn't help himself.

"Something wrong?" Glynnis asked anxiously.

She was returning his stare. "No," he said. "I was . . . looking at you." For a long moment, neither spoke. Then he said, "We'll be together for a long time."

"I know. We'll have to be."

"I'm glad I found you. I lost my wife to the patrol some time back."

"I've never been anyone's wife before. There was Frank, but I was never really what you could call his wife, exactly."

"Many people ever stay with your folks?"

"Not many. Frank only stayed a few days. I liked him. I wanted to go with him."

"Why didn't you?"

She broke off a blade of grass and slowly began tearing it into strips, intently gazing at it. "He just left suddenly without taking me. I guess he thought I was just a stupid brat. That was maybe two or three years ago." Her voice sounded as if she were smiling a little. Nelson thought that strange.

"You ever think much about the sleepers?" he asked suddenly.

"Sometimes. I wonder what it's like in their dreams."

"They like it in their dreams. Those dreams are built for them. They get along happily in their world, grateful for it. That's the word, grateful." He listened for a moment to nightsounds. "But they're helpless. If anything happens, they're asleep and unable to act. If they wake up, they're in a world they don't know how to live in."

"If you were a sleeper, what kind of world would you want to dream about?"

"I don't want to be a sleeper."

"Yes, but if you were. Would you live in a castle?"

He thought on it for the first time. "I don't know," he said finally. "I don't think so. I think I'd travel. Go out to the stars. There's a whole universe out there. Men went out there; they're still out there. I guess they've forgotten us."

"You think they'll ever come back?"

"Some day I think somebody from out there will come back and land on Earth to see what it's like. Maybe they'll try to invade us. We'd be pretty helpless with most of us asleep in our pipe-dream utopias."

"I wouldn't like to be caught and put in a dream," she said. "But I'd like to live in a castle." Nelson gazed at her. She had never known a commune, he realized. If she had, she would have bred when told to and then docilely filed away to her coffin. But she had never been indoctrinated. If she went into the dreams, it would be against her will. But he had to admit that he had some reservations . . .

He moved close to her.

"Maybe some day we can live in a castle. Or go into space to some planet where men live in castles." He stared at the stars. "Out there they must be like gods," he said and his voice sounded strange, even to him.

He looked down at Glynnis. The moonlight was full on her face; she looked fit to be a goddess to those gods, he thought. She was staring off and around at the wilderness; she was saying, "Out here there's trees. And air. I like to look at the trees." He reached over and pulled her face around to him and kissed her. She was startled, but returned the kiss warmly.

She pulled away just far enough to look into his face. She was smiling. "I think I like you better than I did Frank," she said.

Nelson lay awake for a few moments, trying to identify the noise. It was a low humming sound off in the distance. He could feel Glynnis, breathing evenly with sleep beside him. The sky was just beginning to color with sunrise in the east. As quietly as possible, Nelson eased himself erect, still trying to place the noise. He placed it, and realized that he had not really wanted to identify it.

"Quiet," he said as he roused the girl. She opened her eyes wide, and stared at him, confused and uncomprehending.

"What's wrong?"

"Hear that noise?"

"Yes," she said after a second.

"One of the search machines. Probably they've adopted a loose search pattern, or maybe we left some kind of sign somewhere. It's not coming closer, but we'd better get out of here."

They ate hastily, in the awakening light of sunrise. They ran away from the sound of the machine, and it lessened in the distance.

It was the middle of the morning when they heard it again. Nelson judged it to be roughly a mile away and to the west. He waited a minute, listening. It seemed to be describing a search pattern curve that swung in front of their path. He decided to double back and around to miss it.

The undergrowth was thick in this part of the forest. They made their way through bushes and waist-high grasses, being as careful as possible not to leave too many signs of their passing. Glynnis' shorts and thin blouse weren't much protection against the thorns or the recoiling limbs of bushes but she didn't complain. Gradually the forest became mostly trees again. They found a path some animal had made and followed it.

When they came to the clearing, Nelson almost didn't see the thing in the air. He heard Glynnis gasp behind him, and with a start, glanced around. She was staring at something in front of them, and in the air. He looked where she was staring and saw the air robot hovering near the edge of the clearing. It was about two feet long, slender, metallic and smooth. Nelson knew though that it was alert and that receptors built into its skin were registering their presence. It hovered about ten feet above the ground, some twenty feet away from them, making no noise. Sky robots made noise only when they were moving at a fairly good speed. They had fled the noise of one only to be trapped in the silence of another.

Suddenly, Glynnis was shouting, "It's one of them!" Nelson turned to see her level her gun, and before he could stop her a white hot streamer lashed out at the robot and engulfed it.

"No," he shouted, too late. The machine took the blast turning cherry red and bobbing lightly in the air for a moment before energy compensators and stabilizers adjusted to the effects of the blast. The machine turned back to its lustrous silver color and there was a low hum as it righted itself gracefully then swung around, into the center of the clearing to get a better focus on them.

"It doesn't even have a mark on it," Glynnis said, in a low tone, moving closer to Nelson and laying one hand on his shoulder.

"No. But don't worry; it can't hurt us. We've got to figure some way to get out of here and leave it behind." He turned and gently guided her toward the trees. When they were in the dubious shelter of the trees, Nelson stopped and tried to figure a way out. He could see the machine hanging in the center of the clearing on invisible lines of force, turning slightly to find them in the dense growth, then, with one end pointed at them, bobbing slightly with the low breeze.

"What's it doing?" Glynnis asked. There was superstitious awe in her voice that annoyed Nelson.

"Sending a signal to the patrol. We don't have much time before they get here."

"But if the machine can't be shot down what can we do?"

"Hand me your gun." He took her gun and pointed to a vernier control set into the side of the weapon. "This is the intensity control; it's on low." He turned it up. "Now it's on full."

"Will that stop the machine?"

"Not by itself. But if we both move in, blasting together, again and again we might do it some damage."

"All right," she said, taking the gun.

Nelson led the way into the clearing. The machine moved back a little and bobbed to keep them in alignment. Nelson felt the dryness of his throat as he raised his gun to aim at the incurious machine. "All set?" he asked. From the corner of his eye he could see that Glynnis had raised her gun and was sighting.

"All set," she answered.

"O.K." Nelson fired. His blast hit the robot head on. It was absorbed, but almost as soon as it had died down, Glynnis fired. Nelson fired again, catching the machine in an almost steady stream of white hot energy. The machine suddenly caught on to what they were doing. It tried to escape their range by going up, but they followed it. By this time the compensators were already beginning to fail. Haywire instruments jerked the machine back down and then side to side, then into a tree trunk, blindly. It rebounded and dipped low, almost touching the ground before it curved back up. Some of Glynnis' shots were missing, but Nelson made every shot count, even while the robot was darting about wildly.

The machine was glowing cherry red, now, some twelve feet off the ground, unable to rise further, one end pointed sharply upward. Something inside it began screaming, loudly, shrilly, with a vibration that hurt Nelson's teeth. Nelson was firing mechanically. The machine's loud screaming stopped suddenly. Nelson checked his fire. Glynnis fired once more, missing as the machine suddenly dropped about a foot. For perhaps a second the machine remained motionless. Then it died without sound, and fell to the ground, landing with a dull noise and setting fire to the grass under and around it.

For that matter, they had started a major forest fire with their blastings. The trees across the clearing from them were already roaring with flames. Nelson didn't wait to check on the machine. He grabbed Glynnis and pulled her around toward the way they had come. She stumbled, staring back at the machine.

"Come on!" he said, in agitation. She came to life, mechanically, and let him propel her along. The wind was away from them, but the fire growing. They ran madly until they had to stop and fall exhausted to the ground. When he could breathe again without torturing his lungs, Nelson looked back and saw the smoke from the fire in the distance behind them. They were safe from the fire, but their escape was cut off by it. It would, he knew with dull certainty, attract attention.

When he had rested as long as he dared, he said, "We'd better get going."

"I'm not sure I can," she said.

"Well, you've got to. If we stay here, we'll be caught."

They did not pause to eat. It was about midday when they encountered the robot and they walked well into the afternoon, their only purpose being to put as much distance between them and the place where they had shot the robot down as possible. Nelson found himself moving numbly, blindly uncaring of anything but making progress forward. He listened to the humming of an approaching robot for a long while before it registered on his consciousness.

He whirled, drawing his gun, momentarily giving way to the panic that had been threatening to engulf him all afternoon. He saw the machine, high above the trees behind them, safely out of range, he knew. Bitterly, he fought down the urge to fire the gun anyway. It took a tremendous exertion of will to make his arm return the gun to its holster.

"What can we do?" asked Glynnis, a slight quaver in her voice.

"Not a thing," said Nelson; then almost in rage he cried it. "Not one damned thing!"

They both turned back the way they had been going and ran, hoping to find some cover with which to duck the machine. Nelson converted his rage and fear into a strength he had never known he could call upon. He ran on, and Glynnis behind him. And he knew that she, like he, ran despite the rawness in her throat and lungs and cramping of her legs. The only thing he could think of was that he wanted to enter a mausoleum not as a prisoner, but as the head of an army.

He ran blindly, hearing nothing but the machine and his own rasping breath. Then suddenly, he was stumbling over the edge of an embankment, flailing his arms and twisting himself around so that he managed to land on his back. It hurt and the wind went out of him. He was sliding and rolling. Somehow he managed to stop himself. He lay painfully coughing and trying to get his breath. Below him he could see the wild rushing of a river at the base of the sheer embankment. He looked back up. Glynnis had one leg over the edge but had not fallen. Nelson crawled his way back up the slope.

They were trapped by the river. It must be another part of the same river they had spent the night by, thought Nelson. But where it had been calm and shallow, it was now a raging torrential river whose brown, churning waters ran between high, difficult-to-climb cliffs.

There was no need for either to speak. They began looking for a place to cross the river. All the time they searched they could hear the machine behind them, above them, humming safely out of their range.

The sun was low in the sky when they heard the second humming. The humming grew until it was a throbbing that covered the weaker sound of the robot and chilled Nelson.

"The patrol," he said, pushing the girl toward the forest. "Back into the trees. We're going to have to fight it out with them."

They ran into the trees. The throbbing stopped and behind them, Nelson could hear the sounds made by men thrashing through undergrowth. His palms were wet; he wiped them on his shirt front. The impending contact with the patrol gave him a calmness as always, and he picked out a thicket where he believed he could make some sort of stand.

He reached the thicket with Glynnis beside him. Her gun was out. He signed to her to lower the intensity of the gun; she caught on. He watched her face. It was like a mask.

Nelson listened to the sounds of the approaching patrolmen. Five or six, he decided. Plus a guard back at the flier. He'd figure on eight, in all, he decided. Then the first one showed behind some bushes.

Nelson touched Glynnis' arm in a signal to wait. The patrolman looked around, searching too intensely to find anything. He was young. Nelson didn't think he would uncover their whereabouts and for a moment debated letting him pass.

But he didn't want to be surrounded. He pulled his gun up and sighted carefully before squeezing the trigger. In the tenth of a second before the patrolman burst into flames, the blast produced a blast circle that grew to the size of a basketball in his midsection. The patrolman fell without screaming.

The others were there now. Most of them were young and two rushed forward at the sight of their companion's death, to die like heroes. The others wisely sought cover. Nelson decided that the thicket wasn't as safe as he had hoped. One of the patrolmen was doing a good job with an energizer, coming closer with each shot, before Nelson finally saw where he was, and fired at him. Nelson saw the trunk of a large fallen tree and pointed to it for Glynnis' benefit. She nodded.

There was cover most of the way. Nelson went first, crouching low to the ground and running with the ease of a cat. He made the log and began firing to cover Glynnis. He saw her coming, out of the corner of his eye, then concentrated on covering her with fire power. Suddenly the girl let out a startled yell and he saw her sprawl to the ground, tripping over a root. He called her name and without thinking leaped to his feet to run to help her. He was halfway there when the patrolman came into range. Nelson realized what he had done. Glynnis was already on her feet and running. Cursing himself, Nelson jerked his gun around, but it was too late. An energizer blast exploded the ground beneath him and he felt himself hurtling over backwards. He could only see blackness and the bright, quick, flashing of pin-point light in it. Then, he was falling, spinning . . .

Patrol Cadet Wallace Sherman watched the man on the table with mixed feelings; on the one hand, there was pity for a man whose condition was hopeless, and on the other there were the misgivings that come with guarding a criminal. Perhaps it was Sherman's youth that caused him to emphasize those misgivings and move his hand toward his sidearm when the man stirred.

But the man on the table only stirred a little and groaned. Sherman was not sure whether or not the man was coming to. He shouldn't be, Sherman knew. He took a couple of steps forward and stared at the man's face.

The man was breathing normally. His head moved slightly but his eyes were still closed. His face was the palest, softest looking face Sherman had ever seen. It was the face of a man who had never known sunlight, Sherman thought somberly; or at least had not known it in many years. He wondered, vaguely just what kind of life the man dreamed he had. As he was watching the man's face, Sherman saw his lips move and heard him utter something he could not make out. He bent closer to hear better.

"Glynnis"—the man on the table was saying.

"Is he waking up?" Sherman heard a voice asking.

A little embarrassed, Sherman turned around and saw Blomgard standing in the doorway. "Oh, I'm sorry, sir. No. At least I don't think so. He said something; a word. *Glynnis,* I think. Sounds like a girl's name."

Dr. Blomgard came into the room and walked over to the table on which his patient was stretched out. He removed the clipboard from its hook and looked through the sheaf of papers fastened to it. After a few seconds, he said, "Ah, yes. Glynnis. Part of his dream."

"Doctor—," Sherman heard himself saying, then caught himself.

"What, cadet," Blomgard asked, turning around. He was a big man, gray-haired, his hair an unruly mop. His eyes were dark and piercing, but they were softened by the thickness of the white brows over them.

"Nothing, sir—"

"I assure you, that no question will be considered out of place, if that's what is worrying you."

"Well, doctor," Sherman said with some difficulty, "I was

wondering if all this is worth it. I mean a special reserve with the artificial life-dreams for these people. Is it worth the expense and effort?"

Blomgard regarded the question a moment before answering. "Well, that depends on things. We have a fairly dynamic, expanding civilization. This man was born out of step; a natural born rebel. We've reached the stage where, with a little effort on their own part, most people can sooner or later find exactly what they want. There are, of course, exceptions. They can't help being the way they are, but they are that way. It isn't his fault that he would think nothing of blowing up any civilization he found himself living in. This is the solution."

"A drug-induced dream state? Is that a solution?"

"It's a pretty good one. We provide him with a completely fictitious, a totally unreal world in which he will be happy."

"How can anyone be happy like that? I prefer reality."

Blomgard smiled. "Yes, to a larger extent than he does, you do. Or you like what you think of as reality." He picked up the clipboard again and studied the papers on it. "His dream world is one that is designed for his happiness. In it, he sees everyone else as inhabiting the dream-coffins. And he pictures himself as a rugged individualist, going about trying to destroy such a civilization. And of course, he is practically a lone wolf. Not completely, for he would not be happy that way. The man is an underdog."

"I guess it's best," Sherman said.

"It is," the doctor replied, seriously. "We have no right to take his life; nor do we have the right to destroy his personality, however much that personality may be offensive to us. And since most inhabitable planets are, unfortunately, inhabited before we ever get to them, we have more urgent colonies to establish where we can find room. No, this is best. We give him a dream based exactly on his psychological needs; a compensation, so to speak, for the real life we take away from him. For most people only have the right to pursue happiness. In return for a normal life, we've given him a guaranteed happiness."

The doctor let that sink in for a while; but Sherman still had a strong wish that he had pulled some other duty. Perhaps on one of the new outposts, like Deneb.

The doctor glanced at his watch. "Well, the repairs are done with and they should have the nutrient refreshed by now. Let's wheel him on back."

A little gratefully, Sherman moved over to the table.

"You'll be all right, soon enough," the doctor said to the unconscious man on the table. "This interruption will be neatly explained away and remain as merely a memory of a slightly unpleasant moment after things get back to normal. That'll convince you of the reality of your world—if you ever need convincing."

Sherman saw the sleeping man stir slightly and heard him utter sounds again.

"Wheel him out," Blomgard said.

Gratefully, Sherman turned the table around and wheeled it out the door.

From far off, Nelson heard Glynnis calling to him. "Are you all right, Hal?" he heard. "Can you hear me, Hal?"

"I can hear you," he managed to say. He opened his eyes. He saw his gun a few dozen feet away on the ground.

"I thought they had you, sure," Glynnis said quietly. "I got the two of them. Don't ask me how I did it, but I got them."

He sat up, feeling dizzy from having hit the ground with such force. "I don't guess I was much help," he said weakly. "You sure did a fine job." His head ached, but he remembered the fight and being thrown by the impact of the blast. And something else—something distant and alien, like a dream, from the deepest part of his mind. It pestered him a moment, just out of reach of his consciousness, then he shrugged it off as unimportant. He looked around and saw the charred bodies of the patrolmen. "You did a fine job," he told Glynnis, meaning it.

"Can you fly a patrol ship?"

"Huh?"

"We've got one now," Glynnis said. "I shot the guard they left with it, too. Had to."

"I see," he said, marveling at the girl. "I can fly one. I haven't since I was in the commune, though. As long as it's in good condition."

"I guess it is. I didn't hit it with any shots."

"We can go anywhere in the world with that ship," he said getting to his feet. "It doesn't need fuel; it can fly forever. You know what that means Glynnis? We can raise an army, if we want to."

"And we can get into the mausoleums and wake everybody up?"

"Yes. Come on," he said and started toward the flier. But Glynnis grabbed his arm and stopped him. "What is it?" he asked.

"What's it like to live in a world where everyone's awake?" she asked him.

"Why . . . I don't know. I've never lived in one."

"Then why do you want to wake everyone up?"

"It's wrong the way they are now."

Glynnis scowled and Nelson could tell that she was struggling with strange concepts. He felt sympathy for her, knowing how she felt.

"What I mean," she asked finally, "is why is it wrong? What's the reason?"

"Because they can do better. We can save them and show them that; I can lead them back where they belong."

"I see," Glynnis said gravely accepting his words. "All right."

Nelson smiled at her. She looked up at him and smiled back. The patrol ship was waiting for them, not far off.

Together, they marched off to save the world.

Bibliography
Virtual Reality in Fiction

The following timeline traces the roots of virtual reality in science fiction from 1909 to 1992. The majority of the works included here were written before the technology of virtual reality was actualized, with the exceptions of the last few entries.

1909 E. M. Forster, "The Machine Stops"
This story predicts telepresence and what amounts to a computer network, though Forster calls them by different names. Pale, flabby humans live underground, believing the earth's surface is unfit for life, with machines to entertain and take care of them.

1932 Aldous Huxley, *Brave New World,* London, Chatto & Windus; New York, Doubleday
Depicts a society based on conformity and comfort. When citizens get bored or depressed, they pop a few SOMA pills, or go to an ALL-SUPER-SINGING, SYNTHETIC-TALKING, COLOURED, STEREOSCOPIC **FEELY,** WITH SYNCHRONIZED SCENT-ORGAN ACCOMPANIMENT. Every hair on the bearskin rug is "superbly reproduced."

1945 Norman Spinrad, *Riding the Torch,* in *Threads of Time,* ed. Robert Silverberg, New York, Dell
The earth's a burned-out wasteland, but humans entertain themselves with sculpted holo-environments and "sensos" while they search for a new planet to colonize. Eventually, they realize that there are no other planets, but that they have everything they need in artificial reality. As Spinrad's main character asks himself, "Who needs planets? Who needs life beyond the germ we carry? Who needs prime reality at all?"

1950 Ray Bradbury, "The Happiness Machine," in *Dandelion*

***Wine* (1957), New York, Doubleday; London, Hart Davis**
All of the most beautiful experiences in life are recreated inside the box-shaped Happiness Machine—but eventually the characters have to step out of the box and return to their drab everyday lives.

1950 John D. MacDonald, "Spectator Sport," ***Analog Science Fiction/Science Fact***
A time traveler to the future discovers that everyone is saving up for his own personal lobotomy and permanent installation of an artificial reality—Cowboy, Crime and Detective, or Harem series.

1950 Robert Heinlein, *Waldo,* first published in *Waldo, and Magic, Inc.,* NY, Doubleday; as *Waldo, Genius in Orbit,* NY, Avon, 1958
Contains no virtual reality per se, but Heinlein *invented* the idea for telepresence in this book. Actual remote control operation devices are called "waldoes" after the title character.

1953 Ray Bradbury, *Farenheit 451,* New York, Ballentine, and London, Hart Davis (1954)
A housewife spends hours participating in an empty, plotless interactive soap opera.

1954 Arthur C. Clarke, "Patent Pending," in *Tales From the "White Hart,"* New York, Ballantine (1957), and Canada, Random House (1957)
A machine records and duplicates any experience, from sex to a gourmet meal. Ends with the line, "Better sell your TV set before the bottom drops out of the market."

1956 Arthur C. Clarke, *The City and the Stars,* London, Muller, and New York, Harcourt Brace
The privileges of the inhabitants of a sheltered utopian city include adventures in virtual worlds, but they are denied access to the real world outside.

1966 Frederick Pohl, "Day Million," in Rogue Magazine, also *Arbor House Treasury of Modern Science Fiction* (1980),

edited by Robert Silverberg and Martin Greenburg, New York, Arbor House
Lovers live on separate worlds and have sex with computer simulations of one another.

1966 Philip K. Dick, *The Three Stigmata of Palmer Eldritch*, New York, Doubleday, and London, Cape
People forced to colonize a desolate planet escape into a kind of virtual reality that simulates their lives back on earth, while the big corporations who produce the product exploit them for profit.

1968 Philip K. Dick, *Do Androids Dream of Electric Sheep?*, New York, Doubleday, 1968, and London, Rapp and Whiting, 1969
Followers of the religion Mercerism grasp the handles of their "empathy boxes" to "experience" the sufferings of their savior. Androids bitter at being denied the experience expose the empathy boxes as virtual reality, and Mercer as an aging character actor, but this doesn't seem to matter much to humans, who continue to practice their religion as before.

1969 Daniel F. Galouye, *Counterfeit World*, London, Gollancz; as Simulacron-3, New York, Bantam
A man realizes that he is an electronic analogue living in an electronically-simulated world created for marketing studies, and tries to gain some control over his pseudo-life.

1969 Ben Bova, *The Dueling Machine*, New York, Holt Rinehart, and London, Faber (1971)
Instead of wasting lives, money, and weaponry on wars, nations settle their differences by virtual duels. The defeated man loses the war but not his life—until someone begins to sabotage the system.

1975 James Tiptree (Karen Sheldon), "The Girl Who Was Plugged in," in *Warm Worlds and Otherwise*, New York, Ballantine
An early telepresence story. In the future, advertising is outlawed, so corporations devise a scheme to get around the law.

They clone perfect bodies and have teleoperators live glamorous well-publicized lives which involve a lot of use of the corporate product.

1980 Frederick Pohl, *Beyond the Blue Event Horizon,* New York, Ballantine, and London, Gollancz (sequels: *Heechee Rendezvous,* 1984, New York, Ballantine; London, Gollancz, and *Annals of the Heechee,* 1987, New York, Ballantine; London, Gollancz)
People's personalities are translated into computer programs, and they live their lives in computer-simulated worlds. Their existence is indistinguishable, to them, from reality, and they can alter it to suit their wishes. *Beyond the Blue Event Horizon* inspired the product Autodesk.

1981 Vernor Vinge, *True Names,* in *Binary Star 5,* New York, Dell
A cult favorite among computer people. Computer hackers enter the computer network of data in tangible form, perceiving it as a magic land and themselves as their chosen personas.

1981 Larry Niven with Stephen Barnes, *Dream Park,* Huntington Woods, Michigan, Phantasia Press, and London, Macdonald (1983) (sequel: *The Barsoom Project,* New York, Ace, 1989, and London, 1990)
Adults play Dungeons-and-Dragons-like games in a holographic theme park.

1984 James Morrow, *The Continent of Lies,* New York, Holt Rinehart, 1984; London, Gollancz (1985)
"Dreambeans" allow you to experience movies instead of watching them in this satire of the entertainment industry.

1984 William Gibson, *Neuromancer,* New York, Ace; London, Gollancz (sequels: *Count Zero,* 1986, New York, Arbor House; London, Gollancz and *Mona Lisa Overdrive,* 1988, New York, Bantam; London, Gollancz)
Future hackers enter "cyberspace," the visual representation of the computer network of data, directly, via neural jacks to the

brain. Also describes simstims, or simulated stimulations, a virtual form of passive entertainment. *Neuromancer,* the definitive "cyberpunk" novel, has inspired many real-life hackers, programmers, and VR proponents. Fake Space Labs named one invention, a teleoperated camera platform, the "Molly" after the razor-nailed, mirror-lensed antiheroine of the books.

1985 Orson Scott Card, *Ender's Game,* New York, Tor, and London, Unwin
Children are trained intensively by the military on simulators so realistic that it's impossible to tell them apart from actual war. NASA was actually inspired by this novel to hold a conference dedicated to preventing it from coming true.

1989 Dave Wolverton, *On My Way to Paradise,* New York, Bantam Spectra, and Canada, Bantam
During the course of a long space flight to a war on a different planet, recruited mercenaries are turned into hardened soldiers and accustomed to the alien terrain through realistic simulators. They also suffer post-traumatic stress syndrome and other effects of war.

1990 Kim Newman, *The Night Mayor,* New York, Carroll & Graf
A convicted criminal "escapes" prison by locking his mind into his own private artificial reality, The City. It's a film noir world, in black-and-white, bound by censor's codes and inhabited by all the old bit actors and cliches.

1991 Rebecca Ore, *The Illegal Rebirth of Billy the Kid,* New York, Tor
Biogenetic engineering produces "chimeras" for the pleasure of spoiled rich people. The chimeras are conditioned in sensory deprivation tanks with holograms, and perceive the world accordingly; a Billy the Kid chimera, for instance, will perceive a car as a horse or something else that fits his time period.

1991 Pat Cadigan, *Synners,* New York, Bantam
Using well-researched information about current virtual reality

as a base, Cadigan explores the effects VR will have on various human beings. These include an advertising executive trying to create virtual ads which will make the customer feel like a sexy model and a music video performer who acts as a human synthesizer.

Citadel Twilight Books Ordering Information

Thank you for choosing Citadel Twilight Books!

If you like this book, you'll love the other books in this series. Part science fiction, part mystery, part fantasy, the stories in the Citadel Twilight Series draw you into a world with a mysterious twist, a sense of otherness that eludes description.

Ask for these titles at your bookstore. Or to order direct from the publisher call 1-800-447-BOOK (MasterCard or Visa) or send a check or money order for the books purchased (plus $3.00 shipping and handling for the first book ordered and 50¢ for each additional book) to Citadel Twilight, 120 Enterprise Avenue, Distribution Center B, Secaucus, NJ 07094.

Citadel Twilight Books

The Collected Stories of Philip K. Dick
Each volume contains more than 25 short stories from the man considered to be the greatest science fiction mind on any *planet*:

Volume 1--The Short, Happy Life of the Brown Oxford, paperback $12.95

Volume 2--We Can Remember It For You Wholesale *(the story that was the basis for the blockbuster movie Total Recall, starring Arnold Schwarzenegger)*, paperback $12.95

Volume 3--Second Variety, paperback $12.95

Volume 4--The Minority Report, paperback $12.95

Volume 5--The Eye of the Sibyl, paperback $12.95

Divine Invasions: A Life of Philip K. Dick by Lawrence Sutin, paperback $12.95. *The first full-scale bio of the man whose real life was as interesting as his great writing.*

The Science Fiction Writings of Jack London, edited by James Bankes, paperback $9.95. *A surprising collection by the author of* The Call of the Wild *and* White Fang.

The Complete Stories of Robert Bloch
More than 25 stories in each volume, from the author of Psycho:

Volume 1--Final Reckonings, paperback $12.95

Volume 2--Bitter Ends, paperback $12.95

Volume 3--Last Rites, paperback $12.95

Simulations: 16 Tales of Virtual Reality, edited by Karie Jacobson, paperback $9.95. *The most celebrated sci-fi writers (Philip K. Dick, Ray Bradbury, J.G. Ballard and more) plug you into cyberspace.*

Can Such Things Be?: Tales of Horror and the Supernatural by Ambrose Bierce; introduction by Clifton Fadiman, paperback $6.95. *Some of the most chilling and macabre tales in the English language.*

Strange Disappearances by Elliott O'Donnell; foreword by Leslie Shepard, paperback $9.95. *True tales of unexplained disappearances that will baffle even the most hard-headed skeptic.*